Anna

.

The Redemption Series

Book 2

S.J. West

Sandra J. West

List of Watcher Books in the Watcher Series

The Watchers Trilogy

Cursed

Blessed

Forgiven

The Watcher Chronicles

Broken

Kindred

Oblivion

Ascension

Caylin's Story

Timeless

Devoted

Anna

The Redemption Series

Malcolm

Anna

Lucifer (Coming Summer 2014)

Other Books by S.J. West

The Harvest of Light Trilogy

Harvester

Hope

Dawn

The Vankara Saga

Vankara

Dragon Alliance (Coming Fall/Winter 2014)

S.J. West

Anna

CHAPTER ONE

Time. It can be your worst enemy or your best friend. People say time changes all things, but it's ultimately our actions which affect where our lives go and what we become. Time is simply a bystander watching how each individual unfolds their own lives. It has no say in which path we take. It can't guide us into making the right decisions. Only we can change the course of our lives, and in the end, time can only tell us if we've made decisions which were for the better or for the worse.

I listen to the hum of the force field surrounding me. It's almost imperceptible but contrasted against the silence of the stark room I'm in it's become rather annoying. I watch as the red laser beams comprising the spherical prison I'm trapped in whirl around me with maddening speed. As I hang suspended within the middle of my jail, my legs and arms are spread wide apart by an invisible gravity field, presumably meant to prevent me from taking out the silver dagger Levi stabbed into my shoulder. Every inch of my body aches from its awkward positioning, but its pain is dwarfed by the burning tightness inside my chest. My heart cries for those who were unjustly taken from me just when I thought my world had finally been made right with Malcolm's declaration of love.

I had dreamt of Malcolm kissing me since the first night we met. Yet, just when my most fervent dream finally came true, it turned my world into a living nightmare where simply opening my eyes wasn't enough to alter reality. My soul burned with the knowledge that Levi had captured the love of my life because of me.

Through Catherine's paranoia that I would physically betray my vows to her son, Malcolm had unknowingly stepped into a trap neither of us saw coming. The poison she injected into my body every week had rendered him unconscious and now Levi, one of the most sadistic people I have ever had the misfortune of meeting, had him in his grasp. I had no way of knowing what Levi was doing to Malcolm. I also didn't know whether or not he had Lucas as well, but the odds were definitely in Levi's favor.

As soon as the guards phased me back to the palace in Cirrus, they brought me directly to the room I'm in. It was a room I never knew existed until that moment. I assumed it was somewhere in the deepest bowels of the palace where few people ever ventured. My guards made quick work of trapping me in the force field and turning on my revolving laser prison cell. Time was elapsing slowly. I felt sure only two, maybe three hours had gone by since Levi captured us. While I waited for someone to come and tell me the things I needed to know, I felt a flame of hatred towards Levi all but consume my soul. I wanted to tear him to pieces for what he had done to my family. Not only did he hold Malcolm, and more than likely Lucas, prisoner, but he was also the only person in the world who knew where my father was being held.

Even though I now know Lucifer is my biological father, he will never take the place of the man I still think of as my papa. Andre Greco had loved and nurtured me all my life. It didn't matter much to me that half my genetic code came from Lucifer. He obviously didn't care enough to want to raise me himself after my mother's death, and I felt no regret about his absence from my life. Perhaps it was for the best. If he truly is as vile a person as history has made him out to be, maybe my life was made richer by not having him in it at all.

The sound of a cracking whip makes me look up. Levi stands on the other side of the room with his lightning whip firmly grasped in his right hand.

"Have you missed me, my little dove?" He asks, his lips stretching into a manic grin.

"Where is Malcolm?" I demand.

"Still alive," he answers, arching an eyebrow at me and looking rather pleased with himself. "Though, I feel sure he wishes he weren't right about now."

"What did you do to him?" I ask, my voice sounding more like a deadly threat than asking a mere question.

Levi cracks his whip against the floor again and smiles.

"I made him pay the price for kissing my wife."

I stare at Levi for a moment because I want his full attention. I want him to hear my next few words clearly so he never forgets them.

"I *will* kill you one day," I promise.

"Threats, threats, threats." Levi says shaking his head as he walks toward me. "All I ever hear from you are threats, Anna."

"Then be a man and stop hiding yourself behind the people I love to protect your own life," I taunt. "Or are you truly that frightened of me?"

"I'm not exactly scared of you," Levi says, "but I'm not stupid either. Why wouldn't I use the people you love against you if it means I can get what I want?"

"What do you want from me?"

"I want you to do something for me that not even your father could get your mother to do for him."

Levi falls silent. I wait for him to continue, but he doesn't. He just stands there and stares at me with an aggravating smirk on his face.

"Am I supposed to guess what it is you want?" I ask becoming even more irritated. "I'm not a mind reader."

"No," Levi says closing his eyes like he's experiencing

something pleasant. "I'm just trying to enjoy the moment. It's a rare day when I can one up Lucifer. So, please... do shut up and let me bask in my own greatness for a little while."

"Tell me what you want!" I say, not even trying to hide the loss of my temper.

Levi sighs heavily as if disappointed in my impatience with him and opens his eyes.

"I want you to bring me my brothers," he finally says. "I know your Watcher friends have them, and I want them all back."

"I don't know where they are."

"But you can find out."

"And if I bring them to you, what do I get in return?"

"I'll give you Malcolm and that little boy we found hiding in his house."

"What have you done to Lucas?" I ask, praying that Lucas is somewhere safe.

Levi grins. "Oh, I'm using his safety to keep Malcolm in line. I wouldn't want him to just phase away before I had my fun with him, now would I? Unfortunately, I only have the one dagger, and I'm using that one on you."

"And what about my father?"

"Andre?" Levi asks, seeming to want to confirm which father I am talking about. "Oh, I plan to keep him for a while longer. I can't give you everything you want all at once. Plus, if I gave you Andre, what would prevent you from simply killing me and my brothers?"

I hated to admit it, but he had a point.

"I'll need time to find the other Watchers," I tell Levi. "I don't know where they are."

"Unfortunately, neither do I," Levi admits with a dramatic sigh. "They've laid low for so long they don't even exist in the public databases anymore. But, you do know where one of them is."

Jered. I did know where Jered was heading, but I didn't know where Rory and Lora lived exactly. They were the people who were supposed to look after Lucas for us until I could retrieve all of the seals from the princes of Hell.

"Do you know where Jered is now?" I ask.

"Of course I do," Levi replies acting as though I've just asked a stupid question. "But, I'm not going to tell you."

"If you want me to do what you want, wouldn't it be smarter to just tell me where I need to go?"

"Where would the challenge be if I told you everything you

need to know? That's not very sporting of you, wife."

"Stop calling me that," I say unable to keep the disgust out of my voice.

"But, it's the truth."

I choose to ignore Levi and move on with his demands.

"How am I supposed to find Jered if I don't know where he is?"

"Oh, I'm sure you can think of someone who *does* know. Someone you probably want to pay a little visit to again anyway," Levi suggests.

I instantly know exactly who he's talking about.

"And," he continues, "I'll give you a small bit of information just to help you out. Jered is still in the same city as the people he was visiting. In fact, he's trying to figure out what happened to dear Rory and Lora as we speak."

"What did you do to them?" I ask, dreading the answer.

"Oh, they're still alive," Levi says, obviously knowing where my thoughts went. "He just can't find them. I simply needed to delay Jered for a little while. I have no use for those people. They'll be returned to their homes after you locate Jered."

"I need you to do something for me before I gather up your

brothers for you."

Levi crosses his arms over his chest. "I don't think you're in any position to be making demands."

"If you want me to get your brothers, I need to see for myself that Malcolm and Lucas are still alive. I trust you about as much as I want you to take another breath. My life isn't worth living without them in it."

"Awwww," Levi says exaggeratedly, "that has to be the sweetest thing I've ever heard. It's so adorable it's literally turning my stomach inside out."

"I won't do anything until I see them. And I don't just mean a hologram. I want to see them in the flesh."

A twinkle enters Levi's eyes, and I know that can't be a good sign. Nothing gives him pleasure except torture and pain.

"This might surprise you, but that's entirely agreeable to me. Who would you prefer to see first?"

"Lucas," I say, knowing Malcolm will want a firsthand report of Lucas' welfare from me.

"Fine," Levi says, walking over to a control panel on the brick wall of the room at his back and tapping in a combination of letters and numbers.

The force field holding my body suspended in mid-air suddenly releases me into a freefall. The red laser sphere vanishes just before I land on the stone floor beneath me.

I take a few precious seconds to let the soreness in my limbs dissipate. Levi phases over to me and pulls the dagger in my shoulder out. The sucking sound accompanying its removal from my body sickens me slightly, but I'm glad to have it out of my shoulder.

I slowly stand to my feet. "Where is Lucas?"

Levi smiles. "At your house."

I immediately phase home. Unfortunately, Levi phases in right beside me.

I phased to my sitting room. It's still nighttime, and I know for sure now that only a few hours have passed since Levi's unexpected appearance in Malcolm's workshop. I hear a familiar song being hummed by someone I know and trust. I phase to my bedroom and find Millie sitting on the side of my bed singing to a slumbering Lucas. Vala is curled up on the pillow beside him watching over Lucas just like she did me when I was his age. When she notices I'm in the room, she instantly jumps up and runs across the bed, leaping into my arms.

"Where have you been, Anna?" Vala asks, her voice filled with the loneliness she must have felt during my absence.

14

Millie turns around to meet my gaze. She raises a trembling hand to her lips at the sight of me, and I see tears appear in her troubled eyes.

She rises from her seat and walks over to me.

"Oh, my sweet, where *have* you been? We've been worried sick about you."

Millie's gaze soon lands on the bloody wound on my shoulder. She makes an about face and rushes straight into my bathroom. She returns with a Cirrun healing device in her hands.

"Take your jacket off so I can heal you," she instructs.

I place Vala on the floor at my feet and unzip my jacket. Millie has to help me take it off because my arms are still extremely sore from being suspended in mid-air for so long.

"Oh, my poor child," Millie says, pulling my shirt away from the wound, "what has that devil done to you?"

Millie sweeps the black healing wand in her hand over the wound, mending it almost instantly.

"It's nothing I can't handle, Millie," I tell her, looking over her shoulder at Lucas. "Who brought him here?"

"One of the guards brought him about three hours ago," Millie tells me. "He was very upset when he arrived, but Vala and

I were able to calm him down. He seemed to trust me after he saw Vala."

"Lucas said you told him about me," Vala says, sounding proud that I would mention her to Lucas.

I bend down and pick my little friend up in my arms again. "Yes, I did. And I need you to do something for me, Vala."

"You know I will do anything you ask of me, Anna."

"I need you and Millie to watch over Lucas for me while I'm gone. I won't worry about him as much if I know the two of you are taking care of him."

"I'll protect him with my life!" Vala promises fiercely, making me smile in spite of the situation we find ourselves in.

"I know you will," I tell her, rubbing my nose against her little wet one before placing her back on the bed. She promptly pads over to the pillow beside Lucas and sits down again, taking up her position as his protector.

"Lucas kept calling you his mother," Millie says, looking perplexed by the fact. "Why is that?"

"Since he's Malcolm's son, I *will* officially become his mother once we're married."

Millie smiles. "So, you did make that stubborn old fool

finally admit he's your soul mate."

"I'm not sure what changed his mind actually," I say, just now realizing I truly didn't know what happened to make Malcolm accept how he felt about me.

The only thing I did was let him go. Yet, he came back to me with his heart completely open and ready to declare his love. I felt as though there was a piece to the puzzle that I was missing, but there just wasn't enough time to find out what that piece was. In the grand scheme of things, it really didn't matter. Malcolm loved me. That was all I needed to know.

And right now, I had more important things to figure out.

"I have to go back to the surface," I tell Millie. "Levi wants me to do something for him before he'll give Malcolm and the rest of you back to me."

"He has Master Malcolm too?" Millie asks, obviously hearing this bit of news for the first time.

I nod. "Yes, and I have to find Jered. You wouldn't happen to know where some people named Rory and Lora live in the down-world, would you?"

"No," Millie says, looking concerned that she can't help me, "should I know them?"

"They were people Malcolm seemed to trust because he

planned to have them look after Lucas while we dealt with the princes."

Millie shrugs her shoulders. "I'm sorry, my sweet. I have no idea who they are."

"It's ok, Millie," I tell her. "I know someone who will."

I look back to Lucas and walk over to the bed. I bend down and kiss him lightly on the cheek because I don't want to wake him up. I feel sure he would ask about his father, and I don't have any answers for him. It's better to just let him sleep. The sooner I get to work on doing what Levi wants, the sooner we can all be together again. As far as I'm concerned, Operation Family is still in effect, and I will do whatever I have to do to make us whole. I wish I could just phase him somewhere safe, but with Levi so close, it would never work. He would simply follow my phase trail to wherever I went. There isn't anywhere I can hide Lucas safely, not yet at least.

"We'll be back together soon," I promise him. "And don't worry about your dad. I'll take good care of him."

I let my gaze linger on Lucas' sweet, angelic face for a few more seconds before I steel myself for my next visit.

I look over at Millie. "I'll come back for all of you when I can."

Millie nods. "I know, my sweet. We'll be here waiting."

I phase back to the living room where I find Levi speaking with Eliza in hushed tones.

Levi sees me and smiles tight lipped. "Nice visit?"

"Take me to Malcolm," I say brusquely.

Eliza turns to look at me and raises a questioning eyebrow. "You should show more respect to the person you're talking to."

I look at Eliza and realize the person standing in front of me isn't the same young woman who has served as one of my ladies in waiting for the past five years.

"What are you?" I ask, knowing Eliza's soul isn't present anymore. "Are you like Levi?"

"No," Levi answers for her. "This is a changeling. And I've given her orders to snap your precious little Lucas' neck if you try to come back here and rescue him."

I don't feel surprised by this. In fact, I expected Levi to place someone near the people I care about to hold their safety over my head. It was his *modus operandi,* and I was becoming used to it by now.

I look back at Levi.

"Take me to Malcolm," I say more stridently.

Levi rolls his eyes at me. "Oh, very well. As you wish, my little dove."

He grabs me roughly by the arm and phases me into the small confines of a prison cell.

The white walls of the cell are all too familiar to me. I can remember staring at them for hours on end when I was accused of being a traitor to the crown, a crime my father confessed to in order to spare my life. But, these four walls aren't completely white anymore. Patterns of splattered blood cover them in an abstract fashion. To anyone who might not know better, it would almost look like some sort of perverse form of art. Unfortunately, I wasn't naive to the evils of the world. I knew exactly who the blood had come from.

Malcolm hangs suspended in mid-air in the center of the room by an invisible force field, just as I was earlier. His eyes are closed, and his head hangs so low his chin is resting against his bare chest, but I can see his face clearly enough. His silky black hair is a ragged mess of uneven lengths thanks to Levi's rather childishly given haircut. I stare at Malcolm looking for any evidence of where all the blood on the walls could have come from. I can't see any signs of torture on the front of him, and I know that can only mean one thing.

I walk around Malcolm, steeling myself for what I might

find, but nothing could have prepared me for what I see.

Levi used his lightning whip like a master flogger, punishing Malcolm for some phantom crime. Yet, the only crime Malcolm committed was kissing me, loving me, giving himself entirely to me.

I refuse to give into the tears that threaten to reveal the pain I feel as I look at Malcolm. I know Levi is watching me closely, and I won't give him an inch of satisfaction by showing my grief openly. I feel sure he would gain pleasure in my torment and such an emotion is something I will never willing give him. As I study what his lightning whip has done to Malcolm's back, I know for a fact Malcolm can't die, or at least not by Levi's hands.

His skin has been flayed completely away only leaving the remnants of shredded muscles hanging loosely from the completely exposed bones of his spine, ribs and shoulder blades. I literally stand and watch as Malcolm's lungs take in ragged breaths. The small flame of hatred that first ignited the moment Levi phased into Malcolm's workshop now grows to monstrous proportions. It explodes inside my chest like a bomb, all but consuming me.

I phase over to Levi, my hands burst into blue flames without me even having to think about it. I grab him by the front of the neck with one hand, slinging his body up against the blood stained wall at his back. The look of fear which enters his eyes isn't enough to soothe my rage. The only thing that will satisfy my anger is his death.

"I'm going to kill you for what you did to him!"

"You wouldn't dare," Levi manages to strangle out. "If you kill me, you kill Lucas and your father. Can you really live with both of their deaths on your conscience? Do you think Malcolm will still love you after you kill his son?"

"I'm going to kill you," I tell him, shoving my face into his to make sure he hears my words clearly. "Then I'm going to end the life of that changeling who killed Eliza before she even has a chance to look in Lucas's direction, and I'll find my father on my own."

"You'll never find him," Levi says with so much certainty I know he's telling the truth. "And you'll never get to Lucas before the changeling kills him. As soon as you phase home without me by your side, she'll snap his neck."

"I think I can get to her before she even has a chance to look in Lucas' direction," I say, squeezing his neck tighter. "I'm feeling extremely motivated at the moment."

"Anna…don't…"

Only Malcolm's voice can break through the haze of hatred I feel for Levi in that instant. I want to kill him so badly I can taste his death on my tongue like a sweet confection, tantalizing and addictive.

I squeeze tighter.

"Anna…"

Just one thought and Levi would be dead, gone forever from this world.

"Anna…please…"

I tighten my hold on Levi's throat and pull him away from the wall only to throw him as hard as I can against the far wall in the room. The force of the blow is enough to knock him out.

I look up at Malcolm and find him watching me. The pain in his eyes isn't just from the physical torture he's had to endure. I know it's also from the fact that Levi has Lucas. It makes me face the fact that the changeling probably could end his life before either of us could react.

"Malcolm," I say. His name comes out sounding more like a strangled sob because I can't hold in my sorrow over his pain any longer. I walk to him wanting to bring him comfort. Then, I do something that I've never done before. I walk on air.

It's almost like there's an invisible ramp leading from me to Malcolm. He watches me as I float up to him and somehow manages an almost smile.

"I wondered if you would be able to do that," he says before taking in a ragged breath that appears more painful than replenishing.

When I reach him, I cup his face between the palms of my hands and rest my forehead against his, needing the physical contact to prove to myself that he's still alive.

"Oh, Malcolm," I say through a heavy sigh, telling of how helpless I feel. "Why didn't you let me kill him?"

"Not yet," Malcolm says, closing his eyes like my touch is easing the burden of his pain even if it's only a little bit. "He has Lucas and Andre. We need him alive. For now…"

I pull my head away, and Malcolm opens his eyes to look into mine. Mingled with the pain I see in his gaze is his love for me. I want to weep but know that would serve no purpose for either of us. I need to stay strong because I have people whose lives depend on me.

"He deserves to die for what he's done to you," I argue, feeling my hatred for Levi completely burn a small hole in my soul that can never be repaired.

"And he will when the time is right, but that time isn't now. You have to do what he wants."

"So I should find the other Watchers and just give Levi the

princes?" I ask, thinking there has to be a better plan.

"We don't have any other choice. I won't let him kill Lucas."

"Neither will I," I say, resigned to the fact that Malcolm is right. "And I won't let him kill my father."

"Then get the princes and make the deal. We'll worry about the consequences later. Just save our son."

The hate inside my heart is tempered slightly by Malcolm's declaration. I know for certain with his last two words that he thinks of us as a family now.

"I'll protect our son with my life," I promise him. "And he's safe for now. He's being kept at my house here in Cirrus. Millie and Vala will look after him for us."

Malcolm sighs in relief which causes him to grimace slightly. It makes me wonder why he isn't screaming out in pain from his injuries.

"How can I help you?" I ask. "Would a healing wand work on your wounds?"

Malcolm shakes his head. "No. You can't heal wounds made by his whip with that sort of thing. I'll just have to heal on my own."

"Then...your body is able to regenerate?"

Malcolm nods slightly. "It'll take some time, but I'll heal. Don't worry about me."

"That's never going to happen," I tell him, rubbing my thumbs across his cheekbones, feeling completely powerless. "I can't help but worry about someone I love so much."

Malcolm turns his head slightly and kisses the center of one of my palms. He leans his cheek back against that hand and says, "I love you too, but you need to stay focused on what you have to do."

"I'll get it done," I promise him. "I'll make the deal and then we'll sort things out from there."

I lean in and rub the side of my face against his softly.

"I want to kiss you," I whisper.

"Then kiss me, Anna," he urges.

"But what if it makes you lose consciousness again?"

"Then it would be a blessing."

Without hesitation, I press my lips against Malcolm's and pray my kiss has the same affect it did the first time. I hear Malcolm sigh in relief as I caress his lips with mine gently, showing him physically how much I treasure him. I enjoy the sensation until I feel his head completely fall forward, and I know the poison has worked once again. It brings me small comfort knowing my kiss can have such an effect on the love of my life, but at least he can get some rest now while his body heals itself.

"How touching," I hear Levi say snidely beside me. "Really, I feel like I might actually have an emotional moment or something. Oh, wait…no…I think that might just be gas."

I feel my body descend and have no way of knowing how I was able to fly in the first place. Though, I do remember Jered telling me it was one of Jess' gifts from Michael. I have to assume since she's one of my ancestors that's where it comes from. As I face Levi, I find myself desperately trying to reign in my temper.

"If I see that you've laid another hand on him when we make the trade, I promise that when I *do* kill you your death will not be a quick one."

"So many threats, Anna," Levi says with a shake of his head like he's disappointed in me. "Didn't Andre teach you any manners at all?"

"Release Malcolm from this force field."

"And why would I do that?"

"Because if you don't I'm going to smash your face in!"

Levi raises one hand to his jaw line. "The adorable little

27

face of your beloved Auggie? You would defile his body like that, my little dove?"

"You're not Auggie. And you really don't want to test my patience right now."

Levi smiles. "Such a little spit fire you are. I'm going to enjoy taming you, wife."

"I only promised Malcolm that I wouldn't kill you, Levi. I didn't promise anything short of that."

Levi rolls his eyes at me.

"Such theatrics," he says, turning to face the wall behind him. He waves his hand over it to bring up a holographic control panel. After he enters in a code, Malcolm falls to the floor. I go to him and roll him onto his stomach, turning his face to the side so he can breathe easier. I lean down and kiss him on the lips one more time, hoping it keeps him unconscious for a little while longer.

The floor of the prison cell is as cold as I remembered it being. Knowing Malcolm's hot blooded nature, I'm actually grateful for its coolness this time. I pray that it helps him heal faster.

Pray…

I close my eyes and pray to God.

I hear Levi take in a deep, sharp breath.

When I open my eyes, I see God standing across from me. I look up at him as my eyes cloud with tears.

"Help him," I beg. "I swear I won't ask for anything else, just help Malcolm this once."

God looks down at Malcolm. His eyes hold a sorrow only a parent can have when their child is in pain. He studies the damage Levi has done with his lightning whip, but He shakes His head at me.

"I can't interfere with the natural course of events, even when I want to," He tells me. "I'm sorry, Anna."

"Then what good are you?" I ask, feeling angry at God. "If you won't help us, what's the point of praying for you to come?"

"If I healed one person, I would have to heal every person in the world. Otherwise, it wouldn't be fair. Some people are simply meant to die, Anna. Malcolm will not die from these wounds. He will heal them on his own. I cannot interfere with the natural laws of the universe."

I knew he was right, but it didn't make it any easier to go along with.

God turns his attention to Levi.

Levi's shoulders seem to sink lower as he faces his father, but he tries to hold his head up a notch higher in a show of defiance.

"I suppose you're proud of yourself," God says to Levi. Slowly, He shakes His head at the prince of Hell. "But, I couldn't be more disappointed in you, Levi."

"I gave up caring about gaining your approval a long time ago, Father."

"You say that and yet you know you're lying."

Even I could tell that simple fact. In a way, I felt amazed that Levi still cared what God thought about him after all this time.

"The good thing about not being in your Heavenly host anymore is that I don't have to stand here and talk to you if I don't want to."

"No," God agreed. "You don't, my son."

Levi seems taken off guard by God's use of such an endearment, but quickly shakes it off before looking over at me.

"Gather up my brothers and meet me in the desert."

"Desert?" I ask, not understanding what he's talking about. "What desert?"

"Jered and the others will know where to go," Levi says

with a dismissive wave of his hand. "You have until 7am Cirrun time the day after tomorrow to bring them to me."

"And what happens if I can't make it in time?"

"Then I kill the boy!" Levi shouts irritably. "Just do what I tell you, Anna! And don't come back here to visit lover boy unless you want me to end Andre's life. I think you've had quite enough touchy feely time with him as it is."

Levi phases away leaving me alone with God and a mercifully unconscious Malcolm.

I look down at Malcolm's ravaged back.

"I don't want to leave him alone like this," I tell God.

"He won't be alone," God reassures me. "I'm always with him."

I stand to my feet and force myself to look away from Malcolm. Otherwise, I won't be able to leave.

"I won't let anyone hurt my family anymore," I tell God, feeling as though I should warn him that I might do things he won't approve of.

God nods.

"Do what you have to do, Anna," He says. "I know you'll make the right decisions in the end."

31

I take in a deep breath and phase.

I stand in what's left of the room I slept in at Malcolm's house in Lakewood. The house has been reduced to ash now. A few smoldering timbers lay haphazardly against one another marking the evidence of a once happy home. I scan the ground around my feet and breathe in a sigh of relief when I see what I came for.

I bend down and pick up my sword still sheathed in its baldric. Amazingly enough the leather of the baldric isn't damaged and neither is my sword. I remember Jered telling me that archangel Jophiel's vessel, JoJo Armand, had made the baldric to be resistant to fire.

I wipe the soot off of the baldric and slip it on my back, tightening the cinch of the belt around my waist.

I realize I should have asked Malcolm where Jered is, but in those moments with him, I wasn't too worried about it.

I know someone who can give me the information I need.

I just hope, for her sake, she's in the mood to talk willingly.

CHAPTER TWO

I phase to Celeste DuBois's red front door and kick it in. The door slams against the grand staircase inside, sliding down the glossy wooden steps until it comes to a rest against the polished oak floor inside the airy foyer. I probably should have knocked instead of barging in, but I'm really not in the mood to play nice. I pray Celeste answers my questions quickly. Otherwise, I fear what I might do to her in my current state of mind.

I could almost forgive her for betraying Malcolm and me to Levi. She was in love with Malcolm and having him shun her because of his feelings for me must have been devastating not only to her self-esteem but also to her heart. Jealousy was a powerful emotion I could understand. What I couldn't forgive was the fact that she placed Lucas' life in danger by telling Levi where to find us. He was an innocent in all of this, and his life should have never been placed in peril. Her selfish need for revenge could have cost Lucas his life. That, in my eyes, was unforgivable.

I stand within the now empty doorframe, cross my arms over my chest and wait. It takes less than a minute for the residents of the home to wake up and appear at the head of the staircase. The one I've come for is standing dead center among the gathering of scantily clad women, staring down at me with a look of surprise.

Celeste's face is clean of make-up which makes her appear younger in my opinion. Her long blonde hair is braided and hanging over one shoulder. She's wearing a full length, red velvet robe with white lace trim. Her eyes hold a worried look at my unexpected arrival. I'm sure she thought I would be in the hands of the emperor by now, safely tucked away in Cirrus where I couldn't reach her.

"You can't just barge into my home like this in the middle of the night!" She says to me rather indignantly. "We may be lowly down-worlders to you, but we do have some rights!"

"You should choose your words wisely when you speak to me, Celeste, and you should definitely watch your tone. Considering what you did, I could have you executed for treason. In case I need to remind you, I'm empress of these lands," I tell her. "That means I can pretty much do as I damn well please."

"You don't act like any empress I've ever seen," Celeste says scathingly, looking me up and down.

I smile. "I'm a new type of empress," I tell her. "More...hands on."

"Well, *your highness*, I would appreciate it if you left my home. Some of us have to work for a living. Not all of us are fortunate enough to have everything we want handed to us on a golden platter. Now, if you'll excuse me, I need to get some beauty sleep."

Celeste turns her back to me.

It's a colossal mistake.

I unfold my arms and run up the stairs. I say run, but it's more like I fly up them. I'm not even sure my feet ever actually touch a single step. Once I reach the top of the landing, I grab Celeste by her right shoulder and spin her around to face me. I don't completely have my strength under control because my anger is influencing my actions, and I end up spinning her around so hard she falls to the floor with a loud thump onto her backside. The breath is knocked out of her so it takes her a minute to recover enough to say something.

"What the *hell* do you think you're doing?" She demands, breaking my last strand of patience with her.

I grab her by the front of her robe and haul her up off the floor in one fluid motion. My strength surprises her and those around us, causing her girls to slowly back away from me.

Celeste looks at me, but the bravado she showed earlier is nowhere to be seen now.

"There's something different about you. You're more confident...more determined," she says to me, studying my face carefully. I see understanding enter her eye just before they well with tears. "I guess Malcolm told you how he feels about you. The love of a good man can make you feel like you can move mountains. At least, that's the way I felt when I thought he loved me."

Tears slide down Celeste's face, and I find myself pitying her. I know she doesn't deserve such an emotion from me, but I can't help but empathize with her plight. I know what it feels like to love a man but have him completely dismiss your feelings. In my case, Malcolm actually loved me even though he did everything in his power to hide that fact from me. In Celeste's case, he never loved her. Yet, she mistook his frequent visits to her for physical gratification as meaning that he did.

"I'm sorry he broke your heart," I tell her. "But, he was never yours to have, Celeste. He was always meant for me. You need to come to terms with that fact before you let your jealousy destroy what's left of your soul. You'll never be whole again if you let your contempt for him continue to tear you apart. How would you have felt if Lucas had been killed in the attack with the emperor's men? Did you really think you could live with yourself if that happened?"

"The emperor assured me no one would be hurt, least of all Lucas," Celeste says. I know she's telling the truth but have a hard time believing she would be so naïve.

"You had to know Malcolm wouldn't let me be taken without a fight," I tell her, making her face her dark side. "And I think if you're being honest with yourself, you thought he might be killed in the attack so neither one of us could have him."

Celeste squeezes her eyes shut, making her tears wash her cheeks with their salty trails.

"I was so angry," she admits. "I just wasn't thinking straight. I wanted to hurt him. I guess I didn't care who else got injured in the process." She opens her eyes. "Is Lucas all right? He wasn't harmed was he?"

"The emperor has him," I tell her, letting go of the front of her robe, some of my anger dissipating. "And I need your help to get him back."

"What can I do?"

"You knew where we were going after we left here. I need you to tell me where that is."

"Yes, you were on your way to Rory and Lora's house. They live in Baton Rouge."

"What's the quickest way for me to get there? I have to find Jered."

"You'll need to take the teleporter in New Orleans," she tells me.

"Do you have someone who can take me to New Orleans?"

Since it was somewhere I had never been to before, I couldn't simply phase there. The thought had occurred to me that I could phase to Barlow's underground city and use his teleporter, but I wasn't sure if Levi knew about his hideout. I refused to be the one to bring Cirrun forces to Barlow's doorstep and place his people in danger.

"I'll take you there myself," Celeste says. She turns to look at her girls. "Trisha and Madeline, get my buggy ready and be quick about it, no dawdling around like you usually do."

The two ladies quickly make their way down the stairs to do as they are told.

Celeste turns to look at me again. "I need to change my clothes. Are you hungry? I can have someone prepare you something to eat on the way there."

"No, I'm not hungry."

Celeste nods. I'm sure she understands the situation I'm in isn't very conducive to generating an appetite.

"I won't be long," she tells me, turning to walk down the hallway and enter what I presume is her bedroom.

I decide to wait downstairs for Celeste. She's true to her word and reappears less than ten minutes later.

She's dressed rather conservatively considering what she was wearing the first time I saw her when I came here with Malcolm. Her long, red skirted dress still retains the style of 19th century European clothing. The fitted top looks like a jacket with a silky, gold embroidered vest underneath. She slips on a pair of black leather gloves as she walks down the staircase. Her eyes glance in the direction of the door still lying across the lower portion of the steps.

"You're awfully strong for such a little thing," Celeste comments, sounding a bit amused. "The door was unlocked by the way. You really didn't have to kick it in."

"I wasn't in the mood to care," I tell her. "If you'd seen what I have today, I doubt you would have been either."

Celeste looks at me, and I can tell she wants to ask what it is I'm referring to but thinks better of it. I'm sure she knows anything that would make my mood so foul can't be good.

I hear the rattle of the buggy come to a stop outside the home. When I look out the empty spot where the door once was, I see a small black carriage hitched to a black horse.

Celeste and I walk out to the buggy just as the girls who made it ready for us get out of it.

Once we're seated, Celeste clicks her tongue and snaps the reins gently against the horse's rump to get it moving.

"How long will it take to get to New Orleans?" I ask her.

"Thirty minutes normally," she tells me. "But, I think I can get you there in twenty."

She gently flicks the reigns against the horse once more, causing it to pick up its pace.

As we travel down the dark country road, neither of us say a word. Celeste finally breaks the silence with a simple question.

"What did it feel like to have Malcolm tell you that he loves you?"

In spite of myself, I feel sorry for Celeste in that moment. My earlier anger at her has been fully replaced by pity now. I feel sorry for the woman because she gave her love to someone who never could have reciprocated her feelings. It was a fear I had when Malcolm seemed so resolute in denying how he felt about me. When I thought I would have to live the rest of my life without his love, it was like a crushing weight against my heart.

Celeste would never get the reprieve I did. She would always live with the knowledge that Malcolm belonged to someone else. That he gave all of himself to another woman. I very much doubt Malcolm will ever willingly see Celeste DuBois again. Knowing him, he would probably fear what he would do to her after she placed the lives of his son and the woman he loves in danger. Even I had a hard time controlling my temper when I first arrived at her house. I couldn't imagine Malcolm holding in his emotions very well. I think Celeste knew this. I think she knew deep down inside she would never be in the same room with Malcolm ever again. Perhaps she was asking me this question because through me she could at least know what it felt like to have Malcolm's unconditional love.

"It was like having a dream come true," I tell her. "It made me feel whole."

Celeste nods and averts her gaze away from me, returning her attention back to the moonlit road we're travelling down.

"Would you do something for me?" Celeste asks in a quiet voice.

"What?"

"Tell Malcolm that I'm sorry. I never thought Emperor Augustus was someone who would hurt an innocent child. He always seemed to be so kind. I guess you really don't know a person just by what the media tells you and what you see in videos."

Of course Celeste wouldn't know that the emperor wasn't actually Auggie anymore. She had no way of knowing that Levi had taken control of my best friend's body. It was a point I hadn't really considered until now.

"The emperor isn't exactly himself anymore," I say, not daring to tell her the complete truth. "You can't trust him."

Celeste nods. "Yes, I see that now." She looks over at me. "I guess the real question is, can we trust you? We all thought once you and Emperor Augustus took control of Cirrus that the two of you would help us down-worlders. Were we just deluding ourselves?"

"No, you weren't mistaken in your beliefs," I tell her. "But the emperor won't be the one who will be by my side to help fix things. Malcolm will be."

Celeste smiles, a tinge of sad acceptance on her face. "I always thought Malcolm was meant for greater things. I guess he just needed to find the right person to help him become the man he was always meant to be."

"We will help you," I promise her. "We will make things right. You have my word on that."

"I have no reason to trust you," she says, "but for some reason I do. I guess that's the mark of a true leader. You make people who have no reason to trust in your words believe what you say."

"I won't let you down."

Celeste nods, seeming to accept my promise.

The rest of the ride goes by in complete silence. I don't mind the quiet. I have nothing further to say to Celeste, and she obviously doesn't have any more questions she wants answered.

As we approach New Orleans, the city appears like a bubble of light floating within the dark night. I've never actually been in a down-world city before. My father never let me come to the surface with him when he visited here, though those occasions were few and far between.

Celeste maneuvers her buggy through the streets, and I silently observe the decaying city we travel through, taking in everything I can. Cirrun guards patrol along the sidewalks in pairs of two, making me wonder just how many of them are still human now that Levi is in control.

I notice some people huddled in darkened alleyways and near corners of buildings sleeping. I stare at them, not quite understanding why these people don't have homes to go to.

"New Orleans is better off than most of the cities down here," Celeste tells me, obviously noticing my confusion at finding even a few homeless. "Malcolm has spent a lot of his own money trying to keep people here fed and housed. Some people take his offer of kindness and some are just too proud to accept hand-outs."

"Fed?" I ask. "Why wouldn't there be enough food to eat?"

"A lot of what's produced here in the down-world goes directly to Cirrus. The rest of it is used in trade with the other cloud cities. Malcolm has always tried to keep as much as he can down here for us to use, but Empress Catherine seemed to prefer trading our food for things she wanted for herself."

"That will change," I tell Celeste. "I have no intention of living off the backs of hard working people just to stuff the royal coffers."

"Just don't let your newly given powers go to your head," Celeste advises. "A lot of people in powerful positions sometimes start out wanting to help those in need, but change their minds when they realize how much work is involved. Sometimes, it's easier to just let things stay the same."

"I wasn't built that way," I assure her. "I don't back down
44

from a fight. I win."

Celeste looks at me, and I see realization enter her eyes.

"You're exactly who Malcolm has always needed," she says to me, even though it sounds more like she's speaking out loud to herself than telling me something I need to know. "I could never be the person he needs to help him save this world the way he's always wanted to, but you can."

"It's what we were meant to do together," I say, fully realizing how Malcolm and I fit into God's plan for the world. "And we will find a way to do it."

"Of that," Celeste says, "I have no doubt."

Celeste brings the buggy to a stop in front of a five story building which doesn't look anything like the brick and mortar structures we've passed so far. This building is made out of steel and glass, standing out as gaudy beacon of wealth amongst the crumbling city surrounding it.

"I'm sure you won't have any trouble getting help inside," Celeste says.

"Once I get to Baton Rouge, where should I look for Jered? Do you think he would be at Rory and Lora's home even though they aren't there?"

"I would try the home Malcolm has in the city first. It's on

Highland Road. The guards at the teleporter station in Baton Rouge should be able to take you there."

I feel my forehead crinkle at this new information.

"How many homes does Malcolm have down here?" I ask, knowing of at least three now.

"He has one in every major city here in the down-world."

"I knew he was rich, but I had no idea he could afford that much."

"Oh sweetie," Celeste says, like she's just now realizing how little I understand about the politics of the down-world, "he doesn't buy them. They're given to him."

"Why?"

"Because Malcolm is like a king down here. I thought you knew that."

It makes me think of what Levi said to Malcolm at the party the night before our wedding. He asked Malcolm if he thought of himself as the king of the down-world. Malcolm didn't seem to think so, but I now know how the down-worlders actually feel about him. It's simply further proof to me that God does indeed have big plans for us. Maybe placing the world back on the correct path is that something he said only I could accomplish.

I step out of the buggy and turn back around to face Celeste.

"Thanks for bringing me here."

"You can thank me by keeping your promise to change things," Celeste says. "And don't forget to tell Malcolm how sorry I am for what I did."

"I'll make sure he knows."

Celeste nods and flicks the reigns in her hands again to set her horse on its way down the lane.

I turn to face the Cirrun station and walk towards it to start the next leg of my journey, feeling even more determined to do what needs to be done. Nothing is more important to me than putting my family back together, and nothing will prevent me from making it happen.

CHAPTER THREE

As soon as I walk into the station, the guards standing just inside the entrance bend down on one knee before me with their heads bowed in my direction showing complete reverence. I count seven of them in all within the rather sterile antechamber. I decide then and there that one of the things I will do, when everything is said and done, is change any room that is solid white to a different color.

"Empress Annalisse," one guard says, daring to lift his bowed head to meet my gaze. "We weren't told you would be visiting us this evening."

"I need a teleport to Baton Rouge," I tell him not seeing any reason to beat around the bush about why I'm here unannounced. "And I need it now."

The guard immediately rises to his feet.

"Of course, your grace. Please, let me escort you to our teleport pad."

The other guards remain kneeling, and I say nothing to

make them change their position. Once I'm gone, it will be business as usual here for them, and they'll be able to tell their families and friends that they saw the Empress of Cirrus in the flesh that night. It was something I still wasn't used to. I didn't like being placed on a pedestal but, then again, it was that pedestal which would allow me to fix the world I lived in. For so few to live in luxury and have anything they wanted at their finger-tips, while so many went hungry and were forced to work for scraps simply wasn't right. If you worked hard, you should be compensated for it. If you did nothing, then you should reap the rewards of such a lackadaisical life as well. Things shouldn't be handed to you just because of who you are or where you live. You should have to work and contribute to society in some way to have things which made your life easier.

The guard escorts me to a glass room similar to the one Barlow has in his underground hide out.

"Please step on the teleporter pad, Empress Annalisse," the guard instructs.

I step up on the octagonal white pad and watch as he manipulates the control panel.

"Please give my best regards to the emperor," the guard says just as I teleport away.

I arrive in a room almost identical the one I just left. The only difference is the guard.

"Empress!" The guard says in surprise, stepping away from his control panel to kneel on the floor before me.

I'm really getting tired of having people kneel in front of me all the time. I decide that's something that needs to be changed as well.

"Please rise," I tell him. "I need someone to escort me to Overlord Devereaux's home here in the city."

"Yes, Empress Annalisse. I'm new here so I don't know where it is, but I'm sure we can find someone who does. Please, follow me."

I follow the guard out of the room. We pass a few more guards in the hallway, but the quarters are too cramped for them to fall to their knees to show their undying loyalty to me. Though, when we reach the front of the station, the five guards standing there fall to their knees immediately.

"Gentleman," I say to them all, feeling slightly frustrated, "I never want to see you kneel in front of me again. Is that understood?"

They all look up at me like I just spoke in a foreign language.

"If you must do something to show your respect to me," I

tell them, "simply bow at the waist. The kneeling thing may be what Empress Catherine desired from you, but I assure you it is not something I want done every time I enter a room. Is that understood?"

Slowly, the guards stand to their feet, still looking unsure about my order.

"Yes, Empress," they all say in staggered intervals.

"Now, I need someone to take me to Overlord Deveraux's home on Highland Road. Who knows where it is?"

All of the guards raise their hands, and I pick one at random to take me there. I could care less who my escort is as long as I get where I need to be.

The guard quickly comes to stand beside me and places his hand on my shoulder. Before I know it, I'm standing in front of a large home designed in the same style as the one Malcolm had in Lakewood.

"You can leave," I tell the guard.

Without question, he teleports away.

I don't bother to knock on the door. I simply turn the knob and find it unlocked. When I step inside, I shout, "Jered!"

Jered suddenly phases in front of me before I can take a

second step inside the house.

"Anna!" He says, giving me a brief hug. He pulls back and looks down at me like he's baffled by my presence. "What are you doing here alone? Where are Malcolm and Lucas?"

"Levi has them," I say, finding the words hard to say because I feel as though I've failed to keep them safe. "We need to talk."

I tell Jered everything I know. He listens intently and doesn't interrupt me. The only real emotion he shows during my tale is a small smile when I tell him Malcolm declared his love to me and kissed me. After that, however, he simply listens to the horrific events which transpired because of that first kiss.

"What should we do, Jered?" I ask. "Malcolm said to give Levi what he wants, but I'm not sure he was in the best mental state to make that decision."

"I understand your concerns," Jered says gravely, "but Malcolm is right. We should do what Levi wants and worry about the consequences later. This isn't the first time an innocent's life has been used against us to get the princes back. But, we've always managed to recapture them in the end."

"This isn't the first time?" I ask.

"No," Jered tells me, "though in the past we've been able to keep the demand down to one prince at a time. We've never had to give them all up at once."

"Maybe I can take their seals before we hand them over," I suggest.

"I don't think that will work," Jered says hesitantly.

"Why?"

"Because I think you will have to take each of their lives in order to retrieve their seals, Anna."

"Just because I killed Amon and got his seal that way doesn't necessarily mean I'll have to kill them all. I might be able to take them another way."

"I understand your reluctance to slay them," Jered says, "but I want you to brace yourself for the real possibility that it's the only way you'll be able to retrieve the seals."

"Then maybe it's better to have the princes free," I reply. "I don't mind killing if it's in a fair fight. I'm not sure I can do it if they're still in stasis. That's too much like murder."

"Or a justifiable execution," Jered says gently. "The princes have done things that would make you sick to your stomach if I told you about them, Anna. So don't sit there and think that they deserve a fair fight. They don't. They need to be put down like the rabid dogs they are."

Jered's words seem to have so much venom in them that it compels me to ask, "Did you see them do these things? You seem so passionate that they not be given a chance. It's like you judged and weighed their crimes a long time ago and found them past the point of saving."

Jered averts his gaze and looks out one of the windows in the living room we're in. A minute passes by before he says, "I helped them do some of those things, Anna. I'm no saint either, but at least I finally realized I was wrong. They never will."

"How do you know that?"

Jered looks back at me. "Because they're pure evil. There's no way any of them can ever be redeemed."

"Even Lucifer?"

Jered stares at me for a moment as if he's choosing his next words carefully.

"Lucifer had his chance to be forgiven a long time ago. Jess came very close to making him believe he could ask for our father's forgiveness. He chose not to ask for it then. And after he met Amalie..."

Jered falls silent as if the memory of my mother pains him too much to go on.

"What about my mother, Jered?" I ask. "Did she get close

to making him ask for forgiveness too?"

"I believe he wanted to change for her. He truly did love your mother, and if she hadn't died…maybe he would have asked our father for his forgiveness. But, I guess we'll never know for sure."

"Did he blame me for her death?" I ask, some part of me needing to know if Lucifer abandoned me because my entry into this world killed the woman he loved.

"No," Jered tells me. "He didn't blame you for her death. He blamed himself. He felt like his love for her was what killed her."

"Did he even offer to raise me himself?"

"No."

"Then why did he leave me?"

"It was probably one of the most unselfish things I've ever seen him do," Jered admits with a certain amount of reluctance. "Of anyone, Lucifer isn't blind to his own faults and what he is. He knew that if he was the one who raised you, odds were you would become as jaded as he is. Lucifer couldn't stand the thought of corrupting Amalie's last gift to the world with his own hatred and anger. He wanted you to have a better life than the one he knew you would have with him."

"Are you telling me he loves me?" I ask disbelievingly.

"I think he loves you as much as he's able to feel that emotion," Jered says. "And I know first-hand that he can love very deeply. I saw that side of him when he was with your mother."

I swallow hard, not knowing what to say about this new information. But, Lucifer isn't part of my problem at the moment. I stand from my seat on the sofa.

"We should get to work," I say, dismissing the conversation about Lucifer, at least for now. I need to keep my concentration focused. "We need to contact the other Watchers and make sure they know the plan. How do we get in touch with them?"

"We'll have to go to each of them in person," Jered says. "There's no way to safely send them a message and keep their locations from being discovered by Levi."

"How long will that take?" I ask, not feeling very patient about getting things settled before our deadline.

"We have plenty of time, Anna," Jered reassures me. "All we have to do is go to Barlow's and use his teleporter. That way we can keep our travels secret from Levi."

"But why don't we just phase to each of them?" I ask. "Surely that would be faster."

"Faster, but not safer," Jered says gently. "They each have their own lives they want to keep protected, Anna. I understand your urgency. I feel it too, but Malcolm wouldn't want us to jeopardize the lives they've built for themselves just because we were impatient. We have plenty of time to do what Levi wants. Trust me. I want Malcolm and Lucas back just as much as you do. They're my family too."

I suddenly feel guilty. "I know, Jered. I'm sorry. I just thought you guys had a better system set up. Like something for emergencies. For instance, how did you all know to come together and rescue me from Levi after the wedding reception?"

"We were already in Cirrus for your coronation," Jered tells me. "None of us wanted to miss you being crowned empress. We've all waited so long for you to take the throne that we wanted to feel like we were a part of the celebration too. Malcolm left the ceremony early to round us all up because he said he saw something in Levi's eyes that told him he would try to do something to you after the wedding."

"How could he tell? Levi always looks like he wants to do something evil to me."

Jered chuckles at my remark.

"Malcolm just sensed it. Or perhaps he just couldn't bear the thought of Levi trying to consummate the marriage. I'm not sure. But, he was pretty adamant that we get you out of Cirrus that night as quickly as we could. We searched the royal rooms while the wedding reception was taking place to see if we could find anything that Levi might use against you, but we came up empty handed."

"He coated the wine glass with a sedative."

"Yes, we learned that after the fact. As soon as we knew you and Levi were in the rooms we put our plan into motion to get you the hell away from him as quickly as we could."

"You don't know how much I appreciate all of you helping me that night," I say. "Can you believe he wanted me to have his baby?"

The thought makes me shiver involuntarily in revulsion.

"I'm sure that thought is still in the back of his mind," Jered warns. "But, Malcolm will never let that happen. He would tear Levi apart himself before he could ever lay a hand on you."

I can't help but smile at the imagery in my mind of such a thing. I'm not sure if it's Malcolm's protective side that brings a small bit of joy to my heart or the thought of Levi dead which causes me the most pleasure. The happiness doesn't last long though because that image is soon replaced with the memory of Malcolm and his ravaged back.

"I'm going to kill Levi one day, Jered. I can't let him live after the things he's done to the people I love."

"And I won't stop you," Jered tells me. "But don't let your need for vengeance rule your actions, Anna. Hatred will darken your heart faster than anything else in this world and that isn't who you are. You're better than that. Never lose sight of who you are and what you were born to do."

"I feel pretty confident ending Levi's life is something I am meant to do," I say with confidence. "But, don't worry. I won't lose sight of who I am. I won't do anything that would make my father think less of me."

Jered nods like he's satisfied with my answer. "Then let's get started."

He holds his hand out to me, and I place mine into his.

"What about your friends?" I ask Jered. "Do you need to contact them to let them know what's going on?"

"After we get Malcolm and Lucas back, I'll contact Rory and Lora. They don't need to be placed in any more danger than they already have been."

Jered phases us to the exterior entrance of another teleporter station in the middle of a city. I assume it's the station Barlow's teleporter pad is siphoning its energy from. It doesn't matter that Levi knows we phased here. He would have known we were here anyway even if we used the teleporter in Baton Rouge.

"Follow me," Jered whispers, walking along the sidewalk in front of the station and turning down a dark alley beside it.

The alley is a dead end, and I begin to wonder where it is Jered is taking me until he stops beside a metal disk in the cement walkway.

Jered bends down on one knee and sticks his middle finger in a hole in the disk, easily lifting it up.

"Go down the ladder," he instructs me.

I walk over to the hole and peer down to see what's there. The heat and stench emanating from the bowels of the lower level isn't very pleasing.

"Do I have to?" I ask.

Jered grins. "Yes, empress. I'm afraid you'll need to get your shoes dirty during this little part of our adventure together."

I smile at Jered. "Not necessarily."

I float into the air and hover over the hole.

Jered's jaw opens slightly in shock which makes me giggle. I almost feel guilty for laughing. The memory of Malcolm's injuries soon invade the small bit of happiness I have to bring me crashing back to the task at hand. I lower myself down the hole and hover over the waste water within what must be a section of the sewage system beneath the city.

Jered makes his way down the ladder and covers the hole back up before descending almost to the bottom.

"Wait!" I tell him before he steps into the smelly water flowing through the large drainage tunnel. "Can I carry someone while I'm flying?"

"Yes," Jered says.

I float over to him. "Then hold onto me and tell me where we need to go. I don't particularly want you trudging through this mess. There's no telling how long it would be before we could get the stench off of you."

Jered chuckles. "Good point."

I encircle Jered's waist with my arms, and he places his hands on my shoulders. With my strength, holding him to me is easy.

"Which way?" I ask.

Jered directs me through the maze of tunnels.

"Are you sure this is the safest way to get there?" I ask. "Can't they just use our heat signatures to follow where we go?"

"The heat generated from all the waste down here will mask our body heat. Plus there are displacers everywhere."

"Displacers?"

"They're meant to discourage people from staying in the tunnels."

"I would have thought the smell would do that."

Jered laughs. "Some people get desperate when it gets really cold on the surface and don't have anywhere else to go."

"What do the displacer do?"

"When you run into one of them, they transport you to another section of the tunnels. It's a good way to get lost and never find your way back out."

"So how are we going to get to where we need to go if we keep getting displaced?"

"Barlow and his people figured out that if you go through certain displacers in a particular order you can get to their hideout. That way we don't have to worry about anyone following us. They would have to know the exact sequence."

We travel through the tunnels and get teleported at least

ten times by the displacers before we come to a small platform which leads to a metal door on the side of one of the tunnels. Jered makes quick work at breaking the lock on the door and pushing it inward.

"I'm sure Barlow will charge us handsomely for breaking his door," Jered quips as we step inside the small cinderblock room the door was concealing.

"Why don't you like Barlow?" I ask Jered.

"It's not so much that I don't like him," he tells me. "It's more that I don't trust someone who will do whatever it takes to get something they want."

"Wouldn't that just make him tenacious?"

"Aggressively so," Jered replies. "I've known him to kill to obtain certain items."

"Has he ever killed an innocent?" I ask, having a hard time believing even Barlow would stoop so low.

"No, I wouldn't necessarily call the people he deals with innocent, but still, killing for profit just seems like the wrong reason to end a life."

The small room we're in also has a metal disk in the floor. Jered bends at the waist and lifts it up.

"This will lead us straight down to Barlow's teleporter room," he tells me.

The hole isn't big enough for me to carry Jered down with me too. So, I hover over the hole and descend into its black depths alone with Jered having to climb down the ladder behind me.

A small pin point of light at the bottom helps guide me straight to the bottom. Once we're there, I see that we've arrived in the tunnel which connects the room where the teleporter pad is and the tracks leading through the interior of the mountain.

Once Jered has made it down the ladder and to my side, I ask, "How are we supposed to contact Barlow?"

"There's a communicator inside the teleporter room," Jered says, already heading in that direction.

We step inside the glass room and Jered goes straight to the control panel on the glass pedestal. I watch as he manipulates the controls until he brings up a floating image of Barlow's head. The image looks so real it's a little off putting.

Barlow looks at Jered in surprise. "What on earth are you doing in my teleporter room, Jered?"

"I'm here with Anna," Jered informs him. "We need your help."

"I'll be right there," Barlow says without hesitation.

I watch as he turns away and his disembodied head disintegrates into flakes of light.

It doesn't take long before I hear the rattle of Barlow's cart as it rumbles down the tracks. Jered and I stay inside the teleporter room and wait for him to come to us.

Barlow smiles when he sees me, but there must be something about my expression that tells him we're not here on a social call.

"What's wrong?" He asks me. "What's happened to make you look so sad, Anna?"

I tell Barlow everything that's happened, making the story as short but informative as possible.

"That's some major bad luck. I'm so sorry, Anna," Barlow says, truly sympathetic to my plight. "Malcolm finally kisses you and all hell breaks loose because of it."

"Basically," I admit, feeling a bit humiliated by the whole situation.

"And you say you have trackers in your body that go off when the poison is released? Right after you kiss someone?"

I nod. "Yes, that's what I was told. It's how Levi found us in Lakewood."

Barlow looks thoughtful then turns to walk over to the control panel. He soon brings up the image of a young man I haven't met yet.

"Jake," Barlow says to the man, "bring me one of those local EMPs we got in the last trade."

"Sure thing, Barlow," the man says before his image fades.

"A local EMP?" Jered asks. "Do you think that will work?"

Barlow shrugs. "It's worth a try."

"EMP?" I ask, having no clue what they're talking about.

"Electromagnetic pulse," Barlow tells me. "We just bartered for some that will knock out any electronic devices in a foot radius. I'm guessing the little trackers inside you are electronic and not organic ones."

"Why do you think their electronic?" Jered asks, sounding genuinely interested in the answer.

"Electronic nanites can send out a clearer signal than organic ones. The frequency they transmit at is stronger thus giving them a longer range. If Levi was able to detect their signal all the way in Cirrus when they went off, then they pretty much have to be electronic and not organic."

"So your EMP will be able to disable them?" I ask, hoping

this is where Barlow is going with his explanation.

"Yes," he says. "It should. Though, I'm not sure what to do about the poison. I think that will just have to wear off on its own with a little more time."

"I don't suppose you know how long that will take?" I ask hopefully.

Barlow shakes his head. "I have no idea. But, since you said you had to be injected with it once a week, I wouldn't think there should be that much left in your system by now. I would give it a couple more days before you tried to kiss anyone else. Though, I'm sure the reward of your soft lips would be well worth a little cat nap."

I shake my head in exasperation at Barlow. He just grins at me, completely unashamed.

"I'm taken," I tell him. "My heart and body belong to Malcolm."

"Well, if you ever change your mind, you know where to find me," Barlow says with a cheeky grin and wink.

"I can assure you my mind will never change."

Barlow shrugs. "Can't blame a guy for trying."

"No, but Malcolm would probably kill you if you ever tried

to kiss Anna," Jered says with certainty. "Though, he would have to beat me to it."

"You guys are always *way* too serious," Barlow tells Jered. "Can't a guy just joke around with a lovely lady without there being any dire consequences involved?"

"Not when the lady is the Empress of Cirrus and the soul mate of a man who would have no problem at all ripping your head from your shoulders and dumping your body in the nearest ocean for the attempt," Jered says. "Plus, she's family to me and under my protection as well."

Barlow lifts his hands in the air like he surrenders. "Fine, I'll stop making passes at the lovely Anna. I wouldn't want to cause an international incident or inadvertently destroy the universe because I tried to flirt with her."

"Good," Jered says, satisfied with Barlow's withdrawal from flirtation. "I'm glad we've come to a mutual understanding."

I hear the rattle of another cart on the tracks in the tunnel. The young man Barlow instructed to bring the EMP runs into the teleporter room breathing heavily from the exertion.

"Here you go, Barlow," Jake says, handing Barlow a slim black box.

Jake looks in my direction and bows to me at the waist,

"Hello, Empress Annalisse."

I smile. "Hello, Jake."

He grins, looking a little shy at my use of his name so casually.

Barlow slides the lid of the metal box up. In its interior, lies a small silver disk as thin as a wafer. Embedded in its center is a glossy black button.

"It's pretty simple to turn on," Barlow tells me. "All you have to do is press the black button. Just make sure you do it somewhere that doesn't have any electrical devices within ten feet of you, unless you purposely want to ruin them forever."

He slides the box's lid back down and hands it to me.

"I hope it works for you," Barlow says.

"Me too. Thank you, Barlow."

"We'll need to use your teleporter two more times," Jered tells Barlow. "We'll do what we did this time and come down here the back way."

"I'll leave Jake here to help you," Barlow says. "He can get you wherever you need to go."

Jered gives Barlow the coordinates of our first destination.

"Where are we going first?" I ask Jered, as we stand beside one another on the teleport pad.

"Dublin, Ireland. Desmond lives there."

"Ireland is part of the Stratus controlled lands, right?"

"Yes," Jered says, a hitch of hesitation in his voice. "I feel like I should warn you before we get there that the down-world in other parts of the world aren't like they are here, Anna."

"How are they different?"

"They're not nearly as wealthy."

Considering what I saw in New Orleans, I have to ask, "How in the world can they have less? What I saw in New Orleans was disgraceful."

"It gets worse," Jered says. "There are rulers who care even less for their down-worlders. Catherine might have seemed selfish and a bit tyrannical, but she was more generous than most of the royal families."

"Are the two of you ready?" Barlow asks us.

"Yes," Jered says.

"As ready as I can be," I reply.

"Safe travels to you both then," Barlow says before

activating the teleporter and sending us on our way.

Jered's words worry me. I've always known the down-world was in dire straits, but I never knew just how desperate those living in it were in need of the basic necessities. It makes me even more determined to change things for the better. And I have no doubt in my mind that I will make it happen.

CHAPTER FOUR

Dense fog envelopes us upon our arrival. The air all around is so thick with mist I feel as though I just stepped into the center of a cloud. If Jered wasn't standing right beside me, I feel sure we would have lost sight of one another. The loud screech of seagulls in the distance lets me know we must be near a coast line.

"Why is this fog so thick?" I ask him.

"It's not entirely fog," Jered says, looking over at me like he thought I would already know what we're standing in.

"Then, what is it?"

"Camouflage mostly," he says. "Each cloud city is hidden from the down-worlder's view by an artificially produced cloud mass."

"I wasn't aware of that," I admit.

I did know Dublin was centered beneath the cloud city of Stratus, but had no idea the cities below were encased in such an annoyingly heavy amount of murkiness.

"How is it made?" I ask.

"The water vapor given off by the propulsion system beneath the cloud cities produces it. From a distance, it looks like a large pillar of clouds stretching from the ground to the underside of the cities. It helps perpetuate the illusion that the cloud cities are completely surrounded by clouds. When you live in one, you're prevented from seeing the poverty below you. But, this fog is unusually thick. Mostly because it's early in the morning and the natural mist rolling in from the ocean is accentuating the affect. In a little while, it'll dissipate somewhat, at least enough to see through. The city normally just looks like it's surrounded by a thin haze."

"Where is Desmond's place?"

Jered turns around, and I see that we're actually standing in front of some brick steps leading up to somewhere beyond the white mass around us.

"Why don't you use the EMP before we go in?" Jered suggests.

I pull the disk from its box and depress the little black button.

"I didn't feel anything," I say. "How will we know it worked?"

Jered shrugs. "I guess we won't until you kiss someone again. Come on, let's go see if Desmond is up yet."

I follow Jered up the few steps which lead to a rather nondescript blue painted door with a small peep window near the top. Jered raps his knuckles against its center to announce to the occupant inside that he has visitors. We wait a minute but no one readily comes to the door. Jered knocks again.

"Hold onto your horses," I hear a man with a distinct Irish

brogue grumble from the interior. "I'm comin'!"

The door is quickly yanked inward, and I see Desmond again for only the second time in my life.

He's handsome with shoulder length, wavy brown hair and a day's growth of a beard on his face. I assume we just woke him up because he's only wearing a thin, blue cotton bathrobe cinched in at the waist and a pair of black pajama pants. His initial irritation is soon replaced with surprise. When his gaze settles on me, the surprise transforms into unexpected joy.

"Well," he says, running a hand through his hair, "I definitely didn't expect to see the two of you on my doorstep this morning."

Desmond continues to look at me, and I can see his elation falter somewhat after his own words sink in.

"What's wrong?" He asks, coming to the conclusion on his own that we wouldn't be there unless something wasn't right.

"As astute as ever, I see," Jered teases. "May we come in, Desmond?"

Desmond opens the door wider. "Of course. Sorry. Finding the two of you here has knocked me for a bit of a loop."

Jered and I walk into Desmond's home, and he closes and locks the door behind us.

Desmond's residence isn't exactly small but neither is it large in proportion. The interior is narrow with a small, sparsely furnished sitting area to the right of the foyer and a set of black painted stairs which go up one level but also down one level.

"Why don't we go to the kitchen," Desmond suggests. "You can tell me what's going on while I make some coffee. I'm completely useless until I've had at least one cup to wake me up this early in the morning."

Jered turns to me. "When was the last time you ate?"

"Last night at supper," I tell him as my memories quickly backtrack through the events of the night before.

Right after we ate the sandwiches Malcolm prepared for us to eat, Lucas crawled onto my lap and promptly fell asleep. After we put him to bed, Malcolm and I played chess in his study since I lost our bet that I could cook a decent meal. I stop the memories there because I don't want to relive what happened next in that room. The heartache I felt when I told Malcolm I was letting him go is still too fresh. I skip ahead to a happier memory when I was in Malcolm's workshop, and he practically slung the door off its hinges to find me and declare his true feelings. It was the first time he appeared to me just like Desmond and Jered always have, glowing with their devotion.

"Come on then," Desmond says to me with a small grin. "I

can scramble eggs as good as any master chef. It'll fix you up right as rain."

"Honestly, I'm not very hungry," I admit.

"You need to eat," Jered says, sounding strangely similar to my papa in that moment. "You need to keep your strength up. We have no way of knowing what Levi has in store for us. You need to be ready for anything."

Reluctantly, I nod. I know he's right but maintaining an appetite when my stomach is in so many knots is impossible. All I can think about is Malcolm and Lucas, not to mention my papa, Millie, and Vala. They're all in the hands of a maniac, and there's nothing I can,do to get them back safely except give Levi what he wants.

We follow Desmond down the stairs to the lower level of his home.

The kitchen is the only room on this level. There isn't much in the way of appliances except for an old, black wood burning iron stove, a small unpainted table with four chairs around it, and a small sink in the middle of some cabinetry on the outer wall. There is only one door which seems to lead outside to an alley way. Double lines of thin rope hang from wall to wall on one side of the room and are dotted with Desmond's laundry. While Jered and I sit down at the table, Desmond snatches two pairs of underwear hanging from the line and quickly stuffs them into a drawer. I wonder if he thinks I didn't see him do it and have to smile at his show of modesty.

"So tell me what's happened," Desmond says, grabbing what looks to me like a small silver pitcher.

As Jered tells Desmond what's happened so far and why we're here, I watch Desmond make his coffee. He pulls out a silver basket sitting on a metal stem attached to a flat base. He takes the lid off the basket and reaches for a small, white porcelain container on the counter and scoops out tablespoons of coffee grounds from it, dumping them into the basket. He takes the container to the sink and fills it with water then puts the contraption back inside the silver pitcher. After he places it on the stove, he sits down at the table with us and listens to the rest of what Jered has to say.

Desmond sits back in his chair and crosses his arms over his chest after Jered is finished with his story.

"Well," Desmond says, "I can't say I like it much, but I don't think we have any choice in the matter. They're not worth sacrificing our friends for. Maybe this is the way it was always meant to be. Since Anna can kill the princes, it does seem like the perfect time for a good old fashioned fight. They'll finally be put out of their misery once and for all."

"So you don't think I should just try to kill them all while they're in stasis?" I ask Desmond.

Desmond shakes his head and grins. "What fun would that be? And I don't think you're the type of person to kill just for killing's sake."

"If I'm only meant to take the seals from them and return them to Heaven, it might be the easiest way. I could be saving the lives of millions instead of just a handful."

"But you would lose yourself in the process," Desmond says with such certainty it's like he knows me as well as I do. "I don't think you're someone who can kill without being provoked into it. Unless you're telling me in a subtle way that you're truly a sociopath, and I just don't know it."

I let out a small laugh. "No, I can assure you I'm nothing like Levi. I would much rather kill them in a fair fight, if I have to kill them at all."

Desmond chuckles. "That's what I thought, lass."

Desmond looks over at the pot making his coffee. Dark brown water is now percolating up into the glass bubble on the lid. He stands from his chair, takes the pot from the stove and brings it over to the table. After grabbing three cups from a top cupboard, he sets them down in front of us and pours us each a cup of coffee.

"Do you happen to have any sugar?" I ask, never having

acquired a taste for black coffee without something sweet added in to it.

"You might as well have asked if I had any gold spun from straw lying around the house," Desmond says with a good natured grin. "Sugar is a precious commodity down here. As it is, I have to dry out my coffee grounds after I make a pot so I can reuse them a few times."

"I knew the Hallorans were stingy with their down-worlders," I say, "but is Stratus really worse than Cirrus?"

"You heard about the 'accident' right?" Desmond asks me.

"Yes," I say. "Auggie had to come for the double funeral of the emperor and empress of Stratus. It was a tragedy unheard of among the royals."

"It wasn't an accident," Desmond informs me. "I don't have any proof, but I can tell you that Lorcan Halloran orchestrated his parents' untimely demise so he could assume the throne before they changed the law."

"Changed the law?" I ask. "Which law?"

"That only a male heir can ascend to the throne. They wanted to make it so that the eldest child would be the one to take control. I think they both knew Lorcan is off his blooming rocker."

"Too bad they weren't able to do it before they died," I say.

"His older sister is definitely more stable than Lorcan is. The few times I've met her I always felt comfortable around her."

"Kyna Halloran is a rare jewel," Desmond agrees. "How she came from the loins of that family is beyond me. Though, most everyone assumes her mother had an affair with the general of their army. He has the same flaming red hair and green eyes as she does. Plus, she's never displayed the same greed and selfishness of her parents or her brother. Speaking of Kyna," Desmond looks over at Jered, "have you been to see Brutus yet?"

Jered shakes his head. "No, not yet. You're the first one we came to see. Why do you ask?"

Desmond holds up an index finger and tilts it as if telling us to wait just a moment. He runs up the stairs to the second level and returns posthaste with a small tin box.

He hands the box to Jered and says, "Give this to Brutus and tell him he owes me one."

Jered flips the lid of the box open and looks inside. "A neural memo?"

"It's the last message Kyna sent thanking me for what I'm doing down here."

Jered still looks puzzled. "And why would Brutus need such a thing?"

"Because our friend thinks he's found his soul mate."

"His soul mate?" I ask, finding this bit of news interesting. "How does he know? When did he see her?"

"He saw her at your coronation," Desmond says while he walks to the back door and opens it. He reaches down beside it, and I hear the rattle of a chain and the distinctive creak of something metallic being opened. Desmond soon brings in a basket containing a few perishable items of food. I assume he's left them out to keep them cold since I see no evidence of a preserver in his home. Among the items in the basket are a dozen eggs with tan shells.

"Did Kyna see Brutus?" Jered asks, sounding intrigued by this new development as well.

Desmond shakes his head. "No. He was going to introduce himself at the reception, but since we weren't able to attend, he missed his opportunity."

"I'll make sure he gets to meet her," I tell them. "When we have time, I'll introduce them myself. I owe all of you so much. It's the least I can do for him."

"You don't owe us anything," Jered tells me. "I think I can speak for us all when I say we've felt honored to look after your family for all this time. There were probably things we could have handled better in the last thousand years, but overall I think we did what needed to be done."

"Still," I say, "I would love for all of you to find happiness, and if Brutus thinks Kyna is his soul mate, then there's nothing that I wouldn't do to bring the two of them together." I watch Desmond as he grabs a bowl from a cabinet. "Have you found anyone special yet, Desmond?"

"No one that would be soul mate material," he tells me, grabbing an egg out of the basket and cracking it against the counter top before splitting it apart and dumping the contents into the bowl. "But I have high hopes she'll be showing up any minute now."

I can't help but smile at the note of enthusiasm in Desmond's voice.

"And why do you think that?" I have to ask.

Desmond glances in my direction. "Because you're here, lass. Our long vigil is finally almost over. All we have to do now is help you retrieve the seals and our vows will be fulfilled."

"What about Daniel?" I ask. "Is he still waiting to meet the woman of his dreams?"

"Daniel's been married for about eight years now," Jered tells me. "He has four children."

"Four?" I ask in astonishment. "So he met his soul mate?"

Jered shakes his head. "No, he said Linn wasn't his soul mate, but he loves her all the same. Not everyone is lucky enough to find their soul mate. Sometimes people just fall in love and live out content lives with the person they've chosen. I feel sure when everything has been handled, Daniel will ask to become human to live out the rest of his life with Linn naturally."

"Have you thought about doing what Daniel did?" I ask Jered.

I hear Desmond chuckle.

"Jered is a hopeless romantic," Desmond says as he turns around to face us while whipping the eggs in the bowl with a fork. "He'll stay here another thousand years if it takes that long for him to find his one true love."

I look back at Jered and see a heightened hue of color dapple his cheeks.

"I just want to experience that kind of love," Jered says in his own defense. "I don't think there's anything wrong with that."

I place my hand over the one Jered has resting on the table.

"I don't blame you," I tell him. "I can't even compare the feelings I have for Malcolm to anything I've ever experienced before. You should wait if that's what your heart is telling you to do. I'm sure she's out there or, at the very least, will be born soon."

A small smile graces Jered's face at my understanding words.

I look back at Desmond. "And what about you? What are your plans when this is all over?"

Desmond shrugs his shoulders. "I haven't made up my mind yet."

"You've had a thousand years to decide," Jered teases amiably.

"I figure our father will let me know what he wants me to do next. No sense in worrying about something if he's already planned it out."

I can't argue with Desmond's logic. My life had pretty much been planned since the moment my soul was brought into this world. I still had a hard time wrapping my mind around such an idea. Yet, I knew God was telling me the truth when he said I was one of the first souls ever created. I just wish I could remember my time in Heaven.

After Will brought me back to life, he told me we had been playmates there. It was a time in my existence that I wanted to remember. Perhaps there was a reason I wasn't supposed to though. Malcolm did tell me that the living never felt comfortable in Heaven because it was a place they weren't meant to be. I knew I would have to go there one day to return the seals, and in the back of my mind, I wondered if I would be given the opportunity to finally meet my mother.

I let the idea slip away for now. If it was meant for me to meet her one day, I would. I simply had to be patient and wait to see what fate had in store for me.

While Desmond is scrambling my eggs, a frantic sounding set of knocks can be heard coming from the front door upstairs.

"I'll go up and see who it is," Jered offers, standing from his seat and heading up the staircase.

Desmond places the eggs on a plate and sets it in front of me. I hear the overwrought voice of a young boy come from the floor above us and see Desmond's face scrunch up with a worried frown.

Quick footsteps pound down the stairwell and the young man I heard suddenly appears in Desmond's kitchen. He doesn't look any older than ten years old. His cheeks are red not only from the cold outside but from some exertion considering how labored his breathing is. A few wisps of brown hair peek out from underneath his black knit cap. His clothes look far too big for his emaciated frame indicating they were probably hand-me-downs from an older sibling.

"Is something wrong with the baby, Brady?" Desmond asks, walking over to the boy.

"Yes, Dr. Connelly. My ma sent me to come get ya and bring ya back with me."

"Ok, give me a minute to dress and grab my bag," Desmond turns to me. "I'm sorry, Anna. I have to go."

I stand from my chair. "Can we help? Is there anything we can do?"

"I'm not sure there's anything any of us can do," Desmond says without completely explaining what he means. I get the feeling it's because he doesn't want to say more with Brady standing in the room.

"Let us come with you," Jered says. "It might be good for Anna to see how things are here."

Desmond looks worried by this suggestion. "Do you really think it's a good idea?"

Jered nods. "I think she should see for herself what she's fighting to change. Don't you? Plus, we have time. Our meeting with Levi isn't for another 24 hours."

"Hurry up, Dr. Connelly!" Brady says urgently, tugging on one of Desmond's sleeves.

Desmond points a finger at me. "Eat your eggs, lass. We don't waste food down here, and it'll make me worry about you less if I know you've eaten."

"I will," I promise him, sitting back down to finish my breakfast.

Desmond hurries back upstairs, and Brady follows close behind him like he's afraid Desmond might need more prodding to move faster.

"Dr. Connelly?" I ask Jered as he comes back to sit with me while I finish eating. "I didn't know he was a doctor."

"We've all lived so long we can almost be any profession we want to be," Jered tells me. "And don't call him Desmond in front of other people. His name is Devin Connelly down here to help hide his identity. He's done his best to aid the people in Dublin, but there are so many of them in need he simply can't help them all. Princess Kyna sends down supplies when she can sneak them out of Stratus, but ever since Lorcan became emperor, it's been harder for her to smuggle them to Desmond."

"I don't think I'll ever forget the first time I saw Lorcan," I tell Jered, losing my appetite at the memory. "I was eight, and he was ten at the time. Auggie was having a birthday celebration and his mother invited all the children of the royal families to attend. I think Desmond was being too kind when he said Lorcan was off his rocker. He's completely insane if you ask me, talk about a sociopath. I don't have any problem believing he killed his parents. Not after what I saw him do."

"What did you see, Anna? He didn't hurt you did he?" Jered asks, sounding concerned about the eight year old me and what she experienced.

"No, he didn't hurt me," I say, wanting to alleviate Jered's worry. "I went to the rooms he and Kyna were sharing at the palace. It was one of the few times I was allowed to speak to someone new so I jumped at the chance. The door to their suite was ajar and I heard..."

The memory of what I saw that day still haunts me. I had to put my fork down only having eaten half of my eggs. I faintly hope Desmond doesn't get too upset that I can't bring myself to finish my meal.

"I remember peeking through the crack into their room because I heard Kyna crying," I tell Jered. "I saw her on her knees begging Lorcan not to do something. She was crying so hard she could barely breathe. I followed her gaze and saw Lorcan. He was squeezing a puppy by the neck and holding it down on a table in the room. The dog was whining pitifully and trying to squirm away from him, but he wouldn't let it go. Lorcan had a knife in his other hand and told Kyna that she shouldn't have brought her pet to Cirrus because we didn't allow real animals inside our city. Kyna promised Lorcan she would return home with her puppy immediately. That way Lorcan could get all of the attention at Auggie's party. I thought Lorcan was going to accept her offer. I think Kyna did too because her tears stopped and she stood to her feet. Just as she reached Lorcan to take the puppy away from him, he raised the knife over his head and brought it down with such force it stabbed the puppy in the gut up to the knife's hilt. It howled out in pain and Kyna screamed out in misery. Lorcan didn't even have the decency to kill the poor thing. He completely let it go and backed away from the table. The puppy was whining in agony and trying to get away but the knife was halfway stuck in the dog and halfway in the table. I remember just standing there in shock watching Kyna try to get the knife out of that poor dog. When I looked away from Kyna, I found Lorcan staring straight at me with this horrible grin on his face, like he wanted to do to me what he had just done to the puppy. It was almost like he found pleasure in having an audience for his sadism. I ran away as fast as I could. I went straight to Auggie's room and told him everything I saw. He doubled the guards around me for the remainder of the Halloran's stay in Cirrus. I don't think I got a wink of sleep until they were gone. Every time I tried to close my eyes, all I could see was Lorcan staring at me."

"I'm so sorry you had to go through that experience," Jered says.

"Papa wanted to go whip Lorcan after I told him," I say, remembering the only good memory about that time. "I wish he had. Lorcan deserved it and so much more."

"I've heard he's addicted to customized drugs now," Jered tells me. "I think one of them prevents you from sleeping."

"So he's crazier than ever, I guess."

"Well, he's definitely not any more stable."

"We're ready!" We hear Desmond yell down the stairs.

Jered and I stand from the table and make our way up to the second floor.

I wonder what it is Jered hopes I will learn from this little visit through Stratus territory. To tell the truth, I think I already know what I'll end up witnessing. I just hope my heart can take

what it sees.

CHAPTER FIVE

Desmond and Brady walk out the front door, but Jered holds me back before I have a chance to step outside.

"I think you should use another one of your outfit's abilities," he whispers to me, watching Desmond and Brady descend the stairs to the sidewalk while we hang back a little.

"What are you talking about?" I ask.

"If you wish it, you can become invisible while you're wearing your jacket," Jered tells me. "People down here don't need to see the Empress of Cirrus walking around their town. It'll be reported instantly."

Jered had a point. If Desmond was going to keep his life concealed from Levi, my presence in the city needed to be kept hidden as well.

"I just wish to be invisible and it happens?" I ask.

Jered nods.

"And if I want to be visible again I just wish for that too?"

"Yes."

"Sounds simple enough," I say.

I silently wish to become invisible and don't really see

anything happen.

"Did it work? I can still see myself."

"Yes," Jered says with a smile, "it worked. No one can see you besides yourself. Come on. Let's catch up to them."

Just as Jered predicted, the fog isn't as thick now as it was when we first arrived. Jered and I walk a good distance behind Desmond and Brady down the nearly silent city streets. It's still early in the morning and the day hasn't yet started for most of the citizens of Dublin. As we walk, I can't help but notice the stench of decay that permeates the air. After we turn a corner along the sidewalk, I soon learn where the smell is coming from.

A shanty town made of ramshackle buildings put together by what looks like scraps of wood and whatever other items could be easily scavenged comprises a section of Dublin which stretches for as far as my eyes can see. The smell of human waste and death hangs in the air giving it an almost physical presence. I'm thankful I didn't eat all of my breakfast earlier because I know it would have made a sudden reappearance considering how nauseous I feel now.

"Why are people living this way?" I ask Jered in a quiet voice as we walk among the decrepit dwellings.

"It's all they have," Jered replies. "Some don't even have this much here."

"But why would the Hallorans treat their people with such indifference? Wouldn't their citizens be more productive workers if they were properly fed and housed?"

"The Hallorans have never cared how they get their supplies from the down-world. All they care about is getting the things they want in a timely manner. They don't worry about how the people who make their lives easier survive."

"Does every cloud city treat their down-worlders with such apathy?"

"Nacreous is probably the kindest to the people living under their control. The others aren't as bad as Stratus but not as good as Nacreous either. They all fall somewhere in between in their disinterest for the down-world. Sometimes people don't think about others when they're not a part of their everyday lives. It's easy to forget about the down-world especially when it's hidden from view."

"I will never forget," I promise Jered.

Even though he can't see me he smiles at my words.

"I know you won't, Anna. You were built to have a long memory and empathy towards those who are less fortunate. You've been placed in a position of power that will help you use both of those attributes to help you change the shattered world we live in. And I will do everything I can to help you make it a better place not only for your children but for the generations that will come after we're all gone."

Desmond stops in front of a small dwelling that looks slightly larger than the others around it. It still looks as if it's only being held together by the grace of God, but the structure is sturdy enough to withstand the cold wind blowing in from the ocean.

Brady opens the door which is made out of scraps of wood, old rusty metal sheeting and interwoven cloth to prevent drafts from squeezing in through the gaps. Even though Jered can't see me, he holds the door open long enough for me to sneak inside.

A rather plain looking woman stands within the dwelling walking around with a baby cradled in the crook of an arm, wrapped in a once white blanket. I hear no cries from the child and wonder if that's a good sign or a bad one. Instinct tells me it's a very bad thing.

When the woman sees Desmond, I see her shoulders sag in relief. I know then she expects him to work some sort of miracle for the child she holds in her arms, but I fear she may have to face the reality of her situation sooner than she realizes.

"Thank God you're here," the woman says, a desperate sort of hope in her voice. "She's hardly breathing. I don't know what to do for her, Devin."

I watch as Desmond sits the black leather bag he brought

with him on the dusty wooden floor of the shack. By this simple action, my suspicions are confirmed, and I know there is nothing he can do for the babe in the woman's arms.

Desmond walks over to the woman and holds his arms out to take the child from her.

Eagerly, she hands the little girl to him, but I can tell from the look on the mother's face when she looks at Desmond's expression that she knows there will be no reprieve for her little one. A shadow of despair shrouds her features as she's forced to face the truth.

"I'm sorry, Mary," Desmond says. "She was just born too soon. Her lungs aren't mature enough to sustain her."

"How long?" Mary asks, taking in a deep, shuddering breath. "How long does she have?"

"A few more hours at best," Desmond tells her. "I wish there was more I could do, but she'll be drifting off to rest in God's arms soon. All you can do now is hold her until she passes and let her know she was loved in her short life. I'm sorry I can't do more."

"I don't blame you," Mary says, taking the newborn from Desmond and holding the child to her chest. "I blame those people living above us like we don't exist, like we don't matter to them at all!"

Desmond sighs and looks around the small one room home. There are four palettes on the floor on the opposite end of the shack.

"Where are your husband and older son? They should be here with you."

"They're out trying to meet their quota of crabs for those bastards up in Stratus to eat at some party," Mary says, venom in her voice. "I swear to God if I could get that slimy Lorcan Halloran down here I would kill him with my bare hands. None of the royals deserve to live if you ask me!"

"They're not all bad, Mary," Desmond says, trying to sooth the woman's ire. "Some of them want to change how things are."

"Well, they're doing a piss poor job of showing it!" Mary says, tears of frustration and sorrow streaming down her face openly now. "While we and our children are just trying to survive, they're up there livin' high in the clouds without a care in the world. I'm sick of it, Devin! I don't know how much more I can take! I wish I had one of them here in my home to show them what their greed has done." Mary looks down at her dying child. "I wish I could make them watch the pain their selfishness has caused us all."

I tug on Jered's arm, silently telling him I want to go. I can't watch Mary's pain any longer, and I pray Jered understands my silent request.

"I should be leaving now, Devin," Jered tells Desmond. "I'm so sorry for your imminent loss, ma'am."

Mary doesn't seem to hear Jered's words. She's completely lost in her own grief.

"I'm going to stay here with her until the end," Desmond tells us. "Thank you for coming with me."

"See you tomorrow," Jered tells Desmond as a subtle reminder about our rendezvous with Levi.

Desmond nods and turns his attention back to Mary and her dying child.

Jered goes to the door and opens it. He gives me enough time to exit before closing it.

"I need some fresh air," I whisper to him.

Jered walks us through the shanty town until we come to a paved path. The path leads us down a slight slope to a small patch of sandy beach along the coast. The beach is capped on either end by a rocky shoreline. The brisk breeze coming off the ocean acts as a cleansing balm to my lungs.

I silently wish to be made visible again.

"Jered," I say, looking over at him as he stand beside me,

staring out at the ocean. "Even if we help these people, do you think they will still hate us?"

Jered continues to look out towards the ocean.

"I think it will take a few generations for the distrust to fade," he tells me. "Things have been this way for a very long time, Anna. They won't simply forget, and they certainly won't forgive easily. I think there will be some resistance and wariness in the beginning. But," Jered says, tearing his gaze away from the gently lapping waves in front of us to look at me, "I believe all they need is someone they can put their faith into, and I believe that someone is you."

"They have no reason to trust me. They have no reason to believe a word I say even if it is to help repair the damage that's been done to their lives."

"Then you have to give them a reason, Anna. You're a natural leader. People will want to follow you."

"I don't want them to follow me," I say. "I want them to think for themselves."

"And they will, in time," Jered assures me. "But, right now they need a guiding light to bring them out of the darkness. They need a beacon of hope to tell them their lives are worth something. They've lived under the thumb of the hierarchy living in the cloud cities for generations. All they know is what they're told. The people here aren't stupid. They're just worn down by their lives and need someone to show them they're worth more than what they've been told. In the end, that's all people really want. They want to know they matter. They want to know they're appreciated for their efforts."

I look out at the ocean and realize my problems are as infinite as it appears. No end set on the horizon, only a lengthy list of things which need to be fixed.

"It's going to take a long time to make things right, isn't it?" I say, fully realizing the magnitude of the task at hand. My work won't end with the reformation of Cirrus. It stretches far beyond that.

"You won't have to do it alone," Jered assures me. "We'll be with you all the way."

I nod, knowing I will be able to depend on my guardians to help me mend the world. I'm just not sure we'll be enough to handle everything that needs to be done.

I feel lonely all of a sudden. I've come to love Jered as a friend and confidante, but the person I really need standing by my side is Malcolm. I need the strength I feel when we're together, like nothing is beyond our ability to make right.

Jered and I stand in mutual silence for a while before I feel the presence of someone I wasn't sure I would ever see again.

I look to the edge of the sandy beach we're standing on and see Lucifer leaned up against a rock formation.

"I think I have someone who wants to speak with me," I tell Jered.

Jered follows my gaze, and I feel his body stiffen when he sees Lucifer staring at us from beneath his hooded cloak.

"Do you want me to go with you?" Jered asks. I can tell by the tone of his voice that he doesn't really want me to be alone with my biological father. I imagine years of feuding has made Jered overly cautious.

"No," I tell him. "He won't hurt me."

"How can you be so sure?"

"Because if he wanted to, he would have tried something before now. Plus, if he left me with Andre because he didn't trust himself to raise me right, I doubt he's come here to kill the only living reminder left on this earth of the woman he loved."

Jered's stony expression tells me that he still doesn't want me to be alone with Lucifer.

"I'll be here if you need me... watching," he says as a compromise.

I nod letting him know I understand his concerns, and that

I'm grateful he's showing so much self-control. If Malcolm had been there with me, there isn't a doubt in my mind he would have tried to prevent me from going to speak with Lucifer.

I walk up the coastline to where Lucifer is waiting. I can feel him studying me as I approach, and I wonder what must be going through his mind.

"How did you know where I was?" I ask him as I come to stand in front of him.

"Fatherly instinct I suppose," he answers with a shrug. "I assume I can say that now. I doubt you waited very long to have your suspicions confirmed."

"Yes, I know you're my biological father. I know everything."

"I seriously doubt that," Lucifer scoffs.

"What do you mean?"

"Nothing," he says stubbornly. "It doesn't matter."

"It must matter to you or you wouldn't have said it."

Lucifer is quiet and just stares at me. I have no idea what he's thinking. His expression doesn't give anything away.

"Levi tells me you've chosen Malcolm to be your mate." Lucifer say derisively while shaking his head at me. "Anna, you could do so much better than that over-grown man child. Why on earth are you settling for him?"

"Not that it's any of your business, but Malcolm and I are soul mates. I would think you of all people should understand how strong that bond is."

"Yes, I understand its strength," Lucifer says, his voice rising in volume. "But for him to be yours is a completely ludicrous concept! Either that or my father is truly trying to torture me for my past misdeeds."

"Why do you hate Malcolm so much? What has he ever done to you?"

"He exists," Lucifer snarls. "Every breath he takes makes my hate for him grow even more."

"But why?"

"I don't need a reason!"

"Don't raise your voice to me," I tell him, keeping my own steady but forceful. "I won't stand here and be yelled at by you. If you want to talk to me, keep a civil tongue in your mouth, or I'm walking away."

"You act like that's supposed to be some sort of threat."

"I don't think you would seek me out if you didn't want to

speak with me. Why is that anyway? What's your real reason for being here?"

Lucifer is silent.

"I needed to come and confirm a suspicion."

"What suspicion?"

Lucifer reaches out and gently places a hand on my shoulder. His face suddenly looks drawn with disbelief.

"How?" He asks. "How did you get Amon's seal?"

"I'm not completely sure how it worked," I say, realizing my secret mission for God isn't quite so secret anymore. "But after I killed Amon, the seal he carried was transferred to me. You should know that I plan to get them all back and return them to Heaven. It's one of the things I was born to do."

Lucifer remains silent, but I can tell what I just said troubles him.

"How did you know I had it?" I ask.

"I sensed it the last time I saw you," he tells me. "I just couldn't believe it was true. I needed to confirm it for myself."

"Is that the only reason your here?" I ask him.

"No," Lucifer says, letting go of my shoulder and letting

his arm return to his side. "I also wanted to come and warn you."

"Warn me about what?"

"That you can't trust Levi to do what he says. I know what he wants you to do for him, Anna. Once you give him the princes, there's no guarantee that he will keep his end of the bargain."

"I'm not a fool, Lucifer. I understand the risks."

"You're a fool if you think Levi will just give you what you want."

"I may not want the princes released but it's a necessary evil."

"Why?"

"If they're free, it will be easier for me to kill them."

"Sounds a bit bloodthirsty of you," Lucifer quips.

"Why are you warning me about Levi anyway?" I ask. "I thought if anyone would want the princes released it would be you."

"If Levi is the one who orchestrates their freedom, they're no longer my men," Lucifer tells me. "They'll feel loyal to him, not me."

"Is that what you're really worried about? Losing control

over them?"

"Doesn't every great ruler worry about that?"

"I think *great* rulers worry about those who depend on them more than they do themselves."

Lucifer looks at me and then busts out in laughter, like what I said is the funniest thing he's ever heard.

"I can't believe how naïve you are, daughter. But, then again, I suppose I shouldn't have expected more from you since Andre was the one who raised you."

"No one else seemed up for the challenge," I say bitingly. "At least he was man enough to take on the responsibility and not run from it."

"You wouldn't have wanted me to raise you," Lucifer says with so much conviction I know he believes his own words. "Life is much easier to live if you view it through rose colored glasses instead of a hate that eats you up from the inside out. Trust me. I know."

"If you really loved my mother, I don't think you would have allowed yourself to raise me to just become a mirror image of you. You would have wanted better for me."

"I did love your mother," Lucifer says. "I loved her enough to let you be raised by someone she trusted."

"Is that what she wanted?" I ask. "Did she want Andre to raise me?"

"She didn't know what she really wanted," Lucifer grumbles.

I stop a moment to think about what he actually just admitted to.

"She asked you to raise me, didn't she?"

"Like I said, she didn't really know what she wanted. She was in no condition to think logically. I had to do that for the both of us."

"Or maybe you just didn't love her enough to carry out her last wish."

Lucifer leaps to his feet and stands directly in front of me with our faces barely an inch apart.

"Don't ever question how I felt about Amalie!" He roars, his face twisted in anger. "I've killed people for doing less!"

"Is there a problem here?" I hear Jered say behind me.

Lucifer raises his eyes from my face to look at Jered over my shoulder.

"Hello, *Jered*. I have to say that I'm a bit surprised by you."

"Surprised…" Jered says like he's mulling over the meaning of the word. "In what way exactly?"

"Surprised you're giving my daughter such bad advice. You should know better than to trust a word that comes out of Levi's mouth."

"I don't trust him," Jered replies. "But we don't have a lot of options left open to us. Unless you would like to give us a better idea?"

Lucifer grins smugly at Jered. "And why in the world would I do that?"

"Oh, I don't know…to help your daughter save her family?"

Lucifer's grin falters, and he looks back at me.

"I've done all I can for her," he says before looking back at Jered. "The rest is up to you."

Lucifer phases. Just like the first time I saw him, I notice that his phase trail leads to somewhere that is in total darkness.

"Where did he go? Why is it so dark there? It looks more like a hole in space than an actual place," I say to Jered, staring at the void Lucifer has left with his phasing.

Jered doesn't answer me which prompts me to look back at

him.

"Jered," I say, bringing him out of his quiet reverie as he stares at the darkness, "where does this phase trail go?"

Jered drags his eyes away from the black void to look at me. His expression looks haunted. It takes him a few more seconds but he finally answers.

"Straight to Hell."

CHAPTER SIX

"Hell?" I ask, sure I misheard Jered. "You're speaking in literal terms, right?"

"Yes," Jered says, his eyes narrowing on me. "Why does that surprise you? It's Lucifer's domain."

"I guess I just never thought about it," I admit. "I know there's a Heaven and a Hell, but I guess I always considered them faraway places, unreachable except through death." I look at the phase trail again and reach out a hand towards it. "Not real places that I could actually go to while I'm still alive."

"Well, you don't want to go there," Jered says with conviction, putting a hand on my raised arm and making me lower it from Lucifer's phase trail. "And you should never follow him, Anna. Never. There's no guarantee you would make it back out."

"Why?" I ask, looking at Jered. "Would he trap me there?"

"No, not Lucifer directly. It's Hell itself. It loves to play tricks with your mind. You could become lost in your worst memories and never find your way back out again."

"You make it sound like Hell's alive," I say, thinking Jered is over-exaggerating. The look on his face tells me otherwise.

"That place is filled with pain. In a way, it *is* alive because it draws its power from the torment of all the souls trapped there."

"Have you ever been to Hell?" I ask.

"I used to be on Lucifer's side once, remember? I know what he and the others are capable of. I've witnessed it firsthand."

I don't ask Jered to expound on his statement. I get the feeling he would rather keep his past behind him, and I have no intention of making him relive any bad memories just to satisfy my own morbid curiosity.

So, I decide to change the subject.

"Who are we going to go to next? Brutus or Daniel?"

"Brutus," Jered says with a heavy sigh. "I could use a drink right about now."

Something tells me he's not simply wanting to quench his thirst, but I don't ask any more questions.

We phase to the teleport terminal right above Barlow's hideout. It doesn't take me long to fly us through the tunnels this time because I know the way now. As promised we find Jake, Barlow's helper, waiting for us.

"Jake," Jered says when we walk into the glass enclosed teleporter room. "Can the empress borrow your clothes?"

"Uh, sure," Jake says uncertainly, looking confused by the

request. "All of them?"

"No, just your coat, hat and scarf."

"Why do I need his clothes?" I ask.

"Camouflage," Jered says, taking Jake's hat and scarf from him first and placing them on me. He wraps the scarf around the lower portion of my face effectively hiding it from view before putting the black knit cap on my head.

"Are we going somewhere public to see Brutus?" I ask.

"Yes," Jered says, taking Jake's coat and holding it out for me to slip my arms into. "Brutus owns a bar in Kathmandu."

"With the time difference, it should be in the middle of the day in that part of the world. Shouldn't it be empty?"

"Not necessarily. People pass out all the time in bars and just lay down to sleep it off instead of trying to make it to their homes," Jered answers. "This is just a precaution."

"Why don't I just use the jacket to make me invisible?" I ask.

Jered grins looking a bit on the mischievous side.

"Because I want to see Brutus' reaction to you walking into his bar."

"Um, should I be worried about his reaction?"

Jered chuckles. "No. Just humor me. I want to see what he does."

Even though Jered tells me not to worry, I have to admit I am a little bit. From what I remember, Brutus was very…large. He looked like someone who could crush a man's head between his beefy hands without much effort.

Jered gives Jake a set of coordinates, and we're promptly teleported to the next Watcher on our list.

I soon find us standing in front of a two story wooden structure with a set of large ram horns perched on the overhang above the front door. The wind is biting cold and snow pounds us from every direction. I look down and see that we're standing in a snowdrift that reaches up to my knee caps. We've obviously teleported straight into the middle of a blizzard. Jered takes hold of my hand and tugs me forward. I'm not sure if he's holding my hand to lead me where we need to go or if he's trying to make sure I don't get blown away by the elements, possibly both.

We walk up a short ramp to the front door which is just high enough to not be blocked by snow. Jered opens the door and pulls on my hand telling me to go in before him while he holds the door open against the wind's insistence that it be closed.

I step inside and instantly feel the warmth of the interior on the exposed parts of my face. The room we enter is very rustic in design with its outsized, exposed wooden beams which support a cathedral ceiling. The second floor of the establishment is easily visible from the first and marked by a railing all around the room. To the right of us is the bar area which is home to a variety of glass bottles lined up on the staggered shelving sitting in front of a large mirror mounted on the wall. To the far left is a stone fireplace so large it could easily be considered a room all by itself. The heat it produces keeps the interior a warm and toasty temperature even in the face of the blizzard outside.

There are about five people scattered around in different states of slumber. Some are sitting at the round tables in the room slumped forward in their chairs, heads resting against the tops, and some are curled up in front of the fireplace to soak in the waves of warmth it's generating.

Brutus comes in from a room behind the bar whistling a happy tune while he carries in a tray of clean shot glasses. When his gaze settles on me and Jered, he promptly drops the tray he's holding causing the tinkling of broken glass to echo within the room. Some of the slumbering patrons groan their protestations at being awoken by the noise but promptly lay back down to go to sleep.

Brutus comes straight at me.

Before I know it, he's picked me up like a child does a doll, hugging me to him and spinning me around in his arms laughing heartily.

Finally, he sits me down in front of him but squeezes me tightly to him before taking a step back.

"I wish you had warned me you were bringing her here so soon, Jered," Brutus says, moving the scarf hiding the bottom of my face down so he can kiss me on both cheeks.

"We're not here for what you think," Jered tells Brutus, a warning in his voice that all is not well.

Brutus' prominent eyebrows lower. Apparently he knows Jered well enough to understand there's trouble. He crosses his muscular arms over his broad, chest and says, "Tell me."

Jered looks at the patrons in the room. "Are you sure we can speak freely?"

"They're all passed out from drinking all night and into the morning. They've been trapped here by the snow for more than a day. Even if they did hear anything, they would just think it was a dream."

"Got any of that drink left?" Jered asks. "I could use something to take the edge off."

"Always for you, my friend."

Brutus walks behind the bar, being careful to step over the broken glass on the floor, and grabs a small drinking glass from underneath the counter. Jered and I sit in stools at the bar while Brutus grabs a bottle of whiskey from the shelf on the wall behind him. He pours a good serving of it into the glass on the counter and slides it closer to Jered.

Jered takes a long swig, drinking half of the contents. He sits the glass back down and clears his throat to tell Brutus the dire situation we find ourselves in.

After Jered is through explaining everything, Brutus slams his fist against the bar in frustration, making such a loud thud the patrons inside grumble again about keeping the noise down before falling back to sleep.

"Just when we thought this would all be over soon, this happens," Brutus sighs. "I was hoping…"

Brutus doesn't finish his sentence, just shakes his head like his unvoiced hopes were those of a fool. I think I know what he was hoping for. It's the same thing I am. If he's truly found his soul mate in Kyna Halloran, he wants to be with her, just like I want to be with Malcolm.

"Jered," I say, looking over at him, "don't forget to give Brutus what Desmond sent for him."

"Oh yes," Jered says sliding a hand into an inside pocket in his coat and pulling out the small metal box Desmond asked us to deliver to Brutus. The one with the neural memo from Kyna.

Brutus' dismay at having to give into Levi's demands vanishes for the time being. His eyes light up with expectation.

"Is this what I think it is?" Brutus asks, taking the box from Jered.

Jered smiles. "Who knew you would finally find your soul mate? And a princess to boot."

"She could have been the lowliest of scullery maids, and I would still feel the same about her."

I can't help but smile at how Brutus made his declaration of love without actually having to say it in so many words. I knew exactly how he felt.

It was then I sensed the five interlopers into our private moment together.

I know they are standing on the second landing above us. If it hadn't been for the slight flash of light I saw out of the corner of my eye, I wouldn't have known they teleported in. I sense more than see Jered and Brutus tense up.

"What do you normally do at a time like this?" Jered asks in a conversational tone in order to not tip off the men surrounding us that we're aware of their presence.

Brutus shrugs. "Doesn't take much to take care of things. Just enjoy your drink. I'll handle it like I always do." Brutus looks at me. "Would you like some milk while you wait?"

The question catches me off guard, and I assume it's for a purpose.

"Yes, that would be nice," I tell him.

I see Brutus reach underneath the counter like he's getting me a glass, but instead I hear the distinct sound of a sword being drawn. Apparently, I'm not the only one who hears its metallic song.

The people on the second landing suddenly jump over the railing to the ground floor behind us.

"Sorry about this," Brutus tells me with a wink. "I'll just be a minute."

Before I know it, Brutus leaps over the bar to meet his intruders head on with sword in hand.

I turn around swiftly on my stool and reach for the hilt of my sword preparing to help him.

I feel Jered's hand on mine and hear him say, "Don't bother, Anna. Brutus will have this handled quick enough."

I don't feel comfortable just sitting there while Brutus

fights five men alone, but the nonchalant way Jered said his words relieves some of my tension.

I watch as Brutus uses his sword with practiced precision against his five assailants. Three of them try to rush him with their own swords pointed straight out. I suppose they assumed strength in numbers would give them the advantage. Just as they get close, Brutus sweeps his blade against theirs and sheers them clean off, almost to the hilt. They still try to tackle him, but Brutus pounds his elbow into the face of the assailant on the far right, smashing his nose and making the man fall to the ground, shrieking in pain. The one in the middle tries to hit Brutus in the face with his fist, but Brutus grabs his hand, crushing it and making his attacker cry out in agony. The third man raises his hands in a defensive martial arts stance. Brutus just sighs at him and spins on his left foot hitting the man upside the head with a firm roundhouse kick, completely knocking the man unconscious.

The two intruders left seem to have more sense and don't charge Brutus head on. They get on either side of him, hoping to divide his attention. The one in front lunges at Brutus with his sword. The swordplay which follows is exhilarating to watch. It makes me want to jump in and join in the fun. However, it doesn't take Brutus long to have them both disarmed. He smashes their skulls together just hard enough to knock them out but not kill them.

Very little blood is shed, and I think Brutus made his point clearly enough.

The two invaders who are still conscious quickly teleport themselves and their unconscious comrades out of Brutus' bar.

"Sorry about that," he tells me. "They know I keep supplies here. I'm guessing the new black marketer in town thought he could come in and take what he wanted without asking. Next time, he'll think twice about it."

"Next time?" I ask. "You don't think this taught them a lesson?"

"Probably not," Brutus tells me. "It usually takes them two or three times before they understand not to interfere with my business."

"Are they that desperate for alcohol?" I ask.

"No...my other business," Brutus says, looking a little uncomfortable all of a sudden.

"Which is?" I ask, trying to prod him for a clearer explanation.

"I guess you could call me a barterer. I acquire things from people and trade these items to others for certain supplies."

"Brutus," I say putting two and two together for myself,

"are you a thief?"

"I wouldn't necessarily call it *stealing*," Brutus says, apparently not liking the connotation of the term I used. "Think of it as taking from people who have too much. I use those items of luxury to help people who can't survive without the food and other supplies I trade them for. Anyway, it makes me a target for those who want the things I can acquire. Speaking of which, have you been to Daniel's yet?"

"No," Jered tells him. "I thought we would go there last."

"Good, I have some medicine I need you to take to him."

Brutus motions for us to follow him, and he takes us to the room behind the bar.

The room is small and rather ordinary with shelves built into the walls holding miscellaneous items such as glasses and more bottles of alcohol. Brutus closes the door behind us and pushes a recessed button in the wall by the door. I wouldn't have even known it was there it was hidden so well in the knots of the wood panel. I jump slightly because I suddenly feel as though I'm freefalling, but my feet stay firmly planted on the floor as it drops a good ten feet.

"A warning would have been nice," I grouse, feeling a bit disoriented by our descent.

Brutus smiles. "But then I wouldn't have gotten to see the surprised expression on your face. It was absolutely priceless."

I just shake my head in exasperation at Brutus and look around at the hidden room I find myself in. Beneath Brutus' bar is a virtual treasure trove of plunder. Jewels, paintings, and other precious artifacts are all neatly displayed on gray metal shelves within a cement room so big you could fit a good size house into it. Brutus walks off the wood platform we're standing on and goes directly to one of the shelves. He pulls off a medium sized blue box marked with a white cross indicating it contains medicine. He walks back over to Jered and hands him the box.

"You'll get it to him a lot faster than my smuggler can. Daniel told me the kids needed it when I saw him in Cirrus."

"We'll make sure he gets it," Jered assures Brutus.

Brutus walks over to me and gives me another bear hug.

When he pulls back, he says, "And don't you worry. We'll get all of them away from Levi safely."

I nod. "I know. I just wish it was sooner rather than later. I think waiting for the meeting to happen is likely to kill me."

"Oh, I wouldn't count on that," Brutus says. "I have a feeling Linn and Daniel will be able to find things to keep your mind busy, for a little while at least."

"How so?"

Brutus looks over to Jered. "You didn't warn her?"

Jered shrugs. "I thought it would be more fun to watch her expression."

"What is it with you guys and watching my reaction to things?" I ask, completely mystified by why they keep wanting to do that.

"I guess it's because we had to miss so much of you growing up," Brutus tells me, a melancholy smile on his face. "Andre was the one chosen to raise you. He got to watch you experience all the day to day surprises in your life. We loved you just as much as he did, but we weren't able to share in those little moments. They may seem inconsequential to some people, but it's those moments that shape you into the person you will become. Don't think poorly of us for trying to make up for lost time."

Now I feel bad.

I place a hand on one of Brutus' arms.

"No, I understand. I just didn't realize you all felt that way about me."

"You're a part of our family," Jered tells me. "And we knew it was better for you if we didn't confuse you with our presence. Now that you're a grown woman, we can get to know you which is all we ever wanted to do."

"In a strange way, I feel like I already know you," I tell them. "You're so much like my papa. I can see bits and pieces of him in all of you."

"We'll get Andre back," Brutus promises me. "I'm not sure how yet, but we will."

"I know we will," I tell them both. "I have faith that we'll be reunited soon."

Brutus kisses me first on one cheek and then the other.

"And if Malcolm ever gives you any grief," he tells me. "You have four uncles who will knock him into tomorrow to teach him a lesson."

I giggle at the promise.

"I don't think you have to worry about that," I tell him. "I just want to get him back, and make Levi pay for what he's done."

"Oh, don't worry," Brutus says with a look of certainty. "That pompous ass will get what's coming to him. People like him always do in the end."

"Well, we should be going," Jered tells Brutus almost apologetically for having to cut our visit with him short.

Brutus hugs me one more time and then reluctantly lets me

go.

"I'll see you soon," he tells me. "And don't worry. We'll get your family back together."

As I look at Brutus, I realize that my family has just grown with the addition of four very overprotective uncles.

CHAPTER SEVEN

When Jered and I phase back to the teleporter terminal above Barlow's hideout, we're met by an unexpected welcoming party of one.

Christopher, one of the two guards who always escorted me to my lessons with Empress Catherine, is standing there waiting for us. He's holding a medium sized black box tied with a silky red ribbon secured into a bow on top.

"What are you doing here?" I ask. I know he isn't really the Christopher I knew anymore. He's one of Levi's minions now, and his presence can't bode well.

"Emperor Augustus sends his regards," Christopher says to me, handing over the box. "He asked me to bring this to you as an added incentive to do what he wants."

I take the box and feel its weight. It has some weight to it, making me wonder what sort of present Levi has sent. I stare down at it worried over what I might find inside.

"I'm supposed to wait here until you open it," Christopher says. "He wants me to report your...reaction."

I look back up at Christopher and note the concerned expression on his face. It's a fleeting look, and one I probably wasn't supposed to notice. It makes me wonder why he would bother to worry over how the contents of the box will affect me.

"I can open it for you," Jered offers, tucking the box of medicine Brutus gave him for Daniel under one arm and holding out his hands to take the box from me.

"No," I say, pulling on one end of the red ribbon and letting it fall to the snow covered sidewalk at my feet, mimicking a trail of blood against the white.

I lift the lid and look inside the box. I find a piece of black velvet material covering something lumpy. There is a hand written note on a white card lying on top.

In case you are thinking of double crossing me, I thought you might need a little reminder of what I can do to the ones you love…

L

I lift the piece of fabric and almost drop the box on the ground because my whole body goes completely numb.

Lying inside the box, like a broken doll, is Vala. Her head has been ripped from her body and the milky white nutrient which cycles through her system is pooled around her, matting her fur. I have no doubt in my mind that Levi performed the deed himself. Why wouldn't he? His greatest pleasure in life seems to be causing pain. What haunts my thoughts the most is the knowledge that

Vala's last memories would have been filled with fear. She would have fully understood what was happening to her, and I feel an immense sense of guilt over not being there to protect her when she needed me the most. I just hope Levi didn't do it in front of Lucas. But knowing him, he probably made Millie and Lucas watch his cruel act against Vala. He wouldn't have missed an opportunity to teach them what might happen if they tried to cause trouble.

It was a gruesome reminder to me that he could do the same thing to both Millie and Lucas at any time. I'm not sure what Levi truly hoped to accomplish by decapitating Vala and sending me her remains. He probably expected it to frighten me. If that was his goal, he failed miserably.

"I have a message for you to take back to him," I tell Christopher, looking up from Vala to stare straight into his eyes to make sure he doesn't misunderstand a word I say. "Tell Levi that one day in the near future this will be his own fate. Tell him that his *wife* makes a vow to him that his death won't be an easy or a pleasant one. In fact, I plan to make it as painful as I possibly can. Do you think you can remember all of that?"

Christopher bows to me. "Yes, Empress Annalise. I will relay your message."

Christopher phases back to Cirrus to deliver my promise to the monster masquerading as the emperor.

I look back down at Vala and feel the first tears of grief threaten. Memories of my life with her flash through my mind. I can still remember the very first time I ever met my little sentient robotic friend. I was six years old, and she was a birthday present from my papa. Being betrothed to the prince of Cirrus meant I wasn't allowed to have many friends. I was forced to stay mostly to myself for the majority of my life, only being allowed to play with Auggie. My papa knew I needed a friend so he bought me the best one money could buy. Vala had served as a confidante, someone I could share my hopes and dreams with. She knew me as well as anyone in this world, better than most. And now she was gone.

"Come on," Jered says, an urgent quality to his voice. He hastily puts the lid back on the box and takes it from me. "We might be able to save her."

I look up at Jered through my tears and see his face set with grim determination.

"How?" I ask. "Her brain is organic."

"Exactly," Jered says grabbing my arm and phasing us.

We're instantly standing in the middle of what looks like a warehouse full of junk. Cables and metal parts of various items are stacked on and hanging above rows and rows of tables surrounding us. There's a stench in the air that reminds me of burning plasma, but there is also a distinct metallic scent attached to it that irritates my nostrils. The tech surrounding us looks old, nothing as sophisticated as the technology in Cirrus where everything operates on cold fusion. The items around me look like things that might run on old fashioned electricity.

"Won't Levi know where we are?" I ask Jered, wondering why we phased directly to this location.

"This is one of the few places on the planet where Levi can't track our phasing."

"Why?"

"The owner has a jamming device that keeps him completely off the grid."

"Who's the owner?"

"You can meet him for yourself." Jered lifts his head a notch and yells, "Travis! It's Jered. Where are you?"

"Jered?" I hear a startled male voice say from somewhere in the depths of the chaos surrounding us. "One sec!"

The sound of small wheels running along a hard surface can be heard approaching our location. A young man soon emerges out of nowhere. He's wearing a blue and grey plaid shirt and a pair of jeans. Tennis shoes cover his feet, but apparently they have wheels hidden within the soles because he rolls up to us. He isn't tall, maybe five foot seven. His eyes are hazel and he has shaggy, short blonde hair. He looks to be in his mid-twenties, but there is an intelligence behind his eyes that makes him appear much older and wiser.

"What's up, Jered?" Travis asks, a friendly smile on his face. "Long time no see, dude."

Jered hands Travis the black box with Vala's corpse. That's the way I think of what's left of her anyway. There's no telling how long she's been dead. He could have killed her right after I phased from Cirrus or he could have done it a few minutes ago. All I know is her brain can't function very long after being starved of the synthetic nutrients she needs to survive.

"Can you fix her?" Jered asks.

Travis looks confused but takes the lid off the box. I see his eyes light up when he sees Vala.

"*Oh...my...God...,*" Travis says in complete awe, taking Vala's head out of the box. "Is this what I think it is? I've never had the chance to play with a senti before."

"She isn't a toy," I tell him, trying to control my annoyance. I know Travis isn't the one who did this to Vala, but neither am I in the mood for a stranger to treat her like she's an object. "She's one of my best friends. Can you fix her or not!"

Travis looks startled by my outburst.

He stares at me for a moment before asking, "Are you who I think you are?"

"Travis Stokes, I would like to introduce you to Empress Annalise of Cirrus," Jered says by way of introduction.

"Stokes?" I ask, remembering that I know someone else with the same last name. "Are you related to Barlow?"

"Half-brother," Travis says like it pains him to admit such a relationship with Barlow. "We don't really stay in touch that much."

Travis looks back down at Vala. "How long has she been like this?"

"We don't know," Jered tells him. "A couple of hours at most. Do you think you can do something for her?"

Travis sighs. "I'll try. But, I can't make any promises. It's all going to depend on how long ago this happened. Give me a little while so I can see if there's anything I can do."

"Her brain is organic," I tell him, on the verge of tears. "It can't survive very long without being fed the nutrient solution."

Travis nods. "Yes, I know. I understand the tech used to make a senti like this. I've just never been able to work with one before. Sentient robots are super rare and expensive. If I can help her, I promise you I will."

"That's all we ask," Jered tells him. "Do what you can to save her, Travis. We'll make sure you're well compensated for your efforts."

"I would also be in your debt," I tell him, making sure he understands how important getting Vala back is to me. Having the Empress of Cirrus owe you a favor was not a small thing in our society.

"Sure thing," Travis says with a shy grin. "I'll do everything I can to fix her for you, Empress. You have my word."

I nod, satisfied with his answer. It's all I can ask or hope for.

"We'll come back soon," Jered tells him. "If you figure out whether or not you can fix her before we do, let Barlow know. He can get a message to us quickly."

Travis nods.

Jered places his hand on my shoulder and phases us back to the teleport station.

I just stand there when Jered makes to move to the alley by the building. He notices when I don't follow him and turns back to face me.

"Anna," he says, trying to gain my attention. "Don't let him win."

I look up to meet Jered's gaze.

"I have no intention of letting him win," I tell him. "He seems to think the things he does will tear me down. What he doesn't realize is that it just makes me more determined to see him pay for what he's done. I don't just want to kill him now, Jered. I want to make him suffer as much as I can for all the pain he's caused the people I love."

Jered looks troubled by my words and walks back to me.

"Be careful with your hate," Jered advises me. "It can damage you in ways you don't even realize. It can twist you into something that you don't want to become, Anna. Remember who you are. Remember the values Andre taught you. He wouldn't want to see you turn into someone you aren't because of Levi."

"And he wouldn't want me to just sit back and let Levi get away with the harm he's caused others either."

"Levi will get what's coming to him," Jered promises me. "The bad guys always do. Evil will never win over good, Anna. It's not the way the universe is wired to work. At heart, most people yearn to live in peace, not chaos. They almost always choose the noble path in the end."

"But that's not true," I argue. "Look at the princes. They chose to disobey God. They *still* choose to disobey Him. Not everyone wants to be good. Sometimes people just want to be evil because it gives them pleasure to see others suffer. "

"And because of their bad choices they will eventually pay the price."

I stare at Jered for a moment because I'm about to voice something I haven't talked to anyone about yet. It's something we all know, but no one has dared to say what I might ultimately have to do in order to retrieve all the seals.

"If killing the princes is the only way to take the seals from them," I say. "That means I'll have to kill Lucifer at some point, doesn't it?"

Jered's gaze lowers to the ground for a moment. I can see he has been waiting for me to ask this question. When he looks back up at me, he nods.

"Yes, you will, Anna. I don't think there's any way around that eventuality."

"What if I can't?" I ask, thinking it morbid for God to send me down just to kill my own father.

"Maybe you won't have to," Jered says. "Maybe just taking the other six seals will be enough."

I shake my head. "I don't think so, Jered. I think God wants them all back."

Jered stuffs his hands into the pockets of his coat, and I can see this isn't something he wants to be talking about right now.

"Why don't we worry about one thing at a time? Let's just get Lucas, Malcolm, and Millie away from Levi first. Then we can fret about what happens next."

I know he's right, but I also know the thought will remain in the back of my mind until the moment comes when I have to make a choice.

"Come on," Jered says, holding out a hand to me. "Let's make our last visit. I think a trip to Daniel's is just want you need to get your mind off of things for a little while."

I accept Jered's hand, and we walk over to the alley.

"What will I find at Daniel's place anyway?" I ask.

"You'll see," Jered promises. "I would hate to ruin the surprise."

Once we make it down to Barlow's, Jered informs Jake that they might receive a message from Travis for us. I take off Jake's borrowed clothes and thank him for their use. Jered gives him our next set of coordinates, and we're shortly on our way to the last stop on our journey to gather the princes for the trade.

Jered and I are soon standing outside a large building that doesn't look much like a home. It looks more like a place you would run a business out of. It's three stories high with one end of the structure curved, not squared off, and banked with windows. The opposite side has railed verandas on each level. The windows of the building are covered with drawn curtains making it impossible to see what's inside. The sun is setting in the sky, telling me we are in a very different time zone.

"Where are we exactly?" I ask.

"Beijing, China," Jered tells me.

"Cirro territory," I say. "The emperor and empress didn't make it to the wedding."

"No, the emperor has been ill from what I understand," Jered says. "There's a lot of debate about who will succeed him after his death since he has no heir."

"I've heard rumors that the empress might take control."

"It's possible. The people in both Cirro and their down-world love her. In the end, I think keeping your citizens happy is all that matters."

I look back at the building. "Why does Daniel need such a big place to live in? Or does he just live in part of the building with his family?"

Jered holds out an arm for me to take. "Why don't we go in and find out?"

I loop my arm through Jered's, and we walk up to the front door. Jered doesn't even bother to knock on the door. He simply opens it for me. Immediately, I'm bombarded by the raucous laughter of children coming from inside the building.

"Ladies first," Jered says with a mischievous grin on his face.

I take a step inside and find myself engulfed in complete chaos.

A sea of children are crowded together on the first floor. Their ages range from toddlers to teenagers. They look to be in something resembling a line that reaches down a long hallway towards the back of the house.

"Ok, children!" I hear Daniel say somewhere close by, but I can't see him. "It's time to calm down. The sooner you stop playing around the sooner you will all get fed."

I look over at Jered and see him watching me. "I thought you said Daniel and Linn only had four children?"

"Four of their own," Jered clarifies.

"Then who do these other kids belong to?"

"Daniel and Linn run an orphanage," Jered explains. "The other children are their charges."

"What in the world are the two of you doing here?"

I turn to see Daniel walking towards us from the end of the hallway the children are lined up to go down.

As Daniel approaches, I sense an aura of peace surrounding him. When he smiles at me, I feel like everything will be all right, even though I'm not sure if they will be or not.

When he reaches us, he doesn't hesitate to bring me into the fold of his arms for a far gentler hug than Brutus' but filled with just as much love.

He pulls away and looks down at me.

"I didn't expect to see you this soon," he tells me before looking over at Jered. "Is it time to deal with Belphagor now?"

"No, not yet," Jered says. "Is there somewhere we can talk privately?"

Daniel nods. "Sure. Do we have some time though? If we do, I would like to help Linn get the children fed first."

"Yes, we have time," Jered replies. "Is there anything we can do to help?"

"No, they're all pretty good about doing what we ask of

them," Daniel says. "Even if they do look like a disorderly bunch of hooligans at the moment."

"Children! Children! Please calm down!" I hear a woman say as she walks down the staircase which leads up to the second and third floors of the building.

I look up to see Daniel's wife and can easily understand why he fell in love with her. She's absolutely gorgeous, and, just like Daniel, she has an air about her that immediately makes you feel at ease in her presence.

Her face looks like that of a doll. Its paleness contrasts dramatically with her long, black hair which is brushed to the side and hangs over one shoulder. She isn't wearing any make-up but such a mask would only act to obscure her natural beauty.

When her dark brown eyes meet mine, I see instant recognition. A smile illuminates her face, and I know she understands that I'm not just the Empress of Cirrus. I'm someone Daniel has obviously told her about, and I'm special to her because I'm special to him.

She walks directly to me and gives me a hug. I imagine it's the type of hug a mother would give a daughter, though I wouldn't really know how that truly feels.

When she pulls back from me, she says, "Welcome to our home, Anna."

"Thank you. I'm sorry we came unannounced."

"You are welcome here any time, day or night," she tells me truthfully. "Our door is always open to friends and family."

Linn looks over at Jered. "It's been a long time, Jered. We've missed seeing you."

Jered leans in to Linn and kisses her chastely on the cheek. "I'm sorry, Linn. I've been rather busy."

Linn smiles understandingly. "If the two of you would excuse me, I need to help the people who volunteer in our kitchen serve the children supper." Linn looks to Daniel. "Why don't you spend some time with Anna and Jered? I can handle things tonight. I have a feeling they didn't come here for a simple visit."

Smart and beautiful, I thought to myself. I could definitely understand why Daniel decided he didn't need to wait to meet his soul mate. He and Linn may not have had that once in a lifetime connection, but when they looked at one another, anyone watching them could see how much love and respect they had for each other.

"Are you sure?" Daniel asks, holding his hand out to Linn.

Linn slips hers into his so naturally you know they've done it a thousand times before.

"I can handle them," she reassures her husband.

"Why don't I help you?" I suggest. "Jered can tell Daniel what he needs to know."

"Are you sure?" Linn asks, not looking completely convinced I would want to help her with such a chore.

"Sure. How hard can it be?"

CHAPTER EIGHT

An hour later I understand why Linn laughed when I asked that question.

Children are heathens!

After I helped her keep them all in a straight, orderly line to take their turn picking up the plates the kitchen staff prepared, I longed for the little boy I now call my son. Lucas was so well behaved I just assumed most children would be that way. Apparently, I was sadly mistaken. My experience with children was completely limited to Lucas, and I now appreciated his kind heart and intelligence, making me miss him even more.

The one child in the orphanage who seemed most like Lucas was one of Daniel and Linn's own children. Her name was Bai, and she took to me right away for some reason. While I walked up and down the line to keep the rowdier kids from misbehaving, Bai held onto one of my hands and helped me with the names of those who were acting out.

Bai looked to be around the same age as Lucas. Her dark brown eyes and braided pigtails made her absolutely adorable. You could tell she would grow up to be just as beautiful as her mother, possibly even more so. I was glad to see that Daniel had a child close to Lucas' age, and I hoped we would be able to get the two of them together often as they grew up. Lucas would need someone his own age to talk to about a world not many people would ever understand. I didn't want him to feel isolated from others just because he would have to keep secret what he knew about angels and demons. He would need a confidante, and I hoped Bai would be that for him one day.

After the children were fed, it was time to prepare them for bed. Anarchy ensued and some of the children scattered, hiding themselves just so they could stay up a little while longer. Bai was instrumental in ferreting out their hiding places. She seemed to know the best, or perhaps the most frequented, spots. Linn and I soon had all the children tucked into their beds. Bai informed me that her three older brothers liked to sleep in the common room with the other children rather than in their own bedrooms. Bai was the only child who slept in her own room.

"Anna," Bai says, tugging on my hand, "would you like to see my toys?"

I looked around the large common room lined with small beds along all four walls. Linn was tucking in the last of the children, and I saw no reason not to follow Bai to her private sanctuary.

I nod to her. "I would love to see them, Bai."

She pulls me down the hallway and takes me to the room at the end of it.

When we step inside, I see at least one problem Lucas might have with his future friend. I remember thinking when I stepped into Lucas' bedroom in Malcolm's Lakewood home that it was unusually tidy for a six year old. Bai's room was the complete antithesis to Lucas' room. I had to watch where I stepped in fear that I would break a favorite toy.

The first thing she shows me is her treasure trove of paints and art supplies on a small easel that's just her height. It brings back memories of the little birdhouse I was painting in Malcolm's workshop. I enjoyed finding a newfound talent and hoped I would be able to explore it more one day. Malcolm told me that one of my ancestors, Caylin, had been a talented artist and that most of her descendants were able to retain the skill. It was a piece of my lineage that had always been missing.

My thoughts linger on the perfect day we were able to spend together as a family. I suddenly realize that it only happened the day before. Yet, it seems like a lifetime ago. My heart yearns to spend more time with not only Malcolm and Lucas, but also with my papa, Millie, and the other Watchers I have come to know and love. All of a sudden, I feel a great sense of loss and loneliness without having the others near.

"Anna."

I look up to find Daniel peering at me from the entrance to

Bai's room. He smiles at me, and I know one thing for certain.

I am not alone. I have people who have loved me for as long as I've been alive. I simply didn't know they existed until now. They will help me get back the rest of my loved ones and somehow, we'll find a way to defeat those who would keep us apart.

"Linn is making some tea," Daniel tells me. "Would you like to come down for some?"

"Yes, that would be nice."

Daniel walks into the room, being careful not to step on anything.

"And you young lady," Daniel says to Bai, "need to go to bed. If we can find it…"

Bai giggles and throws herself into her father's arms. She says something in a language I don't understand.

"Bai, speak English," Daniel tells her.

"But why?" She asks.

"Because that's the language all of the cloud cities decided we should speak. It makes things easier on everyone if we all speak the same language."

Bai pokes her bottom lip out in an effective pout at Daniel, and I have to hide a smile so it doesn't encourage her behavior, even though I find it irresistibly endearing.

Daniel picks Bai up easily in his arms and takes her to her small bed. After he kisses her on the forehead, he whispers, "Sweet dreams."

I walk out of Bai's room with Daniel, and he quietly closes the door behind us.

"She's adorable," I tell him as we make our way down the staircase from the second floor to the first.

"She's incorrigible," Daniel laughs. "She's just like her mother, always thinking she's entitled to get her own way."

"Well, that's not necessarily a bad thing," I tell him, thinking that it's my mentality too. "It simply means she knows what she wants."

"She wants to visit a cloud city one day."

"I would love it if you and your family could come to Cirrus when all of this is over," I tell him. "In fact, I would like it if you all came to live there with us afterwards."

"That would be nice," Daniel says with great hesitation, "but the children here need us. It seems like as soon as one of them finds a home, another child arrives on our doorstep to take their place."

"At least consider the offer," I say to him.

Daniel nods. "We will consider it."

He escorts me to the back of the house on the first floor. The room we enter is large since it serves as the kitchen and the cafeteria for the children to eat in. Three long tables with equally long benches on either side provide enough space for all the children to eat together at one time. Jered and Linn are already sitting at the table in the middle of the room, opposite one another. I take a seat beside Jered on the bench he's on and Daniel takes his place beside Linn across from us.

"So I assume Jered filled you in on everything?" I ask Daniel.

"Yes, I understand what needs to be done. Don't worry, Anna, we'll get them back. I'm so sorry about Vala though. I hope Travis can repair her for you. If anyone can figure out how to save her, it's him."

Linn pours some tea from the black kettle on the table into my cup. I notice her eyes linger on the shoulder where Levi stabbed me.

"I can mend that for you," she tells me.

It takes me a moment to realize what she's talking about.

Before I can make a reply, she sets the kettle back down

and walks out of the room. She soon returns with a woven basket filled with sewing supplies dangling from the crook of her left arm.

"Hand me your jacket, Anna," she tells me after she sets the basket on the table, "and I will repair the damage."

I shrug off my white leather jacket and hand it to Linn.

I watch as she threads a needle with practiced hands and begins to stitch the two inch slit made by Levi's dagger. I honestly didn't think about the hole until she mentioned it. It feels kind of nice to have someone take care of such a minor detail. It makes me think of Millie. She would have noticed such a thing and fixed it for me too.

I suppose, in a way, Millie has always been cast in the role of a mother figure in my life. My papa was always there for me when I needed someone to hold me or teach me, but Millie took care of my day to day needs without ever asking for anything for herself. She not only provided me with the basic things in life like food and clothing, but she was also a friend to a lonely little girl who had few people she could play with. Millie was the one I went to as a child if I scraped my knee or needed someone to play tea party with me. She was always there when I needed her.

If there was anyone in this world I could entrust Lucas' safety to, it was Millie. I knew she would not only keep him out of harm's way, but protect him from watching anything Levi might do to tear them down. I prayed Levi didn't torture Vala in front of Lucas, but then again, why wouldn't he? He was the worst person I knew, and I hoped I would be the one who ended his life just so I could put an end to his madness. But, I had to admit to myself that there was a small part of me who would gain pleasure from his pain. I tried to quell the murderous side of me seeking revenge, but it seemed impossible.

Once Linn was finished sewing the slit of my jacket up, she walked around the table to help me put it back on.

"Thank you," I tell her, zipping the front of it up. It was a small action but one that made me acutely aware of Malcolm's absence even more.

It took me back to that little beach house where he showed me how to use the zipper for the very first time. It was something I could have figured out on my own, but I wanted him closer and it seemed like a logical thing to ask him to demonstrate. I can almost feel his arms around me now as I think back to that moment. It takes everything in me not to phase back to him. But, I know Levi would keep true to his word and kill my father if I did. I simply had to be patient and bide my time until the trade could be made.

"Don't look so sad," Linn tells me, obviously seeing my sudden melancholy. "You will get them all back soon."

"I think I might have just the thing to perk you up," Jered

says to me, rising from his seat at the table to come stand beside me.

"What do you have in mind?" I ask, curious to know what Jered might think would brighten my mood.

"And ruin the surprise?" Jered asks like I should know better than that by now.

Daniel stands from the table and comes over to give me a hug.

"Try to get some rest," he tells me like a concerned father. "Malcolm would tear us apart if he thought we didn't take good care of you in his absence."

I smile at the reminder of Malcolm's protective side and hope I can experience it again for myself soon.

All I needed to do was get through the next few hours. Then, I could have my family back and possibly find just a little bit of peace, for a time at least.

I knew once we let the princes roam free that our work would just be beginning. The thought of that eventuality should have frightened me. I had no way of knowing what they would do with their new found freedom. I would have to assume they wouldn't be in the best of moods after there long sojourn.

"I'll try," I promise Daniel.

Linn leans over and kisses me on the cheek.

"If you ever need anything, just let us know."

Jered holds out his arm for me to take.

"Ready for the last surprise of the day?" He asks me.

I nod, feeling tired all of a sudden and hoping wherever it is Jered plans to take us it will have a nice, comfortable bed.

Jered phases us to a room that looks similar to the study Malcolm had in his Lakewood home. The dark, polished wood walls are actually built in shelves which are lined neatly with a variety of leather bound volumes. A large wood desk of the same style sits in front of a bank of bay windows with a maroon leather chair to sit in behind it.

"Where are we?" I ask, as I let my tired mind soak in the details of the room, which makes me feel like I'm surrounded by little bits of Malcolm everywhere I look.

"This is Malcolm's home in New Orleans."

I look over at Jered. "Was it safe to just phase here? Levi will know where we are."

Jered shrugs looking completely unconcerned. "I don't think it matters. It's not like he doesn't know about this place. We have to wait somewhere until we can do the trade. I figured here was as good a place as any. Plus, it's filled with Malcolm's possessions which is something I think you need around you right now. It's the best I can do without actually bringing Malcolm to you."

I smile at Jered, marveling at how well he has come to know me in such a short period of time.

"Thank you," I tell him. "It's just what I need."

Jered grins, obviously pleased that he could help me, even if it was only by such a small gesture.

"Why don't you take a look around? I need to go speak with Malcolm's butler, Giles, and let him know we're here. Are you hungry?"

"I could use something to eat," I admit, even though satiating such a small necessity forms a knot of guilt in the pit of my stomach. I'm certain Malcolm isn't being offered water much less food. My kiss has probably worn off by now too. I pray his body had time to heal the majority of the damage done to his back by Levi's whip before he woke up.

"I won't be gone long," Jered tells me as he heads for the door in the room and strolls out.

As I walk around Malcolm's study, I run the tips of my fingers against the leather bound volumes lining his bookshelves. I feel as though I'm getting to know him a little better even though he isn't physically with me. It's apparent books are very important to him since he keeps so many nearby. There isn't a single place in the room where I can't imagine Malcolm being.

I can easily visualize him standing by any of these bookcases thumbing through the pages of a book. I can imagine him sitting behind his desk writing a correspondence or turned around in his chair peering thoughtfully out at the city outside his window. I notice two wing back chairs sitting across from a matching sofa in front of the unlit fireplace and recognize something very familiar, a chessboard. It's the same type of holographic board he had in his Lakewood home. I sit down in one of the chairs and run my hand over it, instantly conjuring up the holograms representing the black and white pieces.

I hear two sets of footfalls approaching the room and run my hand over the board again to turn it off. I stand from the chair just as Jered enters with Malcolm's butler coming in right behind him.

When Jered said he was going to talk to Giles the butler, for some reason I envisioned an elderly man with white hair and a stiff demeanor. The man walking by Jered's side exhibits neither of those traits. He's handsome and looks to be in his late twenties or early thirties. Giles has a serious look about him but not one that is off putting. His short hair and intense eyes are both brown. The mustache and goatee on his face are neatly trimmed, and he's wearing casual clothing consisting of a dark blue cable knit sweater, blue jeans and black rubber boots that reach up to his knees.

"Giles," Jered says as they come to stand in front of me, "I would like to introduce you to Empress Anna."

Giles bows at the waist to me. "It's a pleasure to make your acquaintance, Empress."

I hold my hand out to Giles. He looks surprised by the gesture but doesn't make a big deal out of it.

As he shakes my hand I say, "It's nice to meet you, Giles. Though, I have to admit when Jered said you were Malcolm's butler I was expecting someone much older."

Giles grins like this is something he's heard others say before.

"My family has served Malcolm for a very long time, your majesty. I simply inherited the job from my father like he did from his father and so on."

"Please, Giles, just call me Anna. I have a feeling you and I will be around each other a lot in the coming years. It's good to know Malcolm has had people who have taken such good care of him for that long."

"We've tried our best, Anna," Giles replies with a smile. I think he feels privileged that I'm allowing him to be so informal with me. "Jered said you would like something to eat. Are you hungry for anything in particular?"

"Just something light. I don't have much of an appetite, but my stomach feels like it might rebel against the rest of my body if I don't feed it soon. Something quick and easy will do. So, please, don't put yourself out on my account."

Giles bows to me again. "I'll be right back. Something quick and easy coming up."

Giles walks out of the room, and I look over at Jered.

"Why was he wearing those boots? He looked like he was about to go wading in a river or something."

"He was in the stables cleaning out the horse stalls when I found him," Jered says as his eyes look down at the chessboard. "Do you play?"

"I can play well enough to lose all the time," I say with a sigh of disappointment in myself. Then, I have a brilliant idea. "Do you happen to be any good at it?"

"Yes," Jered says with a small smile. "Anyone who spends much time around Malcolm picks up a thing or two about the game."

"Do you think you could teach me some strategy so I can be better?" I ask eagerly. "I want to be able to play with Malcolm without losing within a few short minutes. I think it disappoints him to not have an opponent who provides a challenge."

"I can definitely try my best to teach you what I know," Jered says, sitting in the chair he's standing by while I retake my previous seat.

Jered and I play for a while until Giles brings some food for us to eat. The meal is a basic one of beef stew with carrots and potatoes. He also brings up a plate of biscuits with some sweet tea to wash it all down with. I surprise myself by eating everything Giles brought up for me. I realize I must have been hungrier than I thought.

"You should probably get some rest," Jered tells me after we eat. "We have a few hours yet before we have to meet Levi for the trade, and I have a few details I need to work out before we meet with him anyway."

"Do you think you're plan will work?" I ask, already knowing what Jered and the others were planning to do to ensure we got everyone back safely.

"I have no reason to believe it won't," he replies. "Come on. You look dead on your feet. You need to get some sleep before the trade."

Jered escorts me to a bedroom a few doors down from the study. As soon as I step into it, I know it's Malcolm's personal bedroom.

"I thought you might like to stay in his room," Jered tells me. "I know Malcolm would want you to."

"Thank you," I say as I walk further into the space, feeling Malcolm's presence surround me like a warm blanket.

"I'll come and wake you if you aren't already up when it's time to meet Levi," Jered promises me.

"All right. Thank you, Jered."

Jered closes the door, and I'm left alone in Malcolm's bedroom.

It's a large room, but it has to be to accommodate the massive four poster bed sitting against the left wall. The bed looks fit for a king with its hand carved wood frame and canopy. Heavy gold and maroon drapes are bunched at all four corners but look like they could be easily drawn together if the occupant lying inside wanted some privacy. I see that Giles has been in the room already because there is a roaring fire in the fireplace providing the space a warmth that is soothing. He must have thought I would want to change into something more comfortable to sleep in also. What I have to assume is one of Malcolm's shirts is lying on the turned down bed covers.

I walk over and pick the blue button down shirt up, bringing it to my nose and inhaling its just laundered freshness. I quickly shed my clothes and put it on. It's too big for me, of course, but it almost makes me feel like Malcolm is holding me. After I slip underneath the covers, I wrap my arms around one of the big, fluffy pillows there and pretend that I'm holding Malcolm instead. I don't find sleep right away. As I look around the room, I notice something white peeking out from underneath a book on the nightstand beside the bed. I reach out a hand and pull on the sheet of paper.

It's a hand written letter, and I notice Malcolm's signature scrawled at the bottom of it. Just as I'm about to return it to its rightful place, not wanting to intrude into his privacy, I happen to glance up to the top of the letter and see that it's addressed to me. I immediately sit straight up in the bed and begin to read it.

Dear Anna,

We met for the first time tonight and the experience has left me shattered. I'm sitting here in my bed wondering what you're doing, wondering if you're thoughts are centered on me as mine are on you, and wondering if I should return to you because not being by your side is tearing me apart. My mind is racing with the implications of our connection and sleep alludes me. I find it almost impossible to believe that someone I've refused to even look at all these years is actually my soul mate. How could I have been such a fool for so long? Yet, perhaps our meeting was destined to be put off until now.

I can't help but think you deserve a man better than me to give your love to, and I don't understand why my father would have you settle for someone with such a checkered past.

I've done some terrible things in my time, Anna. I've tortured those who didn't deserve it. I've killed for sport and menaced the innocent just to see them cower in fear of me. There are literally thousands of sins that I've committed over the years that I had to earn forgiveness for. But, no matter how much good I do, it never seems like enough to make up for the horrors I've perpetrated in my past.

You are a chance at a new beginning for me, a new life. A war is raging inside me right now as I try to decide whether or not to simply accept the gift of you or to turn away from this opportunity and force you to find someone who is more worthy of your love. I feel as though I owe you the opportunity to find happiness with someone else because I'm not completely sure you will ever find it with me. I am not an easy man to get along with. Hell, most of the time I don't even like myself. How could I expect you to love someone who can't even do something as simple as that?

I have a feeling my father wants me to take a leap of faith with you. I'm simply not sure I'm strong enough to do that. I have a lot to work out first, and you shouldn't have to be a part of that. I feel sorry for you in a way. I feel sorry that you got stuck with someone like me for a soul mate. I can't imagine you've done anything in your life to deserve such a miserable fate. I'm not even sure why I'm writing a letter that I have no intention of ever letting you see. I suppose I just needed to find some way to work through my conflicting emotions and sort out what I truly feel and think.

I never thought I could love anyone more than Lilly.

But, Anna, I think I could love you a thousand times more…

Malcolm

I read the letter over and over until my eyes simply can't stay open any longer. I fall into a blissful slumber, clutching Malcolm's letter to my chest and drifting off to sleep with the promise of love from the strongest man I know.

CHAPTER NINE

I wake with a start. As my eyes take in my environment, my mind readjusts to the fact that I'm in Malcolm's bedroom and lying in his enormous four-poster bed. I still have the letter he wrote to me clutched firmly to my chest. I loosen my grasp on the missive and read the very last sentence again.

But, Anna, I think I could love you a thousand times more…

My heart sings with the joy those words bring, and they make me more determined to get my man back.

I quickly put my clothes on, leaving Malcolm's shirt lying on the bed. I hope by that night's end we'll be sharing a bed together. I don't care where it is. All I know is that I want to feel Malcolm's arms holding me close. I need him to tell me everything will be all right and that things will work out as they should.

I still have doubts about handing Levi back his brothers. The smart thing to do would be to kill them all while we still have them, but the results of such an act could destroy me in more ways than one. The simple fact was that it would be murder to kill the other princes while they were still in stasis. In time, I might be able to forgive myself for committing those murders, but I doubted it. In truth, it was the second reason that prompted me to go through with the deal the most. I would never be able to live with myself if Levi killed Lucas, Millie, or my papa because of my duplicity. His torture of Malcolm and execution of Vala was bad enough. Even if I gathered the seals from the princes now and finished God's mission, I would have paid too high a price to get the job done.

No, this was the right thing to do. And Jered's back-up plan to guarantee we got back those we love should work.

As I strap the sword onto my back, I turn to leave the room but notice something else lying on Malcolm's nightstand where I found the note. It's the silver pin in the shape of a lily he wore the night of the wedding celebration. I pick it up and stare at it for a moment. It makes me wonder what happened to make Malcolm finally give me his heart. Or had he completely let Lilly go? I wasn't sure. I do know one thing though. I know I have his love. I have absolutely no doubt about that fact. I put the pin back where I found it and leave the room.

Malcolm's home in New Orleans is as large as any palace. I pass room after room as I make my way down the hallway until I come to one that catches my eye and makes me come to an abrupt halt. The door to this room is unlike any of the others because it's been painted. I stare at the mural, trying to make out what I'm seeing within the gold, maroon, and dark blue hues. The longer I stare, the more images I'm able to make out buried within the painting itself by a skilled hand to make them appear as a cohesive whole, instead of simple portraits which stand out on their own. I see the faces of my Watcher protectors and reach out a hand when

I find Malcolm's visage at the center of them all. I look down the length of the door. Hidden away near the bottom, like the painter didn't want anyone to notice it readily, was an image of Lucifer.

I turn the knob to open the door and step into the room.

Even though the room is filled with furniture, a loneliness permeates the air like it hasn't been lived in for a very long time. I stand in the doorway unsure I want to venture further in until I see something on the nightstand by the wrought iron bed that interests me.

I walk over and pick up a holo-projector. It's a simple gadget used to store captured images and video. I touch the screen of the handheld crystal device and an image from the last video played appears on the display. I feel the salty burn of tears as I look at the woman staring back at me. I had a feeling this was my mother's room, and the smiling picture of her on the screen of the holo-projector has confirmed my suspicion.

I take in a deep breath and touch the image so it will play.

Holo-projectors transform any space you're in to play back videos like you're experiencing them in person. The only thing you have to be careful about is moving around while one is playing. The physical objects in the room don't move. They're simply camouflaged by the projected video. I was always told to stand still while one was on unless I was confident I wouldn't run into anything.

The scene I find myself in is of a sunny day with a clear blue sky overhead. I'm standing in a forest but the trees are bare of leaves. The ground is covered by a light dusting of snow, and the sound of a woman's laughter rings through the still air. I turn around to find my mother running towards me. She's even more beautiful than the portrait I used to have of her in my chambers back in Cirrus. Her dark, wavy brown hair flows behind her like a silky mane as she runs. She reaches up to her dark blue knitted scarf tucked underneath the collar of her coat to pull it just below her chin.

"There's nowhere you can run where I wouldn't be able to find you," I hear a familiar male voice say behind her.

I lift my gaze and see Lucifer quickly catching up to my mother. She laughs even harder when she looks over her shoulder at him. I watch as he grabs the back of her coat to stop her. My mother loses her footing and begins to tumble to the ground, but Lucifer phases in beneath her and cushions her fall. My mother giggles and looks down at him while he smiles up at her with such pure joy it completely transforms his face into someone I almost don't recognize.

"Thank you," she tells him, giving him a quick kiss on the lips. "It probably wouldn't have been a good thing for me to fall in my condition."

Lucifer looks confused.

"Your condition?" He asks. "Are you ill? If you are, you shouldn't be out in this weather. It'll only make things worse."

My mother shakes her head at him and smiles. "No, I'm not sick."

"Then what's wrong?" He asks, lifting a hand to tuck the left side of her hair behind her ear. "Is there anything I can do to help you?"

"Just love me," she replies.

"That I will always be able to do. But, tell me what's wrong so I can do more."

"You've done quite enough, husband," my mother says as her smile turns shy. "In fact, you're the reason I'm in the condition I find myself in."

Lucifer still looks confused, but when my mother's smile practically lights up her face, I can see realization dawn as his expression changes to one of disbelief.

"You're pregnant?" He asks, as if needing her verbal confirmation of the fact.

My mother nods. "Yes. We're going to have a baby girl."

Lucifer rolls his eyes. "And of course our first child will have to be a girl. Your family is famous for them."

My mother pinches Lucifer playfully on the arm, but it seems to actually cause him a bit of pain because he flinches.

"And if we didn't, I might have never been born," my mother reminds him.

Lucifer smiles and lifts his hands to cup one side of my mother's face.

"The day you were brought into this world was the happiest day of my life. I just didn't know it at the time. But when our daughter is born, we can share in that happiness together and be able to relive that memory for the rest of our lives."

My mother lowers her head and kisses Lucifer. He kisses her back fervently, and I look away because I feel as though I'm violating a moment that was meant to only be shared between the two of them.

"I should get you back home and out of this cold," I hear Lucifer say.

I return my gaze to my parents and see them rise from the snow covered ground.

"One second," my mom says, walking over to one of the trees and bending down to retrieve the holo-projector I hold in my

166

hands. She turns around and holds it up to show Lucifer. "I wanted to save the moment to show to our daughter one day. I hope you don't mind."

Lucifer holds out a hand to my mother which she readily accepts.

"Of course I don't mind. I want her to know how happy you made me today."

My mother throws her arms around Lucifer's neck and kisses him soundly on the lips.

The image fades, and I find myself standing in my mother's room again.

I lay the holo-projector back down on the nightstand and leave the room. I'm curious to know what else is on there, but for some reason, I feel like it would be a violation of my mother's memories. I know she wanted me to see that one video and that's enough for me right now. It was strange to see Lucifer so happy. It's a side of his personality I never would have thought existed if I hadn't seen it with my own two eyes. Millie told me once that when Lucifer was with my mother he was a completely different person. What I just witnessed seemed to support her opinion. If he could be that man once, perhaps he could be the man I just saw again one day. Surely even the devil wanted to feel joy in his life instead of anger and hate.

I walk out of the room and firmly close the door behind me.

"I see you found Amalie's room," I hear Jered say.

I look up the hallway and see him walking from the direction of Malcolm's bedroom. I assume he probably went there first to find me which can only mean one thing.

"Is it almost time to meet Levi?" I ask.

Jered nods. "Yes, almost. I was just coming to wake you. Would you like to get something to eat before we go?"

I shake my head. "No, I'm not hungry. Even if I were, I don't think I could eat. My stomach is all tied up in knots as it is."

"Don't worry," Jered says, but I can detect a note of that emotion in his own voice. "We'll get them back."

"Alive, I hope."

"Everything will work out," Jered says with a reassuring smile.

"Even if we get Lucas, Malcolm, and Millie back, there's no guarantee he'll ever release my papa."

"Levi won't kill Andre," Jered says with more confidence. "He knows your father's safety is the only thing keeping him alive. Levi might act brave, but deep down underneath that snarky, all knowing attitude of his he's essentially a coward."

"I know that. And he's the one prince I have no intention of giving a chance to live, Jered. He's done too much for me to allow him to stay alive."

"I won't stop you when the time comes," Jered tells me. "Unfortunately, that time isn't today."

"He's not going to like what we're planning to do," I tell Jered, worried that we might be making a mistake.

"Well, we're not exactly giving him a choice. We know we'll keep our end of the bargain, but Levi doesn't live by any sort of moral code. He'll do what he wants. This way we can keep him on a short leash and force him to do what he promised."

"I just hope it doesn't backfire," I say, worried now about what Jered wants to do.

"If he hurts any of them, he gets nothing," Jered says. "I don't think he'll be that stupid."

"I hope you're right."

Jered looks at the door to my mother's room. "Did you find anything interesting in there?"

"A holo-projector," I admit.

"Amalie liked to watch videos while she was bedridden during the pregnancy."

"I saw the one where she told Lucifer she was pregnant. They looked so happy together."

"I think it broke her heart when he stopped visiting her."

"Stopped visiting her?" I ask in surprise. "Why?"

"He was mad, an emotion Lucifer has always had a hard time keeping under control. He wanted your mother to get rid of you so she wouldn't die."

"He wanted her to abort me?"

Jered nods. "He told her they didn't need to have a child to be happy. He tried to convince her that all they needed was each other. But, Amalie was stubborn. I think she was the most stubborn out of all the descendants, at least that's what Malcolm always said. She insisted that you had a special purpose and had to be born no matter what the cost."

"How did she know I would be the descendant all of you were waiting on to be born?"

"I'm not sure what Amalie knew. She never said anything else about what she thought you were meant to do. All I know is that you were the most precious thing to her and no one else mattered as much to her as you did. I wish you had been given the chance to know her."

"Do you think she would be proud of me? Do you think she

would approve of the way I turned out?"

"Of that I have no doubt," Jered says, an expression of pride on his face as he looks at me. "We're all proud of you, Anna. You've exceeded any of our expectations."

Jered's face looks slightly troubled. "It's time."

He holds out his hand to me and I take it.

"Stay strong," he tells me.

"I will."

Jered phases us.

I'm not sure what I expected the Sahara desert to look like. Being a desert, I suppose I thought it would be covered in sand. Yet, it appears winter has found its way even to this arid climate. We stand on what looks like a snow covered hill, but since I know it's a desert, I think we are actually standing on a dune. The moon is high in the sky casting a ghostly glow around us. Desmond, Brutus, and Daniel phase in at the exact same instant we do.

We all look around but don't see Levi anywhere.

"How predictable," Desmond says with a derisive shake of his head.

"Looks like he did exactly what you thought he would," Daniel comments dryly to Jered.

"I wonder why he thought we would be that stupid." Brutus says.

"I'm sorry," I say. "I feel like I'm missing something important. Why do you think Levi isn't here yet?"

"One of the reasons we're doing this trade the way we are," Jered tells me, "is because we all assumed he would try to see where we phased to retrieve the princes. Like I said earlier, Levi lacks a moral code of any sort. I'm sure he hoped to snatch the princes out from under us just as we phased to retrieve them."

"So he was planning to try to double cross us," I say, realization dawning.

"Looks that way," Desmond agrees. "It's a good thing we've never trusted the slimy bastard."

"Do you think he'll still show up?" I ask.

"Oh, he'll be here," Brutus reassures me. "He doesn't have any choice now."

Approximately a minute later, Levi phases in about five feet away from us. Christopher has an unconscious Malcolm in his arms and lays him on the snow covered ground at his feet. Malcolm doesn't move or even make a sound. Levi has Lucas standing in front of him with his hands on my son's shoulders close to his neck, a subtle reminder to me about how easily he can kill him. Millie stands by Levi with her wrists bound together by magnetic cuffs. Clark, the guard who always accompanied Christopher to take me to my lessons with Empress Catherine, is gripping Millie's left arm so tightly it makes my friend grimace in pain.

"Well, I brought my offerings," Levi says to me. "Where are yours, my little dove?"

Jered tosses Levi a small glass tablet. Levi catches it with one hand. He peers at the device with a confused expression on his face. He holds it up between his index and middle finger to examine it more closely. A cascading array of purple digital numbers play across the screen.

"What's this?" Levi asks, studying the card sized tablet.

"After you give us the three of them," Jered says, nodding his head to my loved ones, "we'll give you the code to unlock the coordinates where you can find your brothers. Then you can go get them yourself."

Levi sneers. "And how do I know you aren't feeding me some bogus locations?"

"Unlike you we actually keep our word," Jered says. "But if you need proof, I've programmed the first coordinate separately from the others. Input code 02201994 for the first coordinate."

Levi inputs the numerical code on the touch screen. One steady set of numbers appears on the screen, and he shows them to Christopher.

"Go there and see what you find," Levi orders.

Christopher looks at the numbers and phases.

Levi looks back over at me.

"How did you like the present Christopher delivered to you?" He has the audacity to not only ask but also smile about it.

"Go to Hell, Levi," I say, not able to keep the contempt I feel for him out of my voice.

"Been there… done that. Completely overrated if you ask me."

"I plan to send you back there permanently," I tell him, finding at least a small bit of satisfaction knowing my threat will become fact one day.

"Wouldn't you miss me just a little bit?" Levi says as if wounded by my words.

"I would miss you about as much as I would miss a boil on my butt, Levi. The sooner I cut you to pieces the better off we'll all be."

I hear snickers beside me and know the boys found my

remark amusing.

"A boil on your butt?" Levi repeats seeming to have only taken in that much of what I said. "And here I have endearments such as 'my little dove' and 'wife'." Levi looks down at Malcolm. "You know this big oaf used to call Lilly his 'dearest'. Do you think he'll come up with a cute little sweet nothing name that means as much for you?"

I knew what he was doing. He was trying to bait me, but I wasn't going to give him the satisfaction of letting it bother me. I had no doubt in my mind about Malcolm's love for me. If I had to share his heart with Lilly, so be it. But he was mine in this lifetime and no one else's.

"He'll be able to call me wife soon enough," I say. "I'm planning to be a widow before long."

"I guess we'll see about that," Levi says, narrowing his eyes at me. "I still have Andre, lest you forget."

"No, I haven't forgotten," I reply. "That's pretty much the only reason I've allowed you to live this long. If it wasn't for him, you would have died the night Christopher brought me Vala."

I look down at Lucas to see what his reaction is to the reminder of Vala's decapitation. He looks sad but not on the verge of tears. He's keeping it together which makes me proud, but it also breaks my heart that he even has to make the attempt.

As if he heard his name spoken, Christopher phases back with one of the princes still in stasis. I see a silver dagger pierced through one of his hands. His clothes look ragged with age from being hidden away for so long.

"I didn't remove the dagger," Christopher tells Levi. "Something's wrong with his seal. I wasn't sure what would happen if I took it out."

Levi looks at the prince's hand and shakes his head in disappointment.

"Well, I guess he might come in handy one day. But, we can't release him just yet."

Levi looks at Jered. "Smart to give me the defective one first."

"Now you see that we're ready to make a deal," Jered says. "Give us Malcolm, Lucas, and Millie, and I'll give you the code that unlocks the rest of the coordinates."

"I can't say I appreciate the way you've handled this," Levi tells us. "I don't like being made a fool of."

"We didn't make you a fool," Brutus says. "You've been one for some time now, Levi."

"*Ha.. ha.. ha,*" Levi says sarcastically.

He hands the glass tablet to Christopher and whispers something to him. Christopher phases the prince he brought and the tablet away. Through his phase trail, I can see he's returned to the palace in Cirrus.

Levi places both his hands on Lucas' shoulders.

"You know," Levi says with a tilt of his head. "I believe I can probably find someone in Cirrus to crack the code for me. But, only I can teach you all a lesson in obedience. This trade should have been a simple one, yet you chose to undermine me. Did you think this was a game? Do you find it amusing to play with my patience?"

With each question, I can see Levi's agitation at us intensify, and his hands are uncomfortably close to Lucas' neck.

"We're only playing the game you started," I tell him.

"You know as well as we do that you wouldn't have kept to your end of the bargain if we had simply brought all the princes here," Jered reasons. "You hoped to get your brothers when we phased to retrieve them from their hiding spots. We all know that, Levi. There's no point in denying it."

"Fine. I won't deny it. I guess I should tell you that I was also planning to make sweet Anna choose which one of these humans I would kill so she could spare the other one's life. But since you've just made it that much more difficult for me to retrieve my brothers, I don't think I'll privilege her with that luxury."

I watch as Levi places one hand underneath Lucas' chin. Lucas' eyes grow wide in fear while Levi smiles at me. I watch in horror as Levi's grip tightens around my son's jaw.

"You shouldn't have tested me," Levi says. "Now I'll have to teach you all a lesson."

CHAPTER TEN

Before I can move an inch or the guys can phase over to Levi, someone unexpected makes an appearance.

Lucifer phases in behind Levi and does to him what Levi had planned to do to Lucas. He quickly grabs Levi's chin with one hand, grips the back of his head with the other and twists. A distinctive cracking sound can be heard as Levi's eyes roll back in his head. His body goes completely limp, and he falls to the ground.

Clark stares disbelievingly at Levi's dead body on the snow beside him and then looks up at Lucifer in trepidation.

"Boo," he says to him.

Clark immediately phases away.

Lucas quickly moves away from Levi and Lucifer to kneel down beside Malcolm, yanking on his shoulders in a desperate attempt to wake him up. Desmond phases to Malcolm and rolls him over onto his back to check his pupils. Daniel and Brutus phase over to Millie while Jered phases us over to Malcolm and Lucas.

"He's just been drugged," Desmond tells us. "I'm sure Levi knew he wouldn't be able to control Malcolm any other way, especially if his plan was to kill Lucas in front of you."

I sit down on the snow and bring Lucas into my arms. He buries his head against my shoulder and begins to cry.

"Are you ok?" I ask him. "Did he do anything to you? Are you hurt anywhere?"

Lucas shakes his little head.

"I want to go home, Anna," he sobs. "Can we please just go home?"

"If you want to leave, I would do it before Levi wakes up," Lucifer advises me.

I look up at Lucifer. He's watching me closely but his expression is indecipherable.

"Why did you help us?"

"Still so naïve, Anna," Lucifer says with a shake of his head. "Who said I did this for you?"

"Then who did you do it for?"

"Myself, of course," Lucifer says. "I couldn't let Levi free his brothers. If I do it, their allegiance stays with me and I have plans for them."

"What plans?" I ask.

Lucifer grins. "You'll know soon enough."

He bends down and grabs a handful of Levi's hair before standing back up with Levi firmly in his grasp.

"Feel free to phase anywhere you want. It'll take Levi some time to wake up."

"Wake up?" I ask, totally confused. "I thought you just killed him."

"No, I did not kill him. I need him for my plans too, even if he is a pain in my ass. Is that close to the same thing as being a boil?"

Lucifer smiles down at me like he expects me to laugh at his little play on my joke. I have too many things on my mind to find it amusing.

"Then he's still alive?" I ask.

"In a manner of speaking," Lucifer answers. "I'm sure your friends can tell you more later. I would suggest you all leave from here. I'll take care of Levi for now so he doesn't bother you. Until we meet again, Anna."

Lucifer phases, and this time when I see the black void his phase trail leads to, I know he's taken Levi directly to Hell.

I tighten my hold on Lucas.

"Where should we go?" I ask, not really talking to anyone in particular.

"Let's go back to New Orleans," Jered says. "It looks like Lucifer has Levi under control. I don't think he'll be bothering us anytime soon, and we can regroup."

I nod and place my hand on Malcolm's arm. Lucas is still clutching me to him. I hug him tightly and phase us all to Malcolm's bed in his New Orleans home. I look over at Malcolm and worry over how still he is. I feel an urgent need to do a more thorough inspection of him.

"Lucas," I say gently. "I think we should check your father to make sure he's ok."

Lucas lifts his tear stained face from my chest and looks over at his dad. He sniffs and nods his head in agreement. We both get off the bed and walk over to the side closest to Malcolm. He's lying on his back, so I gently roll him over onto his left side to check it. To my relief, most of the damage done by Levi's whip has healed itself. There's still some bruising which looks bad, but I'm sure it will fade in record time.

I roll Malcolm back and study his face. I want to kiss him on the lips and have it act like it does in the fairytales where the one sleeping is instantly awoken by true love's kiss, but I know if I pressed my lips against his it would most likely have the completely opposite effect.

"Will he be ok, Anna?" Lucas asks me, taking hold of my hand closest to him, needing my reassurance that his father will be all right.

"He'll be fine, Lucas. I think he just needs some rest."

I tear my eyes away from Malcolm's face and look down at Lucas.

"Lucas," I say. I wait until he looks up at me before I continue. "Are you sure Levi didn't do anything to hurt you while you were in Cirrus?"

Lucas shakes his head slowly. This slight hesitation is a hint to me that he isn't telling me the entire truth.

"You need to tell me if he hurt you," I say.

"He didn't hurt me, Anna. He just killed Vala."

182

Lucas' little shoulders shake as he begins to cry again.

I bend down in front of him and take him into my arms. He rests his head on my shoulder and cries his little heart out.

"It's ok," I tell him, feeling my own pain over Vala's loss unite with his. "There was nothing you could have done to save her."

"I yelled at him to stop, but he wouldn't," Lucas sobs. "I really did try to be brave, Anna."

"Oh sweetie, I know you did. I never had any doubt that you didn't try to stop him. He's just an evil man, Lucas. Bad people do whatever they want no matter who it hurts."

"He was going to do the same thing to me that he did to Vala, wasn't he?"

"He was going to try," I admit, seeing no reason to lie. Lucas is old enough to know what almost happened. And he's smarter than most six year olds. So, lying to him seemed pointless.

"Who was the man who saved me?"

This question was far harder to answer. How much of my connection to Lucifer should Lucas know? How much about Lucifer himself should I warn him about?

"His name is Lucifer," I tell Lucas, finding it hard to

expound much beyond this simple fact.

There's a knock on the bedroom door which saves me from having to come up with more of an explanation.

"Come in," I say.

The door opens and Millie, Jered, and Desmond walk into the room. I stand back up just as Millie rushes over to me for a tight hug.

"Oh, my sweet, we were worried sick about you." Millie pulls back. "I'm so sorry I wasn't able to save Vala. That devil had her in his hands before either of us could react."

"We've taken Vala to someone who might be able to save her," Jered says, even though I wish he had kept that little bit of information to himself for the time being. I didn't want to get Lucas' hopes up over something that was far from a certainty.

"Do you think this person will really be able to help her?" Lucas asks, his voice filled with newfound optimism.

Jered looks down at Lucas, and I can see he realizes the mistake he just made saying what he did in front of him.

"I think he will try very hard to fix her," Jered says. "But there's no guarantee that she can be."

"When will we know?" Lucas asks.

"Well, I'm not completely sure. I suppose I could go see if he knows anything yet though. Would you like to come with me?"

Lucas looks up at me like he's asking for my permission first.

"You can go with Jered," I tell him.

Lucas lets go of my hand and walks over to Jered.

"We'll be right back," Jered says to me. "Hopefully with good news."

I nod, not voicing my worry that Vala was simply too far gone by the time we were able to get her to Travis.

After Jered and Lucas phase, Desmond walks over to Malcolm and does a brief examination.

"Is there anything we can do for him?" I ask Desmond.

"No," he replies after looking into Malcolm's eyes again. "He's merely in a deep sleep. I'm not sure what medication they gave him, but I would wager it shouldn't last more than another hour or two, perhaps less."

"Where are Brutus and Daniel?" I ask.

"Down in the kitchen with Giles preparing something to eat," Millie tells me. "Would you mind very much if I went to help them? I haven't seen Giles since he was a little boy. We have a lot of catching up to do."

"No, go ahead. You should both get something to eat. I'm going to stay up here with Malcolm until he wakes up."

"Like I said, it could be a couple of hours," Desmond warns.

"I understand, but I'm not leaving him."

Desmond grins at me with understanding. "Ok. Come get me if you need me."

After Millie and Desmond leave the room, I pull off Malcolm's boots and tuck him under the covers. I take off my baldric and lay my sword against the wall on my side of the bed. I quickly slip my jacket off and toss it onto a nearby chair. Then, I crawl underneath the comforter with Malcolm. I lay my left hand against his chest and feel the steady tempo of his heartbeat. Its rhythm brings me comfort and reassures me that he's still alive. As I lie down next to him, I can't help but stare at his perfect profile. Even after all he's been through, he still looks as devilishly handsome as ever. I lift my hand from his chest and run my fingers through his hair, noticing that it's matted with blood in spots.

I let my hand drift down the left side of his face and marvel at the man I love. I feel tears threaten, but this time it's not because I'm sad. I'm simply having a hard time believing someone like Malcolm is mine. My life has been a lonely one for the most part. I was only allowed to see certain people and had almost given up hope that I would ever meet a man I could give myself to completely. Then, Malcolm came into my world at the exact moment I needed him to. His touch was the only thing that brought me comfort after killing Amon and absorbing the first seal. As my memories travel back to that moment, I can clearly remember the first time I saw Malcolm's face. It was a moment permanently etched into my memory.

"I will do everything within my power to make our life a happy one," I whisper to him. "Please, wake up, Malcolm."

He doesn't wake up of course, but his continued slumber gives me an idea.

I lay my head on his chest and let the sound of his beating heart lull me to sleep, transporting me to the land of dreams. It's a place where I hope to reunite with my soul mate.

When I enter Malcolm's dream world, I feel out of sorts. It's almost like the drugs inducing his slumber are affecting me as well. Various memories from Malcolm's past swirl around me with no obvious coherency. Flashes of people, some I recognize and some I don't, float in the maelstrom of his thoughts, but no image or scene stays long enough for me to make any sense out of them.

I decide to attempt something to help him, but I have no way of knowing if it will work.

I take control of the dream.

I close my eyes to block out Malcolm's dream world and focus my thoughts on one single moment in our shared past. It's the moment Malcolm was in my room waiting for me to phase there. I had just gone to his bedroom in Cirrus the night of the wedding celebration because I felt his pain through the connection of our souls. Afterwards, I tried to phase back to my own bedroom but was unable to. Malcolm instructed me to follow his phase trail to make it easier to learn how to phase on my own.

When I returned to my room, I found him sitting on the side of my bed waiting for me. The look in his eyes then told me that he wanted me as much as I wanted him. I walked over to him, and he pulled me in close to his body, resting his head against my breasts and closing his eyes as if holding me brought him some much needed peace. I focus on that moment hoping to recreate it again within this dreamscape.

Large, warm hands caress the small of my back, and I feel Malcolm's head come to rest between my breasts.

When I open my eyes, I see that what I attempted to do has worked. Malcolm's incoherent thoughts have been pushed aside, and I'm now in control of what we see.

I pull away slightly which makes Malcolm lift his head and look up at me.

His eyes are slightly unfocussed from being drugged. When a lazy smile appears on his face, I know he can see me and knows who I am.

"Are you all right?" I ask him, concerned not just for his physical well-being but mental stability as well. I can't imagine what he went through during Levi's torture. I'm certain Levi wouldn't have just tried to break Malcolm physically, but mentally and emotionally as well.

"Better now," he answers, his voice sounding tired. "Is Lucas safe?"

"Yes, our son is safe."

Malcolm lets out a deep sigh in relief.

I lean down so my face is only inches away from Malcolm's.

"What can I do to help you?" I ask. "Just name it and it's yours."

"Kiss me, Anna."

I hesitate but then realize there isn't any reason to. We're in a dream, not reality. There's no way I can poison him in this world.

I gently push on Malcolm's shoulders until he's lying on his back. I have to pull the hem of my nightgown up to my thighs before I can climb onto the bed and straddle his waist. I lean over and rest my forearms on either side of Malcolm's head until our faces are only inches apart. He watches me with a look of amusement on his face.

"I almost feel as though I'm being taken advantage of," he tells me, the corners of his mouth lifting in a smile. "Please tell me that I am."

I smile back at him and shake my head.

"No," I tell him. "I would never take advantage of you."

Malcolm sighs in disappointment. "And here I thought I was about to get lucky."

I laugh and lower my lips so they hover just above his.

"You are about to get lucky but with only a kiss."

"I suppose that will have to do…for now."

I tentatively touch my lips to his, kissing his upper lip gently before pressing my mouth over his completely. The sensation is pleasant, but I can instantly tell something is missing. Our physical contact feels buffered in some way. I can feel the warm, wetness of his mouth and the play of his tongue against mine, but something vital is absent.

190

I pull back and look down at Malcolm.

"Why doesn't it feel real?" I ask.

"Because it isn't," he tells me. "We're still in a dream. Nothing compares to reality."

I'm the one who sighs in disappointment this time.

"I was hoping…" I begin to say but can't quite make myself finish.

"That we could be physical with each other here because it's safe," Malcolm finishes for me.

I nod my head. "Yes. I'm sure the poison is still in my system, and we have no way of knowing when it will go away."

"Then kiss me again, Anna. I would rather have a phantom kiss from you than nothing at all."

I lean down to Malcolm again and continue our kiss because he's right. Even this minimal physical contact is better than nothing. I decide to try and make the most out of what we can do to one another.

I run my hands across his shoulders and up his muscular arms until our hands meet. We twine our fingers together like neither one of us wants to let the other go. If it's within my power to control, I plan to make sure we're never separated again. I can't stand not being near him and in my heart, I know he feels the same way.

Malcolm swiftly rolls me over onto my back, pulling my arms higher over my head as he straddles my hips. He kisses his way down one side of my neck, and I tilt my head to give him better access to that part of my flesh. His hands slowly slide down the length of my arms until they come to rest on either side of my breasts. His lips kiss a path down to the valley between my breasts as his thumbs begin to circle their peaks.

"Malcolm…" I sigh. "Will you make love to me?"

Malcolm doesn't answer right away because his mouth is otherwise occupied. He teases one nipple with his tongue through the thin fabric of my nightgown. Apparently, he doesn't want to make the other breast jealous because he slides his lips over to lavish it with the same adoration.

He kisses his way back up to my lips and murmurs against them, "Not here. Not yet."

"Why?" I beg, feeling as though I'll crawl out of my own skin from want if Malcolm doesn't satisfy the burning need I feel to have all of him.

"Because this is just a dream," he says, lifting his head so he can look me in the eyes like he wants to make sure I understand what he's about to tell me. "When I make love to you, I want you to feel everything I do to your body. I don't want to do it here because you would only be feeling a small portion of the sensations. It will be the first time for you, right?"

I nod. "Yes."

"Your first time making love shouldn't be in a dream, Anna. I want you to feel my love physically and know in your heart that you are the only woman I will ever want. If you thought seeing me for the first time made the earth quake beneath your feet, then making love with me will make it seem like the planet itself has exploded all around you."

"You're not making my wait any easier with talk like that," I groan in frustration.

Malcolm chuckles and I feel his hips move against mine.

I gasp slightly at the feel of him between my legs as he proves to me that the wait won't be any easier on him than it is for me.

"Maybe we should stop," I say, albeit reluctantly. "Because this is beginning to feel more like torture than pleasure."

Malcolm kisses the tip of my nose and sits up. He scoots over to rest his back on the headboard, and I go to him, resting my head on his chest while his arms hold me close.

"How are Millie and Vala?" He asks. "Did Levi do

anything to them?"

"Millie's fine. But..."

I find it hard to tell Malcolm about Vala. The uncertainty of her fate is almost more upsetting than if I knew she was dead. A small piece of hope lives in my heart that Travis will find a way to save her.

"But what?" Malcolm gently prods, gliding his left hand up and down my arm in a soothing manner, silently letting me know that I can tell him anything.

"Levi ripped Vala's head from her body in front of Millie and Lucas."

Malcolm's hand stops moving, and I can feel him tense beneath me.

"Is she dead?"

"I don't know yet. We gave her to Travis Stokes to see if he can do anything. Just before I entered your dream, Jered took Lucas to check up on her."

"I'm so sorry, Anna. I know how much you love her."

I try not to cry over the possible loss of my friend, but the tears flow anyway. Malcolm hugs me as I weep, but he doesn't say anything. He just holds me close which is all I really need.

"I hate him," I tell Malcolm. "I hate Levi almost as much as I love you."

"Can you tell me what happened at the trade? How were you able to get us back? What did you have to do?"

I go on to tell Malcolm everything that happened, ending with Lucifer's master stroke to take control back from Levi.

"What did he do to Levi?" I ask. "Lucifer said he wasn't dead even though he broke Levi's neck."

"Lucifer has the ability to trap the souls under his command in the bodies they inhabit, even if that body is dead. It's punishment for disobeying him. Levi will feel Auggie's body start to decay, but he won't be able to leave it until Lucifer releases his soul. Or, I suppose, until you kill him."

"I'll kill him first," I say with heated conviction.

"Be careful," Malcolm tells me, his voice filled with concern. "Don't let your hate control you, Anna. Levi isn't worth you losing your soul over. Lucifer has let his hate control him for a long time now. Don't follow in your father's footsteps."

I look up at Malcolm and see him peering down at me with worry in his eyes. It's the same worry Jered had when we had a similar conversation.

"I won't," I promise him. "I don't think I could ever be like him."

"I don't think Lucifer ever thought he would become what he is either. All I ask is that you don't give into your hate like he did."

"What did he hate so much that would make him go to war against God?"

"He's always despised humanity," Malcolm tells me. "He never understood why it seemed like our father loved humans more than his angels."

"Do you think that?"

"No. I think He loves us all the same. But, Lucifer didn't like it when our father asked us to serve the human race. He considered it beneath us because we were far more powerful."

"I found my mother's room in your New Orleans home. That's where we really are right now. I watched a video of her and Lucifer on her holo-projector."

"The one where she told Lucifer that she was pregnant with you?"

"Yes. How did you know?"

"Amalie loved to watch that one over and over again while she was bedridden. It was one of her happiest memories."

"Lucifer looked so different in it. He looked…happy."

"I think it was one of the few times in his life that he truly *was* happy. Amalie was able to touch a side of him that no one, not even our father, could reach. I didn't approve of them being together, but I couldn't deny the connection they had either. I hoped your mother would be able to change him forever. He's laid low since her death. This is the first time since you were born that he's shown back up."

"He has control of the princes now. What do you think he plans to do with them?"

Malcolm shrugs. "I have no idea, but I'm sure it won't be long before we find out."

I wrap my arms around Malcolm's torso and remain silent for a while. I simply want to be with him and block out all of our troubles, even if it's only for a few precious moments.

Finally, Malcolm kisses me on the top of the head and says, "It's probably time we woke up. There are things we should take care of."

I lift my head and look up at him. His eyes are a lot more focused now which probably means the drugs he was given have worn off.

I sit up and kiss him soundly on the lips one more time.

Malcolm plunges his hands into my hair and kisses me with a ferocity that takes my breath away.

When I pull back, I say, "I have a feeling we won't be able to do that for real yet."

"Probably not right now," Malcolm agrees. "But soon."

"Very soon, I hope," I reply, kissing him again before I force myself to wake up.

When I do awaken, I immediately look at Malcolm's face and find him just opening his eyes.

"How are you feeling?" I ask as I sit up, unable to keep the worry out of my voice.

Malcolm looks over at me and smiles.

"Almost like a new man."

"Your back looks pretty much healed," I tell him, remembering how I found him in the prison cell.

"I told you it would heal on its own. You know...you didn't have to ask my father to come stay with me."

I tilt my head. "How did you know I did that?"

"He was still there when I woke up from your kiss."

"I prayed for him to heal you but he wouldn't."

"And he told you why he couldn't."

"Yes. He told me. It didn't make it any easier to go along with."

"He was right though. If he healed me, he would have to heal every person in the world who asked for it. He can't show favoritism like that, Anna."

"Like I said, I understand that. I just don't like it when it means someone I love has to suffer because of it. There isn't anything I wouldn't do for you. I would sell my soul if I thought it would save you."

Malcolm sits up suddenly and grabs me by the arms.

"Don't you ever say that again," he growls. "Don't even think of it as a possibility, Anna. Promise me."

"I can't promise you that," I tell him truthfully, never wanting to lie to him just to make him feel better. "I would do whatever I had to do to save you."

"But I would never want you to do that, Anna. I would rather die than lose you forever."

"Forever?"

"If you gave your soul to Lucifer in a bargain, you would spend eternity in Hell. We would be separated forever. This life is

199

fleeting. Heaven is a lifetime without an end. Please don't do that to me. Don't make me suffer through forever without you. I've been through enough during my time on this planet. There's no point in going to Heaven if you aren't there to share it with me."

I hadn't really thought about it that way, but Malcolm was right.

"I promise," I say. "I promise I won't do that to you."

Malcolm breathes out a sigh of relief and hugs me close.

"Don't scare me like that again," he whispers, kissing the side of my neck. "I need you too much, Anna."

I pray that I didn't just lie to Malcolm. I understand what he said, and I don't intend to do anything that would jeopardize my soul. Yet, a small part of me wonders if I will be able to keep the promise I just made. If I'm faced with a situation that looks beyond hope, I know myself well enough to realize that I would do everything within my power to protect my loved ones. I would do whatever it took to keep them safe.

CHAPTER ELEVEN

I wrap my arms around Malcolm holding him close.

"Is it bad that I don't want to get out of this bed just yet?" I ask, luxuriating in his warmth simply because it makes me feel happy.

"No," Malcolm says, kissing the side of my neck, "it's not bad at all."

I feel the first tingles of desire and reluctantly pull away from Malcolm.

"I don't want to start something we can't finish," I tell him, hoping he understands it's not his kisses that I'm pulling back from. I just don't want us to have to endure more physical torture than we are already in.

"Well, maybe we can finish it," he says suggestively, leaning in like he's about to kiss my lips.

I phase out of bed to stand on his side of it.

"The others would kill me if I kiss you, and you end up falling back to sleep before they can see you." I hold my hand out to Malcolm. "Come on. Lucas might be back by now, and he needs to see his father."

Malcolm stands from the bed and takes my hand without

further argument.

As we walk out of the room together, I realize how complete I feel with Malcolm holding my hand and walking by my side. Now that he has finally stopped denying how he feels about me and we're together again, I feel like no matter what might happen next we'll be able to face it head on.

Through my travels with Jered, I learned that the other down-worlds are in need of help just as much or more so than the Cirrus controlled lands. Initially, I thought my mission would be confined to the troubles between our own cloud city and down-world. I didn't think that now. I knew I was meant to help those in the other down-worlds too. The people living in all of the cloud cities had become complacent. They didn't care what happened to the down-worlders because they were shielded from the problems plaguing those living below them. It was time the plight within each down-world became known to those in the cloud cities above them. I had a feeling once the conditions the down-worlders were living in came to light, a vast majority of the cloud city citizens would ask the royal families to do something. I wanted to believe in what Jered said about most people desiring to take the noble path through life, that they did indeed prefer peace over anarchy. I too believed that people would choose to do the right thing. Yet, it always seemed to be the few bad apples who preferred chaos over order who were able to turn the world upside down.

"What are you thinking about?" Malcolm asks me as we descend the staircase to the first floor.

"Just…that the world is really screwed up, and I need to fix it," I tell him with a heavy sigh, literally feeling the fate of humankind on my shoulders.

"You don't have to do it alone," he tells me, squeezing my hand as a gentle reminder that he's by my side.

"I know," I tell him. "And I don't have any intention of trying to do it all by myself. If I did, it would either drive me crazy or my attempts would fail miserably. It's not going to be a fast or easy fix, Malcolm. We could spend the rest of our lives just trying to change things and it still might not be enough."

When we reach the first floor, Malcolm tugs on my hand gently and brings me in closer to him.

"And I will remain by your side the whole way," he promises me.

Malcolm lifts a hand to my face, cupping the left side against his palm.

"I've always been strong," he tells me. "But when I'm with you, I feel like nothing is beyond our power to manage. If it takes us a lifetime to transform the world into the place you want it to be, it will be a life well spent. As long as I'm with you, I really don't care what it is we're doing. I know that might sound selfish, but it's the way I feel. I just want you, Anna. You and Lucas are my world."

"According to Lucas we'll have at least two more to add to your list," I tell him, feeling shy all of a sudden at the reminder of the children our son saw us have in the future.

"Ohhhh yes," Malcolm says, grinning as he brings me even closer to him. "I do recall something about babies being mentioned. Did he tell you how many?"

"At least two. He even told me their names, Liam and Lillianna."

"Sounds like names you would give to twins," Malcolm says, mulling this new information over. "You know twins run in your family, especially fraternal ones."

"No, I didn't know that, but then again I don't know a lot about my family's past, especially little things like that."

"Well, at least his vision gives me hope," Malcolm murmurs, as he begins to plant small kisses all over my face, being careful to not touch my lips.

"Hope?" I ask, closing my eyes as I enjoy the tiny explosions his kisses are setting off all over my body.

"Hope that the poison will dissipate quickly so we can get

to work on making babies. I would hate to disappoint our son and not give him the brother and sister he wants so badly. I think we owe it to him to start as soon as possible."

I laugh and pull myself away from Malcolm before either of us loses our heads and throws caution to the wind.

I take one of his hands into mine and say, "Come on. Let's go find the others before I knock you out with a kiss again."

Malcolm groans in frustration but doesn't make an argument.

"Where are they?" He asks.

"Millie said they would be down in the kitchen."

Malcolm takes the lead since I have no idea where the kitchen is located in his mansion. It takes us longer than it should have to finally get there because every so often, Malcolm would stop and bring me into his arms to kiss my face and neck like he just couldn't seem to bring himself to *stop* kissing me. It was pleasurable, of course, but also very frustrating.

Since the moment he entered my world, I've wanted to make love with Malcolm. It was almost like a compulsory need that my body had. I felt like it was probably a combination of my love for him and just plain carnal physical attraction. I mean, who wouldn't want to be with Malcolm in an intimate way? He was everything a woman could desire all wrapped up into one very well endowed package.

"Are you sure we shouldn't give dream world love making a try?" I ask as Malcolm kisses the tender flesh just below one ear lobe. "I'm more than willing to test it out if you are."

"Absolutely not," Malcolm replies resolutely, his voice slightly muffled as he continues his delightful assault on my neck.

I lift my hands to Malcolm's bare chest and push with just enough force to make him back away.

"Then no more of that right now," I tell him, just trying to remember how to breathe. "I can't think straight when you kiss me because all I can think about is taking you back to bed."

Malcolm sighs in disappointment.

"But your skin tastes so delicious, Anna," he tells me, leaning his body into mine again. "I can't seem to get enough of it. I'm not sure how much longer I can wait to taste the rest of you."

I lift my hands to Malcolm's chest and push him away again.

"The rest of me could poison you," I remind him.

"But, Anna…." Malcolm begins until I lift a hand to his lips to stop him from saying another word.

"You know it's true," I tell him, knowing he can't argue against the facts.

I grab one of his hands and pull him forward. "Come on. I want to see if Jered and Lucas are back yet. They may have brought back news about Vala's condition."

This seems to break through Malcolm's desire for me, and we walk hand and hand to the kitchen.

Laughter welcomes us as soon as we enter the room. Millie and Giles are sitting beside one another at the kitchen table giggling about something. Desmond, Daniel, and Brutus are by the stove dishing out food onto platters. I don't see any sign of Lucas and Jered which is a disappointment. I was truly hoping to find out if they had any news about Vala. I needed to know whether she could be saved or if she was truly dead. If she was dead, then I could grieve and move on eventually. But, if we got her to Travis in time, there would be no reason for me to remain upset. The 'not knowing' was wreaking havoc with my emotions.

Millie sees us enter the kitchen first. She smiles broadly and stands from the table to come over to us. Giles follows her lead and comes to stand beside her.

"Good to see you up and about, Master Malcolm," Millie says. "It's been a long, long time."

Malcolm gives Millie a quick hug. "Good to see you again,

Millie."

Giles holds out his hand to Malcolm. "Glad to see you made it back in one piece. Though," Giles say staring at Malcolm, "what the hell happened to your hair?"

"Apparently, Levi thought it was time I had a haircut," Malcolm grumbles, lifting a hand to his shortened locks.

"Well, I can tell you one thing you could use," Desmond says as he places a platter of rolls on the table. "A bath."

"How about you hang in the air and be tortured by Levi for a couple of hours? Let's see how fresh you come out smelling," Malcolm says but with a hint of humor to soften his words.

"I'll fix you up a bath after you eat," Millie tells Malcolm. "I'm sure that brute didn't feed you a crumb while he held you prisoner."

"I don't think making me comfortable was exactly on his agenda of things to do, Millie," Malcolm agrees.

"Then come and eat," Millie looks at me. "I'm sure both of you could use something in your stomachs after what you've been through."

We all sit down at the table and feast on what was prepared. The meal is simple but filling. There is roasted chicken and potatoes, fresh peas and rolls. Desmond opens a few bottles of white wine for us to drink.

While we eat, I ask, "Has anyone heard from Jered and Lucas?"

"Did I just hear my name called?"

I look up at the entrance of the kitchen and see Jered standing there. Lucas immediately runs into the open arms of his father.

"Dad!" Lucas says, throwing his arms around Malcolm's neck, hugging him so tightly I'm not sure Malcolm can actually breathe.

Malcolm sets Lucas away from him a little bit to look him over. Even though you tell a parent that their child is physically fine, it brings them more comfort if they can see it for themselves.

"Did Levi lay a hand on you?" Malcolm asks.

"Not while we were in Cirrus," Lucas answers. "Just in the desert."

Malcolm nods, satisfied with this answer. I already told him what Levi almost did to Lucas at the trade before Lucifer showed up. To say the news upset him was an understatement.

Malcolm picks Lucas up and sits him between the two of us.

Lucas wraps his arms around my waist and squeezes me tightly. I hear him sigh in contentment before letting me go as Millie sets an empty plate in front of him. I watch as Malcolm fills his son's plate for him and can't keep from smiling at how good it feels to have almost everyone I love all in one place.

The only person who is missing is my papa.

The thought of his uncertain fate makes my smile fade. Malcolm must notice my sudden change of mood. He holds his hand out to me behind Lucas' back. I grasp it, finding strength in his touch and knowing inexplicably that everything will work out in the end.

"Malcolm," Jered says, still standing in the doorway of the kitchen, "could I have a private word with you for just a moment?"

Malcolm lets my hand go and walks over to Jered. Jered talks to him in a low voice. It's obvious Jered doesn't want me to hear what's being said. I fear it's the worst of news about Vala. I watch Malcolm closely as he listens intently to whatever it is Jered is telling him.

Malcolm nods his head and says, "Do whatever you have to do."

Jered immediately phases.

As Malcolm walks back to the table, our eyes meet.

"Well?" I ask because I feel sure the conversation had to involve Vala.

"Travis is doing everything he can," Malcolm tells me. "We'll just need to be patient a little while longer."

I'm both disappointed and filled with hope. At least Jered didn't come back saying Vala was gone forever. There was still a chance I would be able to see my little friend again one day. All I had to do was be patient and try to keep my expectations realistic.

The conversation at the table seems to be designed by Desmond, Daniel, and Brutus to help keep our minds off of what we had just been through and what was to come in the near future. They each told us tales about their lives that were both humorous and sometimes sad. It was obvious Desmond had it the hardest of the three. Being one of the few doctors available to the down-worlders in his hometown seemed to mean he had to deal with death on a daily basis. I feel sorry for him, and hope in time we can alter the living conditions of the down-worlders for the better, resulting in fewer deaths.

Daniel seemed to have endless tales involving the children under his care. I felt sure Daniel and Linn would enjoy living in Cirrus, but I could also see how important his work at the orphanage was to him. I had a feeling no matter how hard I might try to get them to, he and Linn would not be moving to Cirrus.

Brutus was chock full of funny stories concerning his exploits in thievery. He made sure to tell Lucas that what he did wasn't right and that you should try to never steal. In Brutus' case, I couldn't chastise him too much. I knew he only stole from those in the cloud cities. Though, he did admit to stealing from an overlord in his own territory once.

It made me wonder what the other overlords in the down-world of Cirrus thought about Malcolm. There was no doubt he was the richest of them all, but I had a feeling Malcolm's wealth was one that had been acquired over a long period of time, not just one lifetime. He had been waiting for me to be born for a thousand years after all. I felt sure he kept himself busy during that time. It would certainly explain how he was able to afford to give so much of his earnings every year in tribute to the Amadors.

After supper, Millie was true to her word and made Malcolm a warm bath in the claw foot bathtub which sat in the middle of a large bathroom connected to his upstairs bedroom. She laid out a pair of scissors and towels for him too.

"You might want to trim up that mess on the top of his head after he washes, my sweet," Millie tells me as she prepares to leave the room.

"Good idea," I reply. "He does look like something the cat dragged in, chewed up, and spit out."

"Thanks," Malcolm grumbles, preparing to take off his pants.

Millie walks out of the bathroom into the bedroom.

"I'll leave the two of you alone," she says with a knowing wink, heading out the door. "I'll tend to Lucas and get him ready for bed. You two take all the time you need with one another."

"Thank you, Millie," I say, as I watch her walk out into the hallway.

When I turn back around, Malcolm is already sitting in the water filled tub. He quickly submerges his whole body into the water to wet his hair. He sits back up and wipes the water from his eyes with one hand. When he opens his eyes, he looks over at me and smiles.

"Would you wash my hair for me?" He asks. Though from the come hither look in his eyes, it seems like he wants me closer for more than just that simple task.

But I can't say no to him. I have absolutely no will power where Malcolm is concerned. I walk over to the tub and pick up a glass bottle labelled shampoo in frosted print from a metal basket hanging on the left side of the tub. I pour some of the clear liquid into my hand and set the bottle back down in its spot. I rub the shampoo between my hands and thread my fingers through to Malcolm's scalp, working the suds into the thickness of his hair. I have to work at loosening the blood matted portions and have to ask him to dunk his head underneath the water to rinse the shampoo out so I can wash his hair a second time.

"This feels nice," Malcolm sighs as I continue to massage his head during the second washing. "I don't think I will ever tire of your touch."

"I hope not," I tell him, "because we'll be with one another for a very long time."

"And it still won't feel like it's long enough."

I smile at the sweet sentiment. Then, swiftly push down on Malcolm's head, forcing him to dunk it underneath the surface of the water again. He bobs back up sputtering.

"Why you little vixen," he says, swiftly spinning around and grabbing me by the waist with both of his hands.

I soon find myself pulled into the tub and laying on top of Malcolm.

"Malcolm!" I shout but can't help but laugh because he's laughing as he holds me to his naked body.

A good portion of the water sloshes out of the tub and onto the bathroom floor from the physical activity, but there's still enough to cover us.

"Now my clothes are all wet," I complain.

"Then maybe you should take them off," Malcolm says without a hint of shame at such a suggestion.

I look up and see the teasing way he's looking at me.

"Then we would both be in trouble."

"But it might be worth it."

"Not if you fall asleep during the middle of it," I tell him.

"I think it's worth a try."

I shake my head. "No."

"Yes."

"No," I say more stridently and phase out of the tub, my clothes dripping wet with bath water now.

Malcolm stands up in the tub not in the least bit concerned that he's completely naked in front of me.

"Yes," he says, only wearing a smile on his face.

I have a hard time not looking down the length of him as he stands completely shameless before me.

I clear my throat because it's a little tighter than before.

"No," I say with a lot less conviction.

Malcolm steps out of the tub and begins to walk over to me. I immediately phase to the bedroom. He walks out of the bathroom to find me. His skin is glistening from the water of his bath and his hair is still a mess, but for some reason, its disheveled appearance makes my heart skip a beat. I find it hard to breathe or even think as he approaches me. The evidence of his arousal at our play is extremely distracting. I try to keep my eyes focused on his face.

"Yes?" He asks hopefully as he draws nearer, and I stand still.

I shake my head, but I can't seem to say no this time.

"At least come over to the bed first," I say, unable to deny him anymore.

"I like the way you think," Malcolm teases, sauntering over to me with an even bigger grin on his face.

"Not for that," I say feeling completely embarrassed now. "And, do you have a robe or something you can put on?"

Malcolm stops walking towards as he looks at me in confusion.

"Why?" He asks.

"So you'll be covered up in case this is an epic fail. Plus, I'm finding it really hard to keep my eyes on your face."

Malcolm chuckles. "Am I the first man you've ever seen naked?"

"Of course you are," I answer, wondering why he even feels a need to ask the question. "Who else would I have seen naked?"

Malcolm shrugs. "I thought perhaps you and Auggie might have played doctor as children."

"Auggie was never interested in that sort of thing with females. We kissed but that was more of a test of our attraction to one another than anything else."

Malcolm places his hands on his hips.

"And did you ever feel an attraction for each other?"

I shake my head. "That was never a possibility for the two of us. All we could ever be was best friends."

"What would Auggie think about the two of us being soul mates?"

"He would be happy for me. All he ever wanted was for me to find happiness with someone I loved, and I've found that."

"I will do my best to keep you that way," Malcolm promises. "There's nothing I wouldn't do for you, Anna. Nothing."

"Then please put on a robe before we try this," I say to him, unable to keep myself from glancing down the length of Malcolm. "And why in the world would Celeste call that you're *Little* Malcolm?"

Malcolm's cheeks grow red, and he starts to chuckle softly. He turns away from me because I think he might actually be embarrassed by my comment. He walks over to a door on the wall behind him and opens it. It leads to a walk in closet. He walks into it but quickly walks back out slipping into a dark green robe. He ties the sash of the robe to close the front opening before coming to stand in front of me.

"Better?" He asks.

"Yes," I say, grabbing him by the arms to change his position so that he's standing near the side of the bed. If the poison is still in my body, he should just fall backwards onto the mattress this way.

"Are you sure it's worth trying?" I ask him, remembering what happened the first time we kissed, and he wasn't able to take in a breath. "Doesn't it hurt to suffocate like that?"

Malcolm quickly pulls me up against him.

"For me, trying is better than the torture of not knowing at all," Malcolm says. "And if this works…the possibilities are endless, Anna."

"I'm getting you all wet," I tell him, realizing my water soaked clothes are drenching the front of his robe.

"Hopefully, you won't be in them long enough for it to matter," Malcolm says in a husky whisper as he brings his lips down closer to mine.

"Please let this work," I sigh as Malcolm touches his lips to mine.

Not wanting to waste whatever time we might have, Malcolm ravages my lips. I involuntarily whimper from the pleasure of feeling him tantalize my mouth with his. I wrap my arms around his waist as we taste and tease one another with our lips and tongues. A small glimmer of hope shines brightly that the poison won't stop us from consummating our love for one another this time. At least until Malcolm stops breathing.

I pull back just as he closes his eyes and falls back on the bed unconscious.

I just stare at him as I stand there breathing hard and feeling completely bereft of hope that we'll ever be able to make love. With a frustrated groan, I go to the other side of the bed and pull Malcolm up by his armpits so his whole body is lying comfortably on the mattress. I grab one of the pillows and position it under his head. Not seeing that it will exactly hurt anything now, I kiss Malcolm's lips one more time before pulling the bedcovers over his body to keep him warm.

I look down at myself and realize I don't have a change of clothes. It suddenly dawns on me where I might be able to find an outfit that would fit.

My mother's room.

CHAPTER TWELVE

When I reach the door to my mother's bedroom, I'm hesitant to enter. I almost feel like I'm invading her privacy. It's a completely silly notion since she's been dead for as many years as I've been alive. Yet, I continue to stand in the hallway with my hand hovering over the door knob, trying to find the courage to enter her room.

"Stop being stupid," I whisper to myself, grabbing the handle and twisting it to open the door, hoping I'm not about to step into a Pandora's Box of memories.

I walk in and close the door behind me. The room is dark now as night falls outside, and I can barely see where I'm going. I walk over to where I remember the nightstand being and turn on the light there. The faint illumination from the old fashioned lamp makes the room appear even more desolate. There's a sadness that hangs in the air, making me wonder if my mother's spirit has truly moved on, or if it lingers here, hiding in the dark corners of the room. I look past the bed and see a door which has been left slightly ajar. I walk around the ornate wrought iron bed and open the door further, finding my mother's closet. I see a chain hanging in the darkness and tug on it. A light embedded in the ceiling switches on. Every item inside the closet is neat and orderly. It's as if someone came in here and lovingly preserved my mother's possessions after her death.

I let the tips of my fingers drift over the clothes on each hanger and can't help but wonder where my mother might have worn each article. I pull out a soft, dark purple turtleneck sweater. I stare at it and wonder what life event she might have experienced while wearing it. Did she wear it while she was pregnant with me? Did she have it on underneath her coat in the video I saw of her and Lucifer? I had no way of knowing, and she wasn't here to tell me the story of her life.

I looked up from the sweater and let my eyes wander around the closet, realizing this was all I had to remember my mother by. I suddenly realize this is the first time in my life I'm able to connect to her in anyway. I'm surrounded by her things. Yet, I know virtually nothing about her. I have no idea what she liked to eat. I don't know what her favorite color was. Did she like to dance? Did she play an instrument? What made her laugh? What made her cry?

She was my mother, but she was also a complete stranger to me.

I quickly find a pair of jeans and a sturdy pair of walking boots to wear. I step out of the closet and over to the chest of drawers across from the bed where I find some undergarments. I quickly change out of my wet apparel and dress in my mother's clothes. They're a perfect fit.

I feel a cool draft in the room and look over at the window to find that it's not completely sealed shut. I walk over to close it and happen to glance outside to the courtyard below. I see someone I didn't expect to seek me out again so soon.

Lucifer is sitting on a wood bench in the middle of the courtyard Malcolm's home is built around. He's staring straight at me like he knew exactly where I was. He has to be here to see me, but I'm not sure why. There's really only one way to find out.

I phase to Malcolm's room and grab my leather jacket. Before I walk out the door, I go to the man I love and tenderly caress his cheek. His breathing is steady now, and I hope he gets some much needed rest after all that he's been through. I fear there will be a lot more that we'll have to endure, but I don't have any doubts that Malcolm and I will meet any challenge set in our path and find a way to conquer it.

It doesn't take me long to find my way out of the house and down to the private courtyard. During the warmer months, I can imagine the enclosure in full bloom with all the rose bushes scattered around and full grown trees now bare of leaves, dusted with snow. Lucifer is sitting underneath a small shade tree watching me as I approach, his expression indecipherable.

I tuck my hands into the pockets of my jacket as I make my way over to him.

I don't say anything to Lucifer, and he doesn't speak to me. I sit down next to him on the bench and hear it creak with the addition of my weight. I look down at my lap going over what I want to say to him in my mind first.

"I appreciate you helping me save my family and handling Levi."

Lucifer doesn't say anything, but I can feel his gaze centered on me. Finally, I turn my head and look at him. His expression gives nothing away about what he's thinking, and I have a feeling he's hiding his emotions from me on purpose. I don't think he wants me to know what he feels when he looks at me, but I'm not sure why it would matter if I did.

"Why were you in your mother's room?" He asks, turning his head to look away from me and up to the window of my mother's room.

"I needed a change of clothes," I tell him.

He looks back at me and stares at the jacket I'm wearing.

"The jacket isn't hers. It used to belong to Jess," he comments knowingly.

"Yes, I know," I say. "Jered told me that you and Jess used to be friends."

Lucifer lets out a harsh laugh but doesn't say anything else

224

on the matter.

"Can you tell me what you plan to do with the princes now that you have them back?" I ask point blank.

"You're rather blunt," he says, looking at me with a wry grin. "You sounded just like your mother. She was never one for beating around the bush much either."

"Are you going to tell me?" I prod.

"All you need to know is this. As long as you don't bother them, they won't bother you."

"You know I can't do that. I'm meant to retrieve their seals and take them back to Heaven."

"My father doesn't need the seals," Lucifer says with a twinge of disgust in his voice. "All he wants to do is cause a ruckus down here that isn't necessary. Either that or he just wants to weaken me by having you kill all my brothers. Do you intend to kill me too, Anna?" Lucifer asks. "Are you really so vicious that you would kill your own father just to do God's bidding?"

I don't have an answer for him. The truth is I'm not sure if I'll be able to kill him if, or most likely, when that moment comes. I'm simply trying to take things one step at a time.

So I decide to change the subject...

"You still haven't said what you plan to do with the princes now that you have them back," I remind him.

"It's none of your concern. Like I said, stay out of their way and they will stay out of yours. I've also told them that this house is off limits to them. You're safe for as long as you remain here."

"How did you get them to agree to that?"

"I told them if they didn't stay away that they would meet the same fate as Levi."

"How do you trap their souls inside the bodies they inhabit?" I ask.

"It's my gift. I can do many things with a soul."

I hesitate for a moment, wondering if this is the right moment to ask him for a favor. Our relationship with one another is just beginning, yet, I have to ask him for the one thing only he can fix.

"Would you do something for me?"

Lucifer leans his back fully against the bench and crosses his arms over his chest with a stern expression on his face as he looks at me.

"What exactly do you want?"

"I want you to revoke your curse on Malcolm."

Lucifer lifts a dubious eyebrow at me. "And why, pray tell, would I want to do that? It gives me an immense amount of pleasure to know he's in so much pain because of me."

"He's the man I love, and I don't want him in pain anymore. Hasn't he been through enough without you continuing to torture him?"

"Not nearly enough, if you're actually asking me that question and not simply being rhetorical. If I could double the pain he's in, it would make me exceedingly happy and probably leave you a virgin for a while longer. Or, at least until you found someone more worthy to bed. Just the thought of that mongrel pawing at your flesh turns my stomach, Anna."

"How do you know I'm still a virgin?" I ask him, not understanding how he could know such a thing about me.

"When you've been involved in as many virgin sacrifices as I have, you tend to develop a sixth sense about that sort of thing," he says in a way that almost sounds like he's making a joke. "You're still as pure as the day I held you in my arms after you were born."

"Wait...," I say, taking in what he just told me. "You were at my birth? But Jered said you refused to see my mother while she was pregnant."

Lucifer doesn't make a response for a long time. Finally he

says, "I couldn't let her leave this world thinking I was mad at her."

"Is that when she asked you to raise me?"

"No. She asked me a hundred times before then, but that was the last time."

"What did she say when you told her no?"

"I didn't tell her no," Lucifer admits. "I promised her I would before she died."

"You lied to my mother on her death bed?" I ask, not sure why I'm shocked that the devil would lie, but considering the relationship he and my mother shared, I have to admit that I am.

"I thought it would ease her mind in those last few moments we had left together. Otherwise, she would have just kept begging me to do it."

"Jered said you didn't want to take me because you were afraid I would become just as jaded as you are. Is that true?"

"Well if Jered said so, it must be true," Lucifer says sarcastically.

"Well is it?" I ask, pressing for the truth.

"Does it matter?" Lucifer asks, fidgeting in his seat like he's getting agitated by my questioning.

"It matters to me," I say, realizing it's the truth. For some reason, I want to know that what he did was for my benefit and not just his own. There's a small part of me which yearns to know for a fact that my father didn't abandon me because he hated me.

"Having Andre raise you was the best thing for everyone involved," Lucifer replies. "He was a far better father to you than I ever could have been."

"Do you know where Levi is keeping him?" I ask, a desperate plea in my voice. "Can you help me get my papa back?"

Lucifer glances over at me but makes no reply. Instead, he bends over to the side of the bench and grabs something off the ground. I know then he has no intention of responding to my heartfelt request.

When he turns back to face me, I see a medium size brown wicker basket in his right hand now. He sets it on his lap.

"I brought you something," he tells me, looking uncertain at how I will react to his unexpected gift.

"What is it?" I ask, staring at the basket's closed lid.

"Levi told me he killed your pet," Lucifer says. "I'm sorry he put you through that, but you can rest assured he paid the price for such an act. I uh...thought you might like this."

He sets the basket between us on the bench.

229

I lift the lid on one side of the basket and gasp at what is laying inside.

"A hellhound puppy?" I ask, closing the lid gently so as not to wake it. "I can't have something like that around Lucas. What if it bit him?"

"Hellhounds aren't born evil," Lucifer tells me. "They're just like any other pet. As long as you treat it with love and respect, it will grow up to be extremely loyal to you and protect those you love. If you treat it with cruelty, it will become vicious and act only in its best interest."

"Why are you giving this to me?" I ask.

Lucifer shrugs his shoulders. "I just thought it might help ease the pain over losing your pet. I know she meant a great deal to you."

Lucifer suddenly stands up from the bench.

"I would advise you to do what I've said, daughter," Lucifer tells me. "Stay away from my brothers and live out your life in peace. Don't pick a fight with them. It's not worth the price you would have to pay to succeed."

"And what would be the price?" I ask, feeling as though Lucifer is warning me about something dire.

Lucifer shakes his head. "You don't want to have to pay it.

Trust my words to you, Anna, and leave things alone."

I feel as though Lucifer is just about to phase. So, I grab his hand before he can.

He looks down at our joined hands, and I see a fleeting moment of confusion pass across his features.

"Thank you," I tell him.

Lucifer meets my eyes and looks at me in surprise, like he wasn't expecting a thank you from me. Then again, I doubt he's done much in his life to be thanked for.

"You're... welcome," he replies, and I can tell by the hesitancy in his voice that he isn't used to saying those two words very often. He gently extricates his hand from mine and phases.

I sigh, feeling slightly disappointed that he didn't stay a little while longer. I have so many questions about my mother, and I feel like he could give me the answers that I need.

"I see you've been given a new friend," I hear God say beside me. "And I think you may have already made an unexpected one."

I look over at God. He's sitting in Lucifer's spot now with a pleased grin on his face.

"Lucifer confuses me," I admit to God. "I don't understand

him at all."

God nods his head, sympathizing with my plight. "Lucifer has a way of doing that to people. Not many people take the time or care enough to understand him. I think your mother and Jess were the only two people who ever got close to discovering the real him."

I look down at the basket and shake my head in dismay at Lucifer's present.

"Malcolm's going to hate it," I say with absolute certainty.

"You could have refused to accept his gift," God reminds me gently.

"Refuse the first gift my biological father gives me?" I say, finding the notion an impossible one. "If I had, he might have taken it the wrong way. I think this might be an attempt on his part to connect with me on some level."

"I would have to agree," God says, sounding pleased with my conclusion. "I think he yearns to know you better. Lucifer has always had a hard time opening up to people. Even when he was in Heaven he tended to use his power to keep his brothers at arm's length. I suppose I shouldn't have made him quite so headstrong."

"He really loved my mother, didn't he?" I ask, but seeking a direct answer to my question isn't really what I'm after. God seems to understand that.

"Lucifer can love just as strongly as he can hate. But his anger towards things and people can cloud his judgment and push him to act out in terrible ways. The line between right and wrong has become blurred to him over the years. I think he simply needs to care about someone more than he does himself to clear his mind and make him want to find himself again."

"Are you hoping I'll be that person for him?"

"Yes," God admits freely. "If he can forge a bond with you, I think he will be able to find the good inside himself again." God looks down at the basket. "And I think this small token of affection might just be the start of his evolution."

I sigh heavily, not knowing if a relationship with Lucifer is what I need at the moment. It could complicate things with Malcolm.

"Will I have to kill him to retrieve his seal?" I ask God, needing to know if that will be the end result of my relationship with Lucifer.

"It depends."

"Depends on what?" I ask, filled with a newfound hope by his answer.

"It depends on Lucifer, and that's all I'm going to say on the matter, Anna. If I divulge too much information to you, all might be lost, and I don't think that's what either of us want."

I feel frustrated by God's reply but keep my mouth shut. It's obvious he has no intention of telling me more. But, his words give me hope that executing Lucifer won't be something that I have to do. Obviously, there's another way. A way I intend to figure out.

"When will I get my papa back?"

"In time."

I sigh in disappointment at another non-answer.

"Can you at least tell me if he's all right? Is he hurt? Is Levi torturing him?"

"He's perfectly safe, Anna. Levi hasn't laid a hand on him. I think he might be scared he'll go too far and accidentally kill Andre in one of his fits of anger. Stop worrying about your father and keep your mind focused on what you need to do. Enjoy the time you'll have here. Andre would want you to do that. Don't spend your energy worrying over him when he's perfectly fine."

I feel a sense of relief with God's words but I know I won't be able to stop worrying about my papa. At least not until he's back with me and my family is made whole again.

CHAPTER THIRTEEN

After God leaves, I phase back to Malcolm's bedroom. He's still peacefully asleep, and I find myself grateful for that small fact. I still haven't decided how to tell Malcolm about Lucifer's first gift to me yet. I'm not sure how I'll explain that it was a present I couldn't possibly refuse to accept.

I walk over to the chair near my side of the bed and sit while placing the basket down on the floor at my feet. I lift the right side of the lid and just stare at the hellhound pup for a minute, studying the way the phantom yellow-orange flames illuminate its coat which helps perpetuate the illusion that the tufts of white hair are moving against an unseen wind. Tentatively, I reach out to stroke the fur on top of its head. Its hair is softer than anything I've ever felt before and makes me involuntarily sigh in contentment. I reach down with my other hand and gently lift the pup out of the basket and lay it on my lap.

The movement wakes the pup, and it lifts its head to look up at me. The hellhound's eyes are a dazzling aquamarine color which takes me by surprise. I remember the hellhounds Malcolm and I fought at the beach house and their eyes were a soulless black, like pieces of marble, cold and hard. If the eyes truly were the windows to the soul, this animal's inner spirit was beautiful. It made me wonder exactly what Lucifer and his brothers must have done to the other hellhounds to extinguish such a brilliant light.

The pup opens its mouth, curling out a little pink tongue while yawning and rolling over onto its back to expose a soft, lily white belly to me. It's completely vulnerable in such a position and looks up at me expectantly, waiting for me to pet it. I immediately see that it's a girl pup as I reach down and gently stroke the tender flesh of its abdomen. It's as if the hellhound is asking me in action form whether or not I accept my newly given role as her master, and after proving that I do consent to the responsibility, she promptly goes back to sleep on my lap.

I continue to stroke her little belly until I feel certain she has fallen back into a deep slumber. I cradle her in my arms and walk over to the bed, gently laying her down on top of my pillow. I take off my jacket and crawl onto the bed to lie down beside Malcolm. It feels a little strange to be lying sideways on a bed, but I don't care. I wrap an arm around Malcolm's torso and breathe in his fresh, clean scent.

He smells like freshly ground cinnamon mixed with vanilla and some other spices I can't readily recognize. I know it's from his shampoo, but for me, the smell of cinnamon from that moment on will forever be linked with Malcolm. It adds to the natural sense of being home when I'm around him and the aroma will always remind me of the man I love.

I snuggle in as close as I can get to Malcolm and rest my head on his shoulder. Just before falling asleep, I feel my new little friend find a spot at the base of my back to nestle up against.

In the world of dreams, I soon find myself standing inside Malcolm's workshop in Lakewood. Malcolm is steadily working on the large birdhouse he was making for Lucas in the real world. When I enter his dream, he doesn't seem to notice me right away. It gives me a moment to secretly watch him as he concentrates on nailing a section of the roof onto the structure. I smile to myself and my heart lurches slightly inside my chest at the sight of him. Every time I look at Malcolm, complete happiness touches my soul, slowly filling it with quiet moments like this that I will never forget.

After he finishes his task, he looks up at me in surprise and smiles.

"Hey," he says. His smile is so bright I know for a fact that my presence affects him in the same way his does me. "I was wondering if you would come."

"Will we always be sharing dreams like this?"

"I honestly don't know," Malcolm says with a confused look on his face, making him look irresistibly adorable to me. "I never thought to ask Lilly if she always shared Brand's dreams when they slept together."

I walk over to Malcolm on the other side of the work table. He puts the hammer in his hand down and instantly brings me in close to his body. I wrap my arms around his waist and lay my head against his chest, just enjoying the dream world feel of him.

After a little bit, I pull back and look up at his face. With the mention of Lilly, it brings to mind a question.

"You know you asked me what Auggie would think of us together, but I haven't asked you what Lilly would say about us being in love."

"She's happy for us," he says, like it's a point of fact and not just conjecture.

"How do you know that with so much certainty?" I ask.

"Because she told me so."

I pull back even further from Malcolm.

"She came to see you?" I ask. Malcolm nods. "When?"

"The night you said you were letting me go," he tells me. "I walked over to her old family home on the lake afterwards, and she found me."

And then the rest of the events from that night immediately begin to fall into place for me.

"She's the reason why you came back to me, isn't she?"

"Yes," he says. "Lilly was never shy about telling me when

I was doing something stupid, and pushing you away was one of the most foolish things I've ever tried to do. She made me realize that the love I feel for you isn't something I should walk away from but run towards."

"I want you to know that I don't expect you to ever stop loving her," I tell him, truly meaning every word. "I'm ok with sharing your heart with Lilly. If there's one thing I learned from your memories of her, it's that she helped you realize what a wonderful person you could be and made you believe in yourself again. I would never ask you to love me more than her."

Malcolm shakes his head at me like he can't believe what I just said.

"My love for you is so different from the love I have for her," Malcolm tells me. He raises a hand and places it behind my neck, almost like he wants to make sure I keep looking into his eyes as he continues. "I won't lie and say I didn't love her very deeply. You know I did, but my love for you goes beyond anything I've ever felt for anyone in my life, Anna. Every time I look at you or even think about you, my heart fills with so much love I'm surprised it doesn't burst at the seams inside my chest. You alone hold my heart Anna Greco. I think you have for a very long time, even before you were sent to Earth. I simply didn't know it until I saw you for the first time. Please, never doubt in my love for you and forgive me for trying to push you away. I thought you deserved someone better than me to give your heart to."

"Deserved someone better than you?" I ask, completely sure I misheard what he said. When he continues to look at me and not say a word, I can tell by the strained expression on his face that it's what he truly thought, and it brings to mind what he said in his letter to me. "That has to be the most ridiculous thing I've ever heard, Malcolm! Why would you even think something like that? It's like you don't even realize how wonderful you are."

"I don't understand how you can say that after the way I treated you, Anna. I can't tell you how much I regret being such an ass to you all that time."

"I knew you were trying to push me away," I tell him. "I just assumed it was because of Lilly."

"It was partially," he admits. "But, mostly I just didn't feel worthy to be the soul mate of someone so perfect."

I let out a half laugh. "I am *far* from perfect."

"Name a fault then," he challenges, like he's sure I'll fail at the task.

"I'm stubborn and opinionated."

"I wouldn't want to be with a woman who didn't know what she wanted."

"I'm hot-headed."

"So am I," he says with a nonchalant shrug of his shoulders. "Next?"

"I'm impatient."

"Patience is overrated. Next?"

"I have a feeling whatever personal fault I admit to you would find a way to make it a positive," I tease.

Malcolm smiles. "There's just nothing you could say that would make me think any less of you, Anna. You need to know that. I'm all in, for better or for worse."

I wrap my arms around Malcolm's neck and kiss him thoroughly. Just like before, it's pleasant enough but not nearly as satisfying as kissing him in the real world. When I pull away, I let out a deep, frustrated sigh.

"I can't wait until we can do that for real and not have you suffocate to death because of it."

Malcolm chuckles and nuzzles the side of my neck.

"It probably won't be too much longer," he says reassuringly, even though I hear a note of doubt in his voice.

The truth is neither of us knows exactly how long it will take for the poison in my body to flush itself out. All I know is that the time in between is bound to make my patience even less manageable.

"Do you come here a lot when you dream?" I ask him.

"I've always liked this workshop," he says, lifting his head from my neck to look at me.

I chew on my bottom lip in worry because I need to tell him what's happened to one of his favorite places. I hate to be the bearer of bad news, but I can't withhold such important information even though I know it will hurt him.

"I have to tell you something about this place in the real world," I say.

"Levi burned it to the ground," Malcolm tells me before I get the chance to.

"How did you know?"

"He gloated about it," Malcolm says with a sad smile. "While he had me, he tried to hurt me in every possible way he could think of, not just physically."

It was what I assumed of Levi. I knew he would try to cause Malcolm as much pain as he could, both physically and mentally.

"Did he say anything to you about me?"

"Of course."

"What did he say?"

"Lies."

"What kind of lies?" I ask, needing to know what was said.

Malcolm shakes his head and looks away from me like he doesn't want to repeat what Levi told him.

I place my hands on either side of his face and make him look at me.

"What did Levi say about me?" I ask.

Malcolm doesn't reply right away, but then he says, "He said there was a darkness inside you that he could sense and hoped to exploit in time. He seems to think you have a lot of your father in you."

"And what do you believe?" I ask, wondering why Levi's words would bother Malcolm so much if he considered them lies.

"When we learned about the prophecy surrounding you, God said that we needed to keep your heart pure. It was almost like a warning."

"He hasn't mentioned that to me," I say. "What do you think it means exactly?"

Malcolm shrugs. "I have no idea."

"Do you think I could ever become like Lucifer?"

"No," Malcolm says adamantly. "Your heart is one of the purest I've ever encountered, and I intend to keep it that way by loving you so much you won't have any room left in there to hate."

"Do you think that's even possible?" I ask. "Because I already hate Levi a lot."

"But you haven't let your loathing for him tarnish your soul, Anna."

I wasn't so sure about that, but I didn't want to upset Malcolm by voicing my concerns over the safety of my soul.

Instead, I hug him close.

"As long as you love me, I don't care about him. I know he'll try to break us apart, but I won't let him. He might be my husband legally, but my heart belongs to you and always will."

"I will always treasure your love, Anna," Malcolm promises hugging me even tighter. "I promise you I will never take it for granted again."

When we let go of one another, I turn to face the birdhouse on the table.

"Do you think you could show me how to build

something?" I ask. "I want us to be able to do things like this together."

I feel Malcolm move up behind me and press himself against me. He leans down and whispers in my right ear, "I can think of a lot more pleasurable things that we can do together."

I smile and roll my eyes. "Well of course we'll be doing that... eventually," I tell him, "but I would like for us to share common interests. I don't only want to be your lover, Malcolm. I want to become your best friend too."

Malcolm backs up a step. "I'll teach you whatever you want to learn, Anna. All you have to do is ask."

"Then teach me how to build a bird house," I request.

For the remainder of the dream, Malcolm shows me how to use the various tools in his workshop, and we work side by side to build a brand new birdhouse, one built with both our hands. I know there's a lot I can learn from Malcolm in the days, months, and years to come in our lives. I just wish the mission God placed in our path was already over. All I want is for us to spend the rest of our lives getting to know one another better than anyone else knows us. I glance over at Malcolm covertly and can't help but smile as I peek at him.

He will be the only man I ever let touch every inch of my body intimately. Since the moment I first saw Malcolm, I've wanted to make love with him. It's odd because sex never really interested me that much before that night. I wanted to experience it, of course. What human doesn't? But, until Malcolm entered my world, I don't think I ever thought about it so frequently. It was almost like not only our bodies but our souls were demanding that we make love to one another to complete this mystical connection between us. I had no problem with that, none whatsoever. I just wish we could begin those private lessons now rather than later.

CHAPTER FOURTEEN

When we finally decide it's time to return to the real world and awaken, I kiss my dream Malcolm deeply one more time before forcing myself to open my eyes and greet a new day.

I wake up first and watch as Malcolm stretches his body out, arms over head, before he opens his eyes and looks over at me.

"Good morning," I tell him, wishing I could kiss him and start our day off right, but I resign myself to the fact that it isn't possible just yet. Instead, I reach out with my left hand to caress the supple flesh of his lips with the tips of my fingers.

"Good morning," he replies, kissing my fingers as they glide over his mouth.

I feel a slight pressure against my hip and look over.

The hellhound pup is wide awake too and propping its front paws across my hip to get a better look at Malcolm. Her little tail is wagging excitedly, and the tip of her pink tongue is sticking out almost like she's smiling.

"What the hell!" Malcolm roars before phasing out of bed and snatching the pup by the back of its neck, pulling it off me.

She whines pitifully at being held at arm's length and in mid-air in front of Malcolm.

I watch in horror as Malcolm begins to wrap his other hand around her neck, and I know he intends to kill my newly given little friend.

"Stop!" I yell at him, phasing to where he stands and pushing his hand away before he can extinguish her life.

Malcolm looks at me in surprise as I place my hands underneath her shoulders and gently pull her from his grasp.

"What the hell, Anna?" Malcolm demands. "It's a hellhound! We need to kill it!"

"No," I growl at him, feeling as protective of the pup in my arms as I do any innocent life. "She was a gift."

The hellhound clings to me and looks back at Malcolm with sad eyes, like she doesn't understand why he was being so mean to her. The pup's body is tense and trembling against me, almost like she's prepared to bolt at the first sign of trouble.

"It's ok," I tell her in a soothing voice, making her lift her head to look up at me. "He just doesn't understand why you're here. He isn't a bad man. I promise."

She seems to trust my words, and I feel her body begin to relax somewhat.

"Anna..."

I look over at Malcolm and see his confusion, silently asking me to explain myself.

"Lucifer gave her to me, Malcolm," I tell him. "She was a gift."

"A gift you should have thrown back in his face!"

The hellhound pup leans its body up against me even more after Malcolm's loud outburst, cautiously watching him.

"Stop yelling," I scold Malcolm. "You're only upsetting her."

Malcolm looks down at the hellhound with a mixture of worry and unease.

"We can't have her around Lucas," Malcolm says obstinately, like that's reason enough to get rid of the dog.

"Lucifer said it wouldn't hurt him."

"And you're just going to believe what the devil tells you?"

"I have no reason not to. I don't believe he would give me something that would hurt me or anyone I loved."

"What was his reason for giving you such a thing in the first place?"

"I guess Levi must have told him what he did to Vala," I

say, a slight lump forming in my throat at the mention of my friend. "He was just trying to replace what Levi took away from me."

Malcolm's eyes narrow on the pup. "I've never seen one with eyes like that before."

"Lucifer said hellhounds aren't born evil. They're made that way by how they're treated. As long as we treat her with kindness and love, she will stay loyal to me and those I care about. I understand your hatred of hellhounds. I truly do. But, this little pup isn't the one who bit you. She's an innocent in all of this. We can raise her the right way and provide her with a safe, loving environment to grow up in. All I ask is that you give her a chance, Malcolm. If not for her sake, then do it for me."

Malcolm's body begins to relax, and he lets out a pent up breath.

"Only for you would I even entertain the idea of allowing a hellhound live inside my house."

I reach out and touch Malcolm on the arm.

"Thank you."

A soft knock resounds on the other side of the door to the room.

"Come in, Lucas," Malcolm says, obviously already

knowing who our early morning visitor is.

I have a feeling this isn't the first time Lucas has come to Malcolm's room right after waking up from his own world of dreams.

The door opens and Lucas peeks his head around its edge. He sees me and looks a little puzzled by my presence in his father's room.

"Good morning, Lucas," I say, wondering why he would find me being in here so peculiar.

"Are you an early riser like us, Anna?" Lucas asks, walking into the room and closing the door behind him. "I tried to figure out which guest room you would be sleeping in, but couldn't find you in any of them. Guess you must have already come in here to say good morning to Dad."

I instantly feel perplexed by Lucas' assumption, then embarrassed. His father and I weren't married yet. In Lucas' young mind, that probably meant we shouldn't be sharing the same bed yet either. The issue becomes irrelevant, however, as soon as the hellhound sees Lucas.

The pup promptly leaps out of my arms, making a mad dash across Malcolm's bed towards our son. Before either Malcolm or I can react, she launches herself at Lucas knocking him down to the floor.

Malcolm and I both phase over to where they are, but I prevent Malcolm from grabbing the pup by the scruff of the neck again when I see Lucas laughing in delight as the hellhound excitedly licks his face.

"Stop it!" Lucas giggles, but does nothing to prevent the pup from kissing his chubby round cheeks as he rolls around on the floor.

Malcolm soon puts an end to their play by helping Lucas to his feet again. The hellhound sits back on her haunches and looks up at Lucas like he's the best gift in the world. Her eyes seem to glow even brighter, and her tail is wagging so fiercely it's producing a slight draft of wind in the room.

"Be careful with that thing," Malcolm warns his son. "It can hurt you very badly if it bites you, Lucas."

Lucas doesn't seem concerned at all about Malcolm's worry and kneels down in front of the pup to pet her head.

"Is it mine?" Lucas asks, enthusiastically.

"It was a gift to me," I tell him. "But I'm willing to share her with you if you like her too."

"What's her name?" He asks.

"I haven't picked one out yet."

"I think we should call her Luna," Lucas announces. "She kind of reminds me of the moon with the way her eyes glow and her coat being so white."

I smile. "I think that's a perfect name for her, Lucas. Luna it is."

Luna seems to accept her name gladly as she jumps up and places her small paws on Lucas' shoulders to continue her tongue bath of his face. Lucas giggles some more in complete bliss, and I remember him telling me how his father never let him have a puppy of his own.

I look up at Malcolm and see a look of resignation on his face at the whole situation. I know he doesn't like the hellhound. I knew he wouldn't even before he met her, but I think for my and Lucas' sakes he will make an effort to tolerate her presence in our lives.

In an indirect sort of way, I feel as though this might also be the first test of Malcolm's patience where my biological father is concerned. Perhaps if he can learn to accept the hellhound into our family, he can, in time, learn to accept Lucifer's permanent connection to me as well. I need for him to understand that getting to know Lucifer is important to me. I want to know more about him and his relationship with my mother, and Lucifer is the only person who can tell me the truth behind their love story.

After Malcolm changes into a pair of grey slacks and silver grey button down shirt, which he leaves mostly unbuttoned and tucked into his pants, we make our way downstairs. In the kitchen, we find Millie, Giles, Desmond, and Brutus already sitting at the table eating breakfast.

"We weren't sure when you would be getting up," Millie tells me, abandoning her spot at the table to make our plates.

"We can get our own food, Millie," I tell her.

Millie waves a hand at me like I'm crazy.

"Don't talk silliness, my sweet. Just sit yourselves down, and I'll have your breakfast in front of you in a jiffy."

Giles rises from the table and helps Millie while we sit down with the others at the table.

After Lucas sits down, he picks Luna up from the floor and sits her on his lap. Obviously, the others were too busy eating to notice the hellhound in their midst when we walked into the kitchen. Desmond is the first to gawk at her, soon followed by Brutus.

"Is that what I think it is?" Desmond asks Malcolm,

looking like he's in absolute shock and openly gaping at the pup.

"Her name is Luna," Lucas tells him proudly. "Anna's sharing her gift with me. Isn't she the most awesomest dog you ever saw?"

"She's...really something..." Desmond says with great hesitation, not sounding sure what he thinks exactly.

"Gift?" Brutus says as though being given a hellhound as a present is the most absurd thing he's ever heard of in his life. "Who in the world would give someone a thing like that as a gift?" Brutus appears to realize the answer his own question. "Oh, never mind, I know who."

"When was Lucifer here?" Desmond asks, having come to the same conclusion as Brutus.

"Last night," I tell them.

"Is that the only reason he came here?" Malcolm asks me, taking one of my hands into his underneath the table. "Or did he want something else?"

"He came to warn me to stay away from the other princes. He said if I leave them alone they will leave me alone. He also told me that this house is off limits to them. If they try to come here, he'll do to them what he did to Levi in the desert."

"Did he happen to say what he and the other princes have

up their sleeves?" Desmond asks. "I seriously doubt they'll simply fade into the background now that they're all back together."

I shake my head as I accept the plate filled with eggs and bacon that Giles hands me.

"No, he wouldn't say," I tell him. "All he would tell me was that I would have to pay a high price to succeed in my mission and that it wasn't worth it."

"I wouldn't put much stock in what he said," Brutus tells me. "Of course he doesn't want you to succeed. Then he would be left with nothing."

"I understand that," I say, "but he seemed sincere in his worry about me. I just wish I knew why he was worried."

I look over at Lucas and see him feed Luna a bit of his fried egg. I'm happy to see Lucas has made a new friend, but seeing the two of them together reminds me of when I first got Vala. I think Lucifer thought having the hellhound would fill the void Vala left behind in my heart, but a new distraction could never replace the years of memories she and I shared.

"Do you have any idea when we'll know if Travis was able to save Vala?" I ask Malcolm, letting go of his hand to pick up my fork and begin eating my breakfast.

"Jered said he would return when he knew one way or the

other," Malcolm tells me as Giles hands him his plate.

I look back over at Desmond and Brutus and ask, "Where is Daniel?"

"He had to get back to the orphanage," Desmond tells me. "He didn't want to leave Linn there to handle everything on her own. When we need him, he'll come back. In fact, until the princes begin to resurface and we know what we're up against, I suggest we all go on with our lives as best we can for the time being. I have a feeling this is the calm before the storm. We might as well enjoy it while it lasts."

There is a lull in the conversation as everyone eats. That is until Lucas voices a question I don't think either Malcolm or I expected him to ask.

"So, are you two courting now?" Lucas asks us.

Complete silence reigns supreme in the room as we all look over at his cute little happy face. He's smiling for all he's worth while he pets Luna on the back and stares straight at me and Malcolm.

"Courting?" I ask.

"You know..." Lucas says like I should understand exactly what he's talking about. "It's when dad takes you out places and brings you flowers and candy and stuff like that. The thing you need to do before you can get married and do whatever it is you gotta do to make babies."

I hear chuckling from the other side of the table and see Desmond and Brutus doing their best to not laugh out loud at what Lucas has said. Desmond lets out a small yelp as I hear movement underneath the table. I'm pretty sure Malcolm just kicked him in the shin to help him find the strength to stop laughing at our son.

"I have *got* to start paying more attention to the books he reads," Malcolm mumbles.

"Well, you know what?" Millie chimes in happily. "I think that's a brilliant idea, Lucas! Anna is a lady after all. She should be treated with the respect she deserves and courted properly."

Lucas watches us expectantly, waiting for an answer from us.

Apparently, he takes our silence as meaning that we *are* courting because his next question is, "Do you have a date planned for today? It sounds like you don't have anything else to do. You might as well get started on it."

I look over at Malcolm and see a thoughtful expression on his face. When his eyes meet mine, it's almost like he's looking at me in an entirely new light.

"Would you like to go out on a date with me, Anna?" He

asks, no humor in his voice like I thought there would be at Lucas' suggestion. He seems totally serious about this courting idea now that it's been presented.

I feel my cheeks flush because I know everyone is watching us and waiting for my answer.

I nod my head and say, "Yes, I would, Malcolm."

Malcolm grins and looks down almost shyly before taking one of my hands underneath the table again and squeezing it lovingly.

I have no idea what the day will bring, but I do know one thing.

It will be a day I'll never forget.

CHAPTER FIFTEEN

After I eat, I get up to put my plate on the counter by the sink. When I spin around, I notice Lucas staring hard at Malcolm.

"What's wrong, Lucas?" I ask him.

Lucas continues to stare at Malcolm and begins to shake his head. "Something has *got* to be done about Dad's hair. It's a mess."

I look at Malcolm and have to agree with my son's sensible conclusion.

"I agree," I tell Lucas. "It does need a trim."

Which I was going to do the night before, but Malcolm decided to stalk me for a kiss instead and completely diverted my attention away from the much needed haircut.

Malcolm stands from his seat at the table and walks over to me to place his own dirty dish on top of mine.

"Then maybe we should go back upstairs so you can cut my hair," he suggests to me, promptly taking hold of one of my hands with his.

"After Anna cuts my hair," he says to all those in the room, "I'll be taking her on our date. So, don't look for us for a few hours."

"I thought you go on dates at night," Lucas says looking confused by the notion of a morning date.

"You can take a lady on a date anytime you want," Malcolm tells him. "This one will last all day though."

"All day?" Lucas asks as his eyes widen in surprise. "That sure is a lot of talking."

I hear snickers come from table but ignore them.

"Yes, it is a lot of talking," I tell Lucas, loving the way his innocent mind works. "It's the only way to truly get to know someone."

"Well you two have fun," Millie tells us, walking over to the sink and rolling up the sleeves of her dress to her elbows. "We'll be giving the house a good cleaning while you're busy."

"Cleaning?" Lucas whines. "I hate cleaning."

"Let's get out of here before she decides we need to help," Malcolm whispers to me, playfully dragging me out of the kitchen like we're making a great escape.

I can't help but laugh.

We continue to hold hands as we head back up the stairs. I catch Malcolm looking at me out of the corner of his eyes, like he's stealing glances at me. I don't say anything about it because each time he does it he smiles. Anything that makes him smile like that is fine with me.

Once we reach his room again, Malcolm allows me to walk in first. After he walks in behind me, he closes the door and turns the lock in the knob.

"I guess you don't want us to be disturbed?" I ask wondering what he has in mind for our time together…alone…in his room…all day…

"Not during our date," he says, walking towards me and taking my hand again. "But first, you need to give me a haircut so I can stop scaring our son."

We walk into the bathroom, and I notice we didn't unplug the tub the night before. The water on the floor has long since dried, but I reach into the cold bath water and pull the plug to let it drain out.

Malcolm sits in a chair by the window in the bathroom while I go grab the scissors Millie left out for me the night before. I walk over to Malcolm and try to imagine how his hair should look once I'm finished cutting it.

"Have you ever done this before?" Malcolm asks dubiously.

"No," I say with a shake of my head.

"Uh, should I have brought Millie in here instead?"

"No. I feel confident I can do it. Worst case scenario we shave your head."

"I would prefer not to be bald," Malcolm admits.

"You worry too much," I say walking behind him and running the fingers of one hand through his hair while holding the scissors in the other to cut with. I make my first snip of his locks and continue to trim the jagged mess Levi left on top of Malcolm's head until it's all even. I left Malcolm's hair at a medium length on top and parted slightly to the right while cutting the sides a little shorter.

"Can you do something for me?" I ask Malcolm as I make the last cut right above his left ear.

"You should know by now that I would do anything for you," he says lovingly.

"Let your hair grow back out," I tell him. "I liked it long."

"You did?" Malcolm asks, resting his hands on my hips as I stand in front of him. "Why?"

Malcolm brings me in closer between his legs as I study his hair with a critical eye to make sure everything is even.

"I liked the way it felt when I ran my fingers through it the first time we kissed. It felt like strands of silk, and I could easily imagine me pulling on it."

"Pulling on it?" Malcolm asks, sounding intrigued by the imagery. "And in what situation would you need to pull on my hair, sweet Anna?"

I smile but say nothing because the scenarios running through my mind are not thoughts a lady should vocalize to a gentleman.

"I guess you'll just have to find out when we start making babies for Lucas to play with," I laugh, remembering Lucas' specific order of our life together.

"Speaking of which," Malcolm says, dropping his hands from my hips. "Are you through with my hair?"

"Yes," I say, taking a couple of steps back, "I'm done."

"Good." Malcolm stands from the chair. "Then it's time I took you to my bed."

I raise a questioning eyebrow in Malcolm's direction.

"Is that your idea of a date?" I ask. "Are we just going to lie in your bed all day, or do you have some other activities planned?"

Malcolm grins. "Unfortunately, we won't be doing anything in my bed that we can't tell our son about."

Malcolm walks over to me and takes the scissors out of my hand, laying them down by the sink while grabbing hold of my other hand.

"Let me explain," he says, tugging me back towards the bedroom.

Malcolm walks us over to my side of the bed, and we sit down. He takes my hands into both of his and holds them like they're the most delicate things on Earth. He glances up to meet my eyes but looks back down at our joined hands without saying a word. He seems hesitant to voice what's on his mind. I'm not sure if he's simply collecting his thoughts to make sure he says the exact right thing or if he isn't sure how I'll take what he has to tell me. So, I simply wait until he's ready to speak.

"What Lucas said at breakfast made me think," he finally tells me. "Anna, you're not like any other woman I've ever had in my life. The way I feel about you goes beyond the physical attraction we feel for one another. The connection between us makes me feel alive for the first time in...well...more years than I care to remember. And I don't want to screw this up. I love you, and I think you deserve to be treated differently from the other women I've had in my life up to this point. I've never had a problem satisfying a woman sexually..."

"Good to know," I chime in, smiling happily at him.

Malcolm grins but shakes his head. "I'm not saying that as a boast. It's just the truth. My point is...I know I can satisfy you physically, of that I have no doubt."

"Me either."

"Anna...," Malcolm says with a half groan. "Please let me finish."

"I'm sorry. Please go on."

"I don't want our relationship to be built on sex alone. Last night in our dream world, you said you wanted to become my best friend. Well, I want that too. In order for that to happen, I think you deserve to know as much about me as you can. Or, at least as much as I can show you. I don't want there to be any secrets between us. I don't want you to feel like you ever have to keep anything from me to spare my feelings. You and Lucas mean everything in this world to me, and you both deserve to have all I have to offer."

Malcolm takes in a deep, shuddering breath, and I know the next few words will be hard for him to say.

"I think for the first time in my life I want to do everything right. I don't want to rush what we have growing between us, and I think every moment we spend together strengthens our bond. Plus,

I want to be a better role model for Lucas than I was to my first son."

"Your first son?" I ask. "Where is he?"

"He passed away a long time ago," Malcolm says, pain over the loss entering his eyes making me wish I hadn't asked the question.

"I think you're a wonderful role model for Lucas," I tell him, squeezing his hands with mine to emphasize how much I believe in my words. "I don't think he could have asked for a better father than you. I see the love you have for him, and I think it's one of the most beautiful things about you."

"I could be a better father," Malcolm says confidently. "And I hope to do that by showing him how a man should treat a woman once you give her your heart. I want to erase the way he saw me treat you back in Lakewood because I never want him to act that way towards someone he loves and plans to spend the rest of his life with."

I have a bad feeling I know where this conversation is going.

"You're going to make me wait, aren't you?" I ask, secretly hoping he says 'no', but already knowing he will say...

"Yes. I want to court you Anna Greco, and...I can't believe

I'm about to say this to you...but I want us to wait until we're married before we make love. I don't want to have any regrets later on and think that I should have handled things better. I want to do things right the first time. I want to treat you with the level of respect I think you deserve. You're not just some woman I want to have sex with, Anna. You're the love of my life, and you are not someone I ever want to take for granted. You deserve the best of me, and that's exactly what I plan to give you."

"So…does this mean I'll have to kill Levi first?" I ask, knowing that will probably be far in the future, at least as long as he keeps my father prisoner.

"Do you remember what I said to you in Cirrus about what constitutes a real marriage?" Malcolm asks.

I think back to that particular conversation.

"Yes. You said a real marriage was one of the heart."

"And did you give your heart to Levi the day you got married?"

"Absolutely not," I say, shivering in disgust just at the mere thought of such a thing.

"Then you're not really married to him," Malcolm tells me. "Having a marriage certificate means nothing, Anna. When we marry, I plan to make my vows to you in front of my father. He's the only one who can truly make us one."

"And how long will you make me wait for this wedding and wedding night to take place?"

"Well...I haven't even properly proposed yet..."

"The answer is yes!"

Malcolm chuckles. "I do appreciate your enthusiasm, but that was not a proposal of marriage, Anna. Let me do this right for you, for us. I don't want either of us to ever regret not enjoying this time together. When we do make love, I want that moment to be engraved into your memory for the rest of your life as being one of the happiest."

I love the fact that Malcolm wants to treat me differently from the other women he's known during his many years on Earth, but I also know myself pretty well. If I didn't still have the poison in my system, he would be hard pressed to keep me off of him.

"All I ask," I tell him, "is that you not make me wait too long. Like I told you earlier, patience isn't a virtue that I possess, and I've wanted to make love to you since the very first night we met."

"Have you now?" Malcolm says, grinning at me with a pleased look on his face at this revelation. "Well, I didn't know my charms swept you off your feet so quickly."

"The moment I saw you, Malcolm," I confess.

Malcolm brings me into his arms and kisses the side of my neck.

"I promise," he whispers in my ear, his warm breath tickling it, "that I will make the wait worth it for you, Anna."

I sigh and close my eyes praying that I survive Malcolm's courtship of me with my sanity intact, but I highly suspect it will bring me to the brink of insanity instead.

"So what are we going to do in your bed all day?" I ask him as he pulls away from me.

"I want to show you my life, at least the important parts. Like I said, I want you to know everything about me. I don't want to hide anything from you. Let me take you back to our dream world so I can show you who I was, who I am, and who I hope to be one day."

"I would love that, Malcolm," I tell him, feeling like he's truly opening up to me in a way he probably never has to anyone else, not even Lilly.

"Since we're being so truthful with one another," I tell him. "I have a confession to make."

"Confession?" Malcolm asks, looking completely intrigued by my turn of words.

"I read the letter you wrote to me," I say, turning my head and nodding towards the nightstand on his side of the bed. "I didn't know what it was at first, and I almost put it back. Then, when I saw that it was addressed to me, I had to read it. I'm sorry for invading your privacy like that."

Malcolm tightens his hands around mine lightly.

"I'm glad you read it," he tells me. "I'm glad you know how I felt when I first saw you. And that's a moment in my life I want to share with you too."

"Then take me," I tell him. "Show me everything."

Malcolm and I lie down on his bed. I rest my head against his chest and listen to the steady beats of his heart as I prepare myself to take a walk through Malcolm's memories.

CHAPTER SIXTEEN

The sun shines brightly in the sky overhead. I have to lift a hand to shade my eyes from its reflective glimmer off the white, sandy earth at our feet. I wasn't disoriented at all by our location on the dune. In fact, I knew exactly where we were, even though the sand was covered with snow the last time I saw it.

"This is where we met Levi to make the trade," I say, looking over at Malcolm.

"This place, especially this particular spot, is holy to us Watchers," Malcolm tells me, taking hold of my free hand in our dream world. "It's where we first came to Earth in the human forms we chose. We all arrived here eager to help humanity progress further in their advancements with our added knowledge. Before we came down, we spent a great deal of time observing human behavior."

"Why did you watch them before you came to Earth?"

"Mostly, we wanted to learn which disciplines needed the most help in order to push humanity further along in its evolution," Malcolm tells me. "All of us had our own specialties. Mine was architecture. I wanted to start this journey with you here because this is where my Earthly life began, and I felt like you should see the moment of our arrival."

Malcolm looks out onto the vast expanse of desert in front of us, and I follow his gaze and watch as the first moment of his life on Earth unfolds.

As one, a group of Watchers appear before us. They're all dressed in black feather cloaks, black leather pants and matching boots with silver buckles on the sides. As I scan their faces, I notice a trend among the Watchers. They're all handsome and seem to exude a certain self-confidence that makes them even more attractive. Malcolm from the past is standing in the front row of the group and, to my eyes at least, stands out from the crowd.

"I love the outfits," I tell him, ogling Malcolm's memory of himself with an appreciative eye. "Do you still have yours?"

"Yes," Malcolm says, looking over at me with a smile on his handsome face. "Why do you ask?"

"Because I definitely want you to wear it for me one day," I say.

Malcolm chuckles.

"Your wish is my command," he tells me.

"How many of you were there in the beginning?"

"Two-hundred of us came to Earth."

Suddenly one of the Watchers phases in beside us. I

recognize him as Mason, Jess' husband and leader of the Watchers before Malcolm was given the responsibility.

"Brothers," Mason says to the crowd of angels in front of him. "Today is the day we have all been preparing for. We've been sent here by our father to help the humans progress further than they have so far, but remember, we are only meant to help them in their technological and cultural advancements. Be an inspiration to them, but don't try to take them forward before they're ready. We are their guides to the wonders our father has in store for them, and that is all we are meant to be. Now, go to the places you have chosen to spend your time and may God bless the work you are about to do."

As quickly as they came, the Watchers vanish.

"Where did you choose to go?" I ask Malcolm.

The scenery changes and I find us standing on a small, grassy knoll now instead of the dune. I notice a group of twenty men tugging on thick ropes wrapped around a large rectangular slab of stone. They grunt as they use their combined strength to pull the stone up the small hill towards a deep hole dug into the summit. I see Malcolm and some other men urging the laborers on to keep pulling the stone up towards the hole.

"This is where I decided to come," Malcolm tells me. "This part of the world would later be known as the north-western region of France. The humans were entering the Neolithic period and beginning to use large stones to build various structures."

"What are you building here?" I ask.

"It's a dolmen. Basically, it's a burial chamber made of free standing stones and covered with a capstone. But, that's not why I brought you here," Malcolm says, pointing to something in front of us.

I look to see what he's pointing at and find that it isn't a thing at all but a woman.

She is petite in stature with beautiful long blonde hair which reaches down to her waist. Her skin is pale with just a hint of pink. Her face is beautiful with its delicate bone structure, but it's her eyes which draw me completely in. They're an amazing cornflower blue, and I can honestly say I've never seen eyes like hers before in my life. Just by watching her facial expressions and the way she carries herself, I can tell she has a sweet temper and probably never even thought to raise her voice to anyone in her life.

"Who is she?" I ask, staring at the woman as she lugs a wooden bucket full of water up the hill beside the men.

"Her name was Mina, and she was my first wife."

I watch Malcolm's memory and notice the past him openly

staring at Mina, not seeming to care if anyone else takes notice of his diverted attention. By the small stretch of Mina's pink lips, it's obvious she knows he's watching her and enjoys being able to hold his interest.

"What made you fall in love with her?" I ask, noting what a stark contrast Malcolm's first wife is to me. It wasn't just the physical disparities that made us distinctive from one another either. Mina's demeanor gave the impression that she had a sweet and calm personality. How could Malcolm love someone as brash and temperamental as me when he chose a woman like her to be his first wife?

"Mina emanated a natural serenity around her that almost everyone she came into contact with felt," Malcolm reminisces, his voice taking on a far off quality as he answers my question. "The war with Lucifer and his followers in Heaven was hard on all of us who had to fight in it. It took a lot of time for some of us to recover and even longer for others to come to terms with what happened. For me, Mina was like a healing balm on my soul. She was so caring and nurturing to not only me but also to all those around her. I was immediately drawn to her and her to me. At the time, I didn't care that God ordered us to refrain from becoming emotionally and physically involved with humans. All I could think about was the way Mina made me feel, and I didn't see why it would be wrong to love her as long as she felt the same way about me. So, I asked her to marry me, and we were wed the next day."

Malcolm's memory changes location to the interior of a small one room cottage. I see Malcolm sitting naked on the side of a small bed crying like he had lost all hope. Mina is lying underneath the covers of the bed and simply looks like she's in a deep sleep.

"That next morning after the wedding, I couldn't wake her up. I knew something was wrong, but I didn't know exactly what was happening at the time. I had a feeling then that my father was punishing me for going against his orders. It wasn't until the hunger for blood hit that I understood the full strength of his wrath. My father has never been one to take disobedience lightly, and his punishment for us was fitting to our crime. Those of us who married were rewarded with the death of our wives by the birth of children cursed because of our sin."

Time rapidly passes within the little cottage, and I watch as Mina's body withers away but not from decay. It's almost like something is slowly eating her from the inside out and only leaving behind an empty husk of skin and bones.

The memories finally stop and I stand to see past Malcolm holding a small bloody creature in his arms. What's left of Mina is still lying on the bed, but her belly looks like it exploded from the inside out.

"Our children took what nutrients they needed from the body of their mothers and then clawed their way out of the wombs once they were ready to be born," Malcolm tells me in a detached voice. "The instant my son was born I knew I couldn't live among humans anymore and still take care of him. So, I phased us to a remote cave in the Himalayan Mountains."

Our surroundings change to a cave where a single fire is burning at its center. There are a few furnishings around such as a cot and a table, but little else is present to provide for a comfortable life. A small wooden cradle is set beside the cot, and I see past Malcolm reach into it and pull out what appears to be a healthy looking baby.

"I was relieved when the sun rose and the thing that clawed its way out of Mina transformed itself into something that looked human," Malcolm tells me. "But every night I had to endure his cries when he transformed back into the creature I had doomed him to become. Every time I had to watch Sebastian suffer through the change, my rage towards my father grew just as my hunger for human blood did. I hated Him for a long time. And, I finally decided I'd had enough. If He wanted me to become a monster, so be it."

We're soon standing in what looks like an Egyptian bazaar from a time in Earth's history I've only read about. Vendors are vigorously hawking their merchandise to passersby, desperately trying to make a sale. I see past Malcolm leaning up against a wall near a stall where colorful fabrics are being sold. He's shirtless and only wearing a white cloth skirt around his hips with a blue and gold silk sash tied around his waist. His skin looks paler than those of the people milling around the bazaar, causing him to stand out to my eyes. The expression on his face is a mask of complete control as he watches a group of women browsing the fabrics of the nearby merchant. If it wasn't for the predatory glint in his eyes, I would have thought he was completely bored with the goings on around him.

"I attempted to live among humans without eating them," Malcolm tells me. "I initially came here to just help build the pyramids at Giza, but the longer I stayed around humans the more intense my hunger for their blood became. It finally got to a point where I didn't care about my soul anymore. All I wanted to do was hurt my father for what He had turned me into and for the curse he placed on Sebastian for a sin I had committed."

I watch as past Malcolm pushes away from the wall he was leaning against and approaches one of the women he's been watching. It doesn't take him long before he has her separated from her friends and walking away with him willingly.

In an instant, we're standing on top of a pyramid. Past Malcolm is holding the woman against him with his face buried in the side of her neck. The woman is completely limp in his arms, and I hear a rhythmic sucking sound as Malcolm drinks her blood.

"This was the first time I fed on a human," Malcolm tells me, his voice filled with disgust as he watches himself become a monster he would later come to hate.

"Why are you showing me this?" I ask, averting my eyes away from past Malcolm to the man I love standing beside me.

Malcolm tears his eyes away from his memory self and looks down at me. The pain of watching himself murder a helpless woman is written clearly on his face. I squeeze the hand I hold tighter trying to reassure him that he isn't that man anymore.

"You don't have to relive these moments," I tell him. "You don't have to show me this."

"Yes," Malcolm says with a small nod of his head, "I do. I need you to understand who I was because that person is still inside me, Anna. He'll never completely go away, but I've learned how to forgive him for what he did. I can't erase the pain I caused others, but I can strive to be a better man and continue to rise above who I was so that part of me is only a distant memory."

I glance back at past Malcolm.

"What did it feel like to kill her?" I ask.

Malcolm sighs heavily. "Her blood tasted like the sweetest nectar. It made me feel invincible and fed the monster growing inside me, making him think he could kill at will and not have to pay a price for it later on. I went on a killing spree after this moment that didn't stop for many years."

"And where was Sebastian during this murderous rampage of yours?"

"I kept him safe," Malcolm says. "It was my only redeemable quality during that dark period of my life. I made sure he never killed anyone because I didn't want his soul to be damned because of me. I had already ruined his life enough. I wasn't about to be the reason his afterlife was doomed as well."

Malcolm takes me to a moment in his past that I've already seen. It's the night he first met Lilly.

"Why are we here?" I ask him as I watch past Malcolm study Lilly as she crosses the street in front of him. "I've already seen this."

"I want to show you the memories that changed who I was," Malcolm tells me. "This is a moment that changed my life forever."

"Yes," I say, "I know. I felt what it did to you the last time I saw it."

"I didn't know it then," Malcolm tells me as he watches his past self take hold of Lilly's arm, "but I would come to realize this was the moment my real life on Earth began. If it hadn't been for Lilly, I never would have been able to experience the happiest years of my life."

The scene quickly changes, and I find us standing inside a home with a Christmas tree in the corner. Malcolm is knelt down in front of it.

"Are you sure you have a gift for me under here, dearest?" Malcolm asks, while he scans the presents. "I still don't see it."

"It's there, Malcolm," a very pregnant Lilly says to him with Brand standing by her side as she watches him with amusement. "But you can't open it until tomorrow morning. That's the rule."

Past Malcolm sighs heavily and stands up. He turns to face them both.

"All I seem to be able to find are gifts for Caylin," he halfheartedly complains.

"I've been a good girl, Uncle Malcolm."

I see a little girl with brown hair and grey eyes walk from the back of the house into the living room with a half-eaten cookie in her hand.

Malcolm changes the scene, and I literally begin to see years of his life flash by.

"It was the first time I felt the power of family," Malcolm tells me as his life with Lilly and Sebastian's families fade in and out. "We were all so happy during the years that followed. I didn't even mind the occasional brawl with Lucifer, at least until I was bit by his hellhound."

Malcolm only briefly shows me a glimpse of that fight and the moment he was bit.

"I asked Lucifer to take his curse off of you when he came to see me," I tell Malcolm. "But he won't."

"He never will," Malcolm tells me with certainty, freezing the moment his physical torture began. "He's been trying to make me beg him to take my soul for years. I think it frustrates him that I've never given in. If it wasn't for my promise to Lilly to stay alive until you were born and help you retrieve the seals, I might have given him my soul to end the pain by now. But with you in my life," Malcolm says, turning to fully face me, "I have a whole new reason to endure it."

My vision grows blurry as I try to hold in my sorrow over the pain Malcolm has to live with.

"I would give anything to help you," I tell him.

Malcolm shakes his head. "You've already given me everything, Anna. Don't you realize that? I've lived with this pain for a thousand years. But your love for me is something I never expected to be gifted with. It overshadows everything else. The pain is still there, but it's finally been made bearable because my love for you pushes it so far back in my mind I can almost forget about it."

Malcolm lifts our joined hands to his heart.

"You live here now," he says, emphasizing his words by lightly tapping our hands against his chest. "And you always will."

I feel a tear slide down my cheek at the sweetness of his words because I know they are the truth. Malcolm leans in to kiss the tear's wet trail away.

"I didn't say that to make you cry," he tells me, pulling back.

Before he can, I wrap my arms around his neck and kiss him deeply. It may only be a dream world kiss, but I want him to know how much I love the fact he's sharing his life with me so unreservedly.

"Thank you for not giving up," I whisper against his lips as I end the kiss. "Otherwise, I wouldn't have been able to experience happiness like this."

"You're welcome," Malcolm grins. It's not a cocky smile, but one telling me he's glad he didn't give in to his pain too.

Malcolm kisses me on the forehead and turns his body

away from mine to show me more of his memories.

We're back in the desert once more. The Watchers are again dressed in their formal wear and kneeling with one knee on the sand. I watch as Caylin walks among the watchers and see her come to stand in front of my papa and Daniel.

"This is the moment when Caylin chose those of us who would watch over the princes and wait for you to be born," Malcolm tells me. "I didn't want to admit it at the time, but I knew I was one of her chosen even though she refused to tell me."

"Thank you for staying here so long and waiting for me," I tell him, unable to imagine my life without him in it.

"It hasn't been easy," Malcolm admits. "Especially when we lost so many that we loved."

We leave the desert.

I see an old man sitting in a rocking chair on a front porch of a nice looking two story home. The man looks to be in his eighties with more wrinkles on his face than I care to count, but the ones around his mouth and the corners of his eyes seem to be more prominent than the rest. They hint at a life spent in laughter and true happiness.

I see past Malcolm walk out of the front door of the home carrying two cups in his hands. He hands one of the cups to the man in the chair.

"Thanks, Dad," the old man says, making me gasp because I realize this is an older version of Malcolm's son.

"Anytime," Malcolm says, sitting down in a matching rocking chair angled toward Sebastian's.

"Malcolm," I say, looking over at him, "you don't have to show this to me."

I can only imagine the pain this memory must be causing him.

Malcolm nods his head. "Yes, I do."

I look back and watch.

"Dad," Sebastian says, his voice raspy from age, "can you do something for me?"

"You know I would do anything for you, Sebastian. I love you."

"Then, I want you to have more children one day."

Past Malcolm keeps his expression blank as he replies, "I don't see that happening."

"But you're such a great father," Sebastian argues. "Even when you were at your worst, you always made me feel loved.

With the curse lifted, you can have normal children with a woman now."

Malcolm shakes his head. "I would have to be in love with a woman to have children with her, Sebastian. I fear my chance at happiness like that has long since passed."

Sebastian leans in toward his father and places his age spotted hand on Malcolm's arm.

"Don't close your heart off to others," Sebastian almost begs. "There's so much good inside you, Dad. It would be a sin for you not to share yourself with someone. I know you always loved Lilly, but she wasn't the one you were meant to be with. I think you know that. Just promise me that you won't stop trying to live after we're all gone. I know you'll want to shut people out to spare yourself the heartache over losing them. But, you should know better than anyone that this life isn't the end. We'll all be together again one day in Heaven."

"That knowledge doesn't make losing you in this life any easier," Malcolm tells his son. "I have no way of knowing when I'll be able to see you again."

"I know, Dad," Sebastian says letting go of Malcolm's arm to lean back in his chair. "But if and when the time comes that you find someone to love, don't push her away. I want you to experience the joy of being a father the way it was meant to be.

You sort of got cheated out of that with me."

"I regret what happened to you because of me," Malcolm says, almost like a confession. "You never should have been put through all those years of pain."

"It was all worth it in the end, Dad," Sebastian says with a content look on his face. "I've had a wonderful life, and even if I were given the chance to change what happened, I wouldn't."

"Why?"

"Because if I changed one single moment, the life I've had might not have ever happened. I wouldn't have met Abby at just the right time, and without her, I wouldn't have had my children. Having them and you in my life makes it all worth it to me, Dad. I wouldn't change a thing."

My Malcolm faces me again. "I tried to keep Sebastian's words in mind, but after a few hundred years, I gave up hope of meeting anyone. All I wanted to do was finish our mission and finally find release in death. Then, something unexpected happened and changed the way I started to feel about my life."

Our location morphs into one I recognize, Malcolm's study in his New Orleans home. Past Malcolm is sitting behind his desk staring out the window at nothing in particular. I can tell he has something else on his mind besides the activity happening outside his home on the busy street below.

There's an insistent knock at the door.

"Come in," Malcolm calls out to the visitor, turning around in his chair to face the new arrival.

Jered opens the door and walks in. He's carrying a baby swaddled in a blue blanket on one arm.

"He's here," Jered says to Malcolm.

"Have you made arrangements with Daniel and Linn for them to take him in?"

Jered closes the door behind him and walks over to Malcolm's desk.

"Yes," Jered says hesitantly. "Though I disagree with your decision."

"It's better for him in the long run," Malcolm tells Jered.

"Better for him or for you?" Jered asks, a challenge in his voice. "Marcus and June specifically stated in their will that they wanted *you* to take care of their son, Malcolm. How can you just toss him aside so easily?"

"I'm not tossing him aside," Malcolm defends. "I'm giving him a better life than what he would have with me."

"I think you're just scared to care about anyone too deeply," Jered challenges. "You haven't let anyone get close to you in years. Don't you think it's time you started caring for someone else besides yourself?"

Malcolm quickly stands to his feet and places his hands against the top of his desk, leaning in towards Jered. The anger on his face is just as evident in his voice as he says, "I will live my life the way I see *fit*, Jered. I don't need you telling me what I should do."

Jered sighs but not in defeat.

"Then do one thing for me, and I'll leave you alone. I won't bring the subject up ever again."

"If it will shut you up, name it."

Jered walks around the desk and holds the baby out to Malcolm.

"Spend one hour with him. If you feel nothing for him after that, I won't say another word on the subject."

"Should I get that in writing?" Malcolm quips, eyeing the baby warily.

"No, I will keep to my word. You have my promise."

Malcolm takes the child from Jered.

"One hour," Malcolm reminds Jered.

Jered nods and leaves the room.

I watch as Malcolm looks down at the child he holds in his arms.

"Hello, Lucas," Malcolm says. "Jered seems to think we should become acquainted with one another. What do you think about that?"

Lucas lifts his little fists into the air and makes a happy gurgling sound.

Reluctantly, Malcolm begins to chuckle. He sits back down in his chair and begins to talk to Lucas about all the reasons why he would make a horrible father.

"Obviously," my Malcolm says, "I decided to keep Lucas with me. But, that moment changed the way I viewed my life. I had someone who needed me to keep them safe, and I pledged to Lucas that day to do just that."

Then Malcolm changes the scene to one I remember quite well. It's the night Amon attacked me, and I killed my first prince of Hell. It was also the night the connection between our souls opened up, telling Malcolm that I needed him.

I see myself lying on the stone floor of the veranda as my body writhes in agony. I can remember how blinding the pain was until I felt Malcolm's first touch. I feel my head tilt of its own accord when I see myself the way Malcolm saw me that night.

"I glowed to you?" I ask, sure that something must be wrong with my eyes.

"Yes," Malcolm tells me, "you did."

"But I didn't even know you. We hadn't met before this moment. How could I have already been devoted to you?"

"When Lilly came down to set me straight, she told me that you've known me for a very long time. On one of her trips to Heaven, you apparently told her that you would take good care of me when you came to Earth."

"I wish I could remember that," I say, finding it hard not to stare at my glowing form.

"I knew that night that you would change my life forever," Malcolm tells me. "I just refused to admit it to myself."

The scene changes quickly to the moment I rolled over on my bed and looked at Malcolm for the very first time. Even though I knew what I was thinking in that moment, you would have to be a fool not to see the love I held for him just from viewing the expression on my face.

"You knew I loved you," I say to him, watching the past Malcolm turn from me and walk away.

I couldn't see his expression back then, but I can now. He looks confused and slightly shocked because of the way I'm looking at him. All the clues about our bond were there for him to see, yet he still tried to deny how he felt about me. At least until Lilly came down from Heaven and made him realize what a fool he was being.

Malcolm looks at me and says, "Now you know about my past and my present. Our future is writing itself, but I want to show you what I hope it will look like within the next few years."

Malcolm turns me so I'm facing away from him and brings my back up against his torso. Our surroundings slowly fall away to be replaced by the two of us standing on the veranda of the highest tower of the palace in Cirrus. The clouds drift by on the ever present artificial wind, and I feel Malcolm's hands move against my belly, but something feels funny about the action.

I look down and see that I'm pregnant. Malcolm has clothed me in a loose fitting sleeveless lavender gown. I hear the sound of children's laughter and look to the side of us to see a slightly older Lucas playing with a little boy and a little girl who can't be much older than two years old.

Malcolm leans down and kisses my bare shoulder tenderly.

"How many children do you see us having?" I ask, leaning further back against him as I let myself revel in his dream of our future together.

"As many as you will let me have," he murmurs against my neck.

I close my eyes and smile.

"Then we may need a bigger palace."

Malcolm chuckles and my heart warms with joy.

It's a perfect future. And I, for one, plan to make sure it comes to pass.

CHAPTER SEVENTEEN

When we wake up, I wrap my arms around Malcolm because I never want to let him go. I feel him stroke my hair and gently run his fingers through the long strands. We just lie there in the quiet of the room, simply enjoying being close to one another. It's a perfect moment for me until I feel the muscles just below my abdomen begin to cramp. I wince from the unexpected pain.

"Are you all right?" Malcolm asks, his voice filled with concern.

I sit up in the bed and feel the twinge happen again. It's an odd sensation, unlike anything I've ever experienced before.

"I'm having muscle spasms for some reason," I tell him, placing my hands over where I feel the pain.

"Is it your time of the month?" Malcolm asks me.

I look at him in confusion. "My time of the month for what?"

"You're a woman…" Malcolm replies like this statement alone should be enough of a hint. Apparently my continued confusion is showing on my face. "Women of childbearing age normally have a monthly cycle…"

"Oh, that," I say realizing what he's talking about. "I've

never really had many of those."

"But your twenty-one, Anna. This sort of thing should be a normal part of your life by now."

"I did have one right before I turned thirteen," I say, recalling that eventful day in my young life. "But I haven't had one since."

"Didn't you think that was peculiar?"

"Honestly, I was just relieved it went away. It's not exactly something I wanted to experience again."

Malcolm looks concerned about this piece of information.

He gets off the bed and holds a hand out to help me up also.

"Let's go talk to Millie," he says. "She has to know the reason why."

As we walk out of the room, I ask, "Do you think something's wrong with me?"

Malcolm glances at me, and I see the worry in his eyes.

"It's not natural for someone your age not to experience a monthly period. Didn't any of your girlfriends ever ask you why you weren't having them?"

"The only real friend I had was Auggie, and it wasn't

exactly something he would have asked about."

When we make our way downstairs, we find Giles mopping the wood floor of the foyer and Millie dusting the furniture ahead of his progress.

"Millie," Malcolm calls out, "can we have a private word with you?"

Millie leaves her dust rag on the small table by the front door and walks over to us wiping her hands clean on the bottom of her white apron.

"Is there a problem, Master Malcolm?" Millie asks, looking from Malcolm to me with worry.

Malcolm tugs me along as we walk into the adjacent sitting room with Millie following close behind.

Once we're well out of earshot of Giles, Malcolm turns to Millie and asks, "Why has Anna only had one monthly cycle in her life?"

"Oh…that," Millie says, looking a bit sheepish. I have to assume it's because she's having to discuss such a private matter with Malcolm. "Empress Catherine told us it would be a side effect of the shots." Millie looks at me. "Do you feel it coming, my sweet? Have the cramps started?"

I nod. "Yes. What do I do?"

297

Millie shrugs helplessly. "There's really nothing that you can do except let it happen. But we will need a few supplies for you to handle the...a... effects of it."

"Wait a minute," Malcolm says, "I want to make sure I understand you correctly. Did you just say the shots prevented Anna from having her cycle?"

Millie nods. "Yes...at least that's what we were told."

Before I have a chance to react properly, Malcolm has me in his arms and is kissing me on the mouth with an urgency that makes me tingle from the top of my head to the tips of my toes.

"Oh my," I hear Millie say, sounding flabbergasted by our public display of affection. "I'll leave the two of you alone... to discuss this."

Malcolm continues to kiss me and realization hits. He isn't passing out. The fact that I started my cycle is proof that the poison is finally out of my system. I wrap my arms around Malcolm's neck firmly and phase us directly to his bed. He instantly notices the change in our surroundings and pulls away from me breathing hard.

"Anna," he says tenderly, "this doesn't change anything."

"It changes everything for me," I say, bringing his head back down to mine, not intending to let him out of his bed until

298

after he makes love to me.

Malcolm pulls away again. "Anna…"

"Stop talking so much," I tell him, pulling his head back down to mine again.

I know Malcolm wants to make love as much as I do. I can feel the evidence of his adoration pressing into me.

We kiss for a long time, but Malcolm doesn't do anything with his hands to encourage the hope I have that he intends to go further than just kissing.

I finally break the contact of our lips to look into his eyes. They're filled with pent up desire for me, making him look almost drugged, but there's also a look of grim determination on his face.

"Could we just make love once?" I suggest, thinking it's a reasonable request. "And then you can do all the courting of me you want."

Malcolm shakes his head, completely shattering my hope of spending the day in his bed in various compromising positions.

"Please don't make this any harder on me than it already is," he says. "I meant what I said to you this morning, Anna. You don't deserve anything less than the best of me."

I sigh in resignation because I know there won't be any

changing his mind, at least not yet.

"If that's the way you want it," I say, unable to hide my frustration and disappointment.

"Anna," Malcolm murmurs, looking down at me with so much love and tenderness it makes my heart tighten inside my chest, "don't be mad."

I sigh again. "I'm not mad, Malcolm. But I won't lie and say I'm not disappointed. I meant what I said earlier too. I've wanted to make love to you since the moment we met. And I don't say those words lightly. I can honestly say that I've never felt like that about anyone I've ever met. You saw the evidence of my devotion to you when you first saw me. And considering what Lilly told you, I can only imagine that I've loved you for a very long time, even while I was in Heaven. My body, mind, and heart have belonged to you for who knows how long. I've already waited so long to be with you. But, I guess I can hang on a little while longer if it's that important to you. All I ask is that you not make the wait totally unbearable."

"It won't be unbearable," Malcolm promises, smiling at me. "I plan to make it the most memorable part of your life thus far, Anna. I can tell you I love you a million times over, but let me show you with my actions just how much you mean to me."

"Couldn't you do that just as easily by making love to me

sooner rather than later?" I tease, knowing it won't change his mind.

Malcolm chuckles. I like feeling the vibrations from his laughter against my chest. It's a little thing, one most people would take for granted. To me, it's one of the most magical things in the world. It has the power to make me feel content.

"Trust me, I want to make love to you so badly right now I'm almost ready to give into your request. But I know I would end up regretting it because I would be disappointed in myself for not giving you the experience of a lifetime."

I wrap my arms around Malcolm's neck and simply bring his head down to mine to hold him close.

"All right," I say. "I promise to try and keep my hormones under control during this courtship of ours. I can see how important it is to you."

"Thank you," Malcolm whispers in my ear, kissing me just below the ear lobe.

"If you don't want me to just strip you down naked right here and now," I tell him, "we need to get out of this bed and do something else to take my mind off of doing just that. What else did you have planned for us to do today?"

Malcolm lifts up slightly and looks at me.

"I plan to perform a miracle," he says unexpectedly.

"Did you achieve sainthood and not tell me about it?"

"I'm not sure showing you how to cook will count towards sainthood in my father's eyes, but it should. Like I told you before, there hasn't been one descendant in a thousand years who could cook an edible meal. I plan to break that trend with you, sweet Anna."

"Considering the colossal disaster I made of the roast, I think a miracle might just be in order."

Malcolm laughs and gets off of me and the bed.

"Come on my future, sous chef. I'll start you off on something easy."

Malcolm and I go down to the kitchen and pick up a little boy and hellhound on our way. When Lucas learns about Malcolm's plan, he looks surprised.

"Wow," Lucas says, "I didn't know you were that brave, Dad."

I grab Lucas and begin to tickle him mercilessly under his arms. Luna yaps like she's laughing at our play.

Malcolm decides to start me off with something easy, a soup. He shows me how to dice potatoes, and we place these in a large pot of boiling water. While they are cooking, he grabs some sausage from his preserver and helps me cook the meat in a skillet on the stove. After the potatoes are tender from boiling, I add in the sausage, some kale and some fresh cream to thicken the soup.

"Well done," Malcolm says, hugging me around the waist when we're finished. "I'll have you cooking a real meal all by yourself in no time."

"Mmmm, is that lunch I smell?" I hear a familiar voice say from the entrance of the kitchen.

Malcolm and I turn to see Jered walking towards us.

I know what his presence means. He has news about Vala.

I take in a deep breath and ask, "Was Travis able to save her?"

Jered smiles and the tightness of worry inside my chest loosens.

"Why don't the three of you come and see her for yourself?" Jered says. It's only when he looks at Lucas that he notices the hellhound pup sitting on my son's lap.

"Is that what I think it is?" He asks apprehensively.

"Yes," Malcolm says in mild disgust. "It's exactly what you think it is. A gift to the lovely Anna from her *other* father."

"And why are we allowing it to stay here?" Jered asks sounding confused by the hellhound's continued presence.

"Because I want it," I tell him.

"Good enough reason, I suppose," Jered replies, still looking doubtful about the hellhound's trustworthiness. "Anyway, Travis is waiting for us."

Lucas walks over to me and Malcolm. I place my hands on his shoulders and Malcolm phases us to Travis' workshop.

Jered phases in beside us and says, "Follow me."

We follow Jered through the maze of tables, hanging wires and metal parts until we come to an area of the workshop that looks a little neater than the rest. Travis is standing beside a steel table with a large dog I've never seen before laying on top of it. The dog appears to be asleep as Travis manipulates a blue-green 3-D hologram of a brain which is hovering above it.

"Where's Vala?" I ask Travis.

"What?" Travis says in surprise, looking between Jered and Malcolm. "I thought one of you would have told her before you even brought her here."

"Anna," Malcolm says beside me, taking hold of my hand which does nothing but make me nervous. Obviously, he thinks what he's about to tell me might be upsetting. "Travis wasn't able to save Vala's body. He had to use what nutrients were left in it to minimize the damage done to her brain."

I look at the dog lying on the table and the blue-green holographic image of a brain floating over it.

"Are you telling me that body has Vala's brain in it?" I ask.

"Sure does," Travis says proudly. "And let me tell you, I felt lucky I was able to save as many of her memories as I did."

"What kind of dog body is that?" I ask.

"Well..." Travis says, scratching his head. "I couldn't find a body like the one she had before. They stopped making that model years ago. Most people now a days want a dog that can be a personal companion *and* guard them. This is the newest Akita model. Thank God Malcolm's so rich, or we wouldn't have been able to get her a new body."

"How much did you pay for it?" I ask Malcolm.

Malcolm shrugs. "I honestly don't know. I just told Jered to pay whatever he needed to." Malcolm looks over at Jered. "What exactly *did* I end up paying for it?"

"Your home in New York," Jered says and pauses for a moment before saying, "your home in Florida, and your home in California."

"I guess the seller wasn't interested in money?" Malcolm muses.

"No, they wanted property. They wouldn't take anything less."

Malcolm shrugs. "Easily replaceable. I'm just glad you were able to find a body at all."

I stare at Vala's new form and wonder what she will think about being so much larger. Her coloring is close to the same orange and white coat she had as a Pomeranian. I just hope the shock of finding herself in a different body won't be too much for her.

"How many of her memories were you able to save?" I ask.

"Not sure yet," Travis admits. "We'll have to wake her up to find out, but from what I can tell from her brainwave activity the damage should have been minimal. That's one reason I wanted you here before I woke her up. If she doesn't recognize you, then we know the damage is more severe than I thought. Plus, she'll be a little disoriented in this new body."

I let go of Malcolm's hand and walk to the table to stand by Vala. For some reason, I'm hesitant to touch her new body, but I force myself to take hold of one of her paws like you would a sick person's hand. If I'm feeling a little unsettled about her new form, I can only imagine what her reaction will be to it.

Out of the corner of my eye, I see Lucas get a little closer to Malcolm's side as they both watch what happens next.

"Are you ready?" Travis asks me.

I take in a deep breath and nod my head. "Wake her up."

Travis taps the hologram of Vala's brain and it vanishes from sight.

I watch Vala's face and see her slowly open her slightly slanted brown eyes. She looks around until she sees me.

"Anna?" she says, her voice sounding different, not quite as high pitched as it once was.

"Vala," I say, "I need you to listen to me very carefully before you try to move. Ok?"

"Ok...Anna," she says, already sounding like she knows something isn't quite right.

I'm sure she can feel the difference in her body. I know by the hesitancy in her speech pattern that she can hear the difference in her voice.

"What is the last thing you remember?" I have to ask, needing to know if her last memory is of Levi separating her head from her body.

Vala is silent for a moment, and I can see by the movement

of her eyes that she's trying to think back.

"I remember Levi coming to see us and snatching me out of Lucas' arms…" she says, hesitating like she's doing her best to remember what happened after that. "I'm sorry, that's all I remember, Anna. What happened next?"

"You have nothing to be sorry about, Vala," I tell her, silently thankful she can't remember the pain or fear from having her head ripped off. "I'm the one who should be apologizing for not being there to protect you."

"Anna, what happened?" Vala implores. "I feel funny. Did he do something to me?"

"Vala," I say, hoping to ease her into her new reality as gently as I can, "Levi tried to kill you, but a friend of mine was able to save your brain. He had to use parts of your body to keep your brain alive though."

"My body?" Vala asks, slowly moving the paw I hold and lifting it out in front of her so she can see it. "Am I in a new body, Anna? Is that why I feel so odd?"

"Yes," I tell her, "but the important thing is you're still alive. This body is a lot bigger than what you're used to, Vala. It will take you some time to adjust to it."

Vala lowers her leg and rolls over onto her stomach. She

looks around at her surroundings. Her eyes focus on me then turn to see Lucas and Malcolm.

"Are we safe now, Anna?" Vala asks, looking back at me. "Are we away from Levi?"

"Yes," I tell her. "You're perfectly safe now, and I plan to keep you that way."

Vala turns her head as far as her neck will allow to view the rest of her new body. I see her eyes widen in surprise, but she doesn't exactly look alarmed by her new state of being.

Slowly, she looks back at me.

"I'm big," she says in amazement. "I always wanted to be bigger."

"Then you're ok with it?" I ask. "You're ok with this new body?"

Vala stands up on the table and turns her head to look at her fluffy, curly Q tail as she wags it.

"I love it, Anna!"

She makes to jump into my arms but thinks better of the action.

"Oh," she says sounding slightly disappointed, "I guess I can't do that anymore."

"I can hold you," I tell her. "But I'm not sure it would be very comfortable for either of us."

"No, probably not," she admits.

Vala turns to look at Lucas.

"Who do you have there, Lucas?" Vala asks, staring at the latest addition to our family.

Lucas walks up to Vala. "This is Luna, and she's a hellhound. Anna's dad gave it to her."

"Is Lord Andre back as well?" Vala asks me, hope in her voice.

"No," I regret to inform her. "Lucas is talking about my biological father."

"Oh, yes, Lucifer."

"How did you know about him?" I ask Vala, caught off guard by her knowledge.

"Lord Andre mentioned him to me a few times. I was to tell you about him if, for some reason, Lord Andre wasn't around, and you needed to know about your true lineage."

"It seems my father used you as his backup memory for a lot of things," I say, remembering that it was Vala who showed me where to find my sword in my father's office. "Is there anything

310

else that you need to tell me?"

"Not that I can think of at the moment," Vala says, lowering her head a little like she's trying to recall if there actually is something else that she needs to tell me. "Some of my memories seem a little hazy."

"They might come back to you later," Travis says to Vala. "Or, they might be lost forever. It's hard to know for sure."

Vala turns to look at Travis.

"Vala," I say, "this is Travis Stokes. He's the friend I was telling you about who was able to save you."

Vala holds out a paw to Travis. He looks at it for a second before shaking it.

"Thank you, Travis," Vala tells him. "I appreciate your assistance in my recovery."

Travis looks a little embarrassed. I'm sure he isn't used to talking to dogs, even though Vala is so much more than that, at least to me.

"You're welcome, Vala. I'm just glad I was able to help you. You're very unique."

"Thank you," Vala says, taking his words as the compliment they were meant to be.

Vala turns back to me. "Are we going home now, Anna?"

"Yes, but not to the one in Cirrus," I tell her. "We'll be staying with Malcolm and Lucas in one of their homes in the down-world."

"The down-world?" Vala asks, sounding intrigued by such a notion. "That'll be a new adventure for us."

"Yes, a very new adventure," I tell her, hugging her around the neck.

I smile as tears of joy and relief come to my eyes. My family is almost all back together.

Now all I need is my father to make the circle complete.

CHAPTER EIGHTEEN

When we return to Malcolm's home, we eat the soup we prepared for lunch at the kitchen table. Vala watches the flaming hellhound within our midst with blatant curiosity.

"Why doesn't she speak?" Vala asks as she lies beside my chair while I eat.

Luna is eating some food Millie gave her in a small bowl over in a corner of the room.

"Animals don't talk," I tell Vala.

"Oh," Vala says like the distinction between herself and the hellhound should have been obvious to her before my statement. "Sometimes I forget I'm not real."

"You're very real," I say, leaning down to scratch her between the ears.

Vala tilts her head to the side, enjoying my attention. I smile down at her filled with joy to have one of my oldest friends back by my side. I look over at Malcolm who is sitting next to me and suddenly feel the urge to kiss him all over his face for providing a way to make this happy moment possible.

While we're cleaning up the table after our meal, Millie says, "I've tidied up a room for you to sleep in upstairs, my sweet.

I plan to go buy you some clothes of your own as well. Is there anything you would like in particular?"

"Just something comfortable," I say, feeling the cramps which started earlier in the day intensify. "And don't forget to get those other supplies for me while you're out."

"Oh, they're on my list," Millie assures me with a worried look on her face. "In fact, I'll go out straight away and get some things for you. Then, I'll bring them back here before I go shopping for your clothing. You might need them sooner than I thought."

"Thanks," I tell her, trying to hide the pain I feel, but apparently I'm not fooling anyone.

Malcolm comes up to me and sweeps me off my feet to cradle me in his arms like I'm a child.

"What are you doing?" I laugh, looping my arms around his neck.

"Taking care of you," he tells me, kissing the tip of my nose. "Come on. You should rest."

"I don't want to sleep," I tell him. "I'm not tired."

"I didn't say anything about sleeping," he replies with a smile which makes me hopeful we're going to go back to his bed and make out again. That is until he turns to Lucas and the dogs to

314

say, "Come on Lucas and Vala," Malcolm lifts an eyebrow at Luna, "and you too mongrel. Let's try to make Anna more comfortable."

"Are you sick, Anna?" Lucas asks in a worried voice as he picks Luna up in his arms and follows us out of the kitchen.

"No, not really," I say, not wanting to go into any details about what's actually wrong.

"It's a woman thing," Malcolm tells him off-handedly.

"Ohhhh, ok," Lucas says, like this simple sentence explains everything.

I look at Malcolm for an explanation as he begins our ascent up the stairs.

"I've always told Lucas that women are mysterious creatures we men aren't always meant to understand," Malcolm tells me with a wink.

I just shake my head and roll my eyes at Malcolm which makes him chuckle.

Malcolm takes us into his study and sits me down on the leather sofa in there. Vala hops up beside me and rests her head in my lap. I stroke her fur while I watch Malcolm light a fire in the fireplace. Lucas goes over to a set of cabinets on the wall by Malcolm's desk and pulls out a bag of tinker toys. He brings the

315

bag over in front of the sofa and dumps them out not too far in front of me.

"I'll be right back," Malcolm tells me after the fire is lit. He phases out of the room but soon returns with a soft brown blanket in his hands. He walks over to a bookshelf and grabs a book before walking back over to the sofa.

"Vala, would you mind moving for just a moment?" Malcolm asks her.

Vala jumps down off the sofa while Malcolm drapes the blanket over my lap. He then sits down next to me and brings me up against his side. I lift my legs from the floor and lounge against his warmth while Vala jumps back up and nestles in the open space between my legs and the back of the sofa.

I look at the book Malcolm has in his hands. It's a copy of Great Expectations by Charles Dickens.

"I've never read that one," I admit.

"It's a classic," Malcolm says, opening the book to its first page. "There are probably a lot of books in here that you might like. This is a personal favorite of mine."

"Why?"

"It's about a boy who thinks he's being given everything he could ever want only to find out that it's not what he thinks at all."

"Is there a love story?"

"Yes, but…I don't want to ruin the ending for you."

"Will you read it to me?" I ask.

Malcolm smiles and kisses me lightly on the lips. "That was the plan, my love."

I snuggle in closer to Malcolm and smile as he begins to read to me.

It's not so much the story which instantly captures my interest, but the way in which Malcolm reads the story to me. Both Vala and I laugh when he voices the character of Miss Havisham, the wealthy old spinster. As the story unravels, I begin to feel sorry for Estella and Pip being played as pawns in Miss Havisham's sadistic game of hearts. At one point, Lucas becomes interested in the story as well and grabs Luna to place her in his lap as he sits closer to his father's feet. We take little breaks in between chapters for small snacks Malcolm goes to the kitchen to prepare. One such snack ends up being mugs of hot cocoa. When I taste mine, I notice it's been spiked with a splash of alcohol. I look up at Malcolm in surprise.

"I thought it might help ease the ache a little," he tells me with a small, sympathetic grin.

I find that it does in fact take the edge off quite well and marvel once again at the thoughtfulness of the man I'm in love with.

We spend the whole afternoon and most of the evening in the study with Malcolm reading to us. At the beginning of this day, I remember thinking that Malcolm would make this day one I would never forget. I was right. It was one of the first times in my life I felt the fullness of a family of my own. I thought about the future Malcolm showed me and smiled. My heart yearned for that future so badly I was ready to cut down anyone who got in the way of it happening quickly. I understood I would have to be patient and wait for our lives to unfold on their own, but that knowledge did nothing to lessen the need I felt to have it sooner rather than later.

By the time we got to the end of the story, Lucas was curled up in front of the fire with Luna nestled up against him, snoozing peacefully. It was well into the night, but I didn't want to go to bed just yet. All I wanted to do was hold onto Malcolm forever.

"You should get some sleep," Malcolm says, kissing the top of my head as he holds me close.

"Not yet," I beg, almost sounding like a child asking for permission to stay up just a little while longer.

Malcolm stands and scoops me up into his arms again.

"You know I'm fully capable of walking," I tease him.

He smiles. "I know that. But, then I wouldn't be able to hold you so close."

I rest my head against his shoulder, loving the fact that Malcolm is doing everything he can to show me his love. I realize he's right. Actions can speak louder than words sometimes. And the way he showed how much he cared for me that day lit my heart on fire with the knowledge that he truly did love me. He would do anything for me, and I hope he knows I would do anything for him.

"What about Lucas?" I ask Malcolm as we walk out of the study.

"I'll come back for him after I tuck you into bed," he tells me, kissing me tenderly on the lips. "He'll be fine with Luna watching after him."

"I see you've decided to use her name instead of calling her mongrel," I comment, noting the difference in Malcolm's attitude about the hellhound pup.

"Lucas is taken with her, and she seems to love him too," Malcolm says in resignation. "I guess I can't exactly hate something my son loves so much."

"You're a good father," I tell Malcolm, such a thought making me think about my own and bringing tears to my eyes.

I try to hold back my sobs, but Malcolm hears me sniffle. When we reach the door to the room Millie made up for me, Malcolm rests me on my feet and takes me into his arms to provide a shoulder to cry on.

"We'll get Andre back," Malcolm promises me fiercely. "I promise you that, Anna."

I know Malcolm will do his best to hold true to his promise. I try to hold onto God's words that Levi hasn't harmed my father, but it doesn't prevent me from worrying.

Considering what Lucifer did to Levi, I wouldn't be surprised if Levi simply killed my papa out of spite. Though, he knows I'll kill him for sure then. There would be nothing to hold me back, and Levi's death is at the top of my to-do-list.

I finally pull back from Malcolm and wipe away my tears. He leans down and kisses me on the lips.

"I want to make your future one in which you never have a reason to cry," he tells me.

I smile at the sweet sentiment, but we both know such a future would be impossible to achieve. It was just part of human nature to become upset by certain things. Sadness was happiness' counterpart. You couldn't have one without the other. It was just like you couldn't have peace without war or good without evil.

I lean into Malcolm and tug at the front of his shirt as we kiss. It's not a kiss filled with passion but one filled with an undemanding love where the joining of our lips isn't rushed. We're simply enjoying the taste of one another and marveling in the fact that we can kiss without any adverse side effects.

"God you taste good," Malcolm moans, forcing himself to pull away with me. "Too good in fact."

He leans behind me and opens my door for me.

"I should say goodnight here," he says with his words but his arms pull me against him once more. "But, you make it really hard for me to want to let you go."

He kisses me deeply before forcing himself to pull away from me again.

"Good night, sweet Anna," Malcolm says, kissing me lightly one more time before turning away and walking down the hall back to his study.

I look down beside me and see Vala staring up at me. I had completely forgotten she was with us.

"I'm sorry you had to watch that," I tell her, feeling slightly embarrassed. "I forgot you were here."

"Don't be sorry, Anna," Vala says walking into my bedroom. "I'm just happy to see you finally find someone you can love. It's been one of your heart's desires for a long time now."

I close the door behind me. There is a white nightgown laid out on the bed for me, and I assume Millie was probably the one who left it out. As promised, she came back after lunch with supplies for my little problem and returned again right before dinner with some new clothes for me to wear. I quickly shed the clothes I borrowed from my mother's closet and slip into the sleeveless nightgown. Just as I am pulling down the covers to get into bed, I notice something lying on the pillow next to mine. It's a paper flower, but the petals have words written on them telling me it's actually a note.

I climb into bed and pick the flower up. The handwriting is in Malcolm's hand. I hate to unfold the flower, but I desperately want to see what he wrote. I gently pull two of the petals outward and soon have his letter to me laid before my eyes.

To My Love,

This day has been one of the best in my life, and it's all because I was able to spend it with you. Anna, when I'm with you, I feel like I can truly be myself and not have to hide the real me. Even if I make a mistake, I know you won't judge me for it because of your love. I can't express in words how much you mean to me because words filled with so much joy and love simply don't exist.

I want you to know that today was only the start of a host of days we will have together during our lives. I plan to do my best to make the next one better than the last until your life is filled with only beautiful memories.

I love you, Anna. You are the caretaker of my heart, and I know it couldn't be in more loving hands.

Yours forever and always,

Malcolm

I read the note again and again until Vala asks, "Why are you crying, Anna?"

I wipe my tears of happiness away and let Vala read the note.

"Oh," she says with a nod of her head, "he's good."

I laugh because I totally agree with her.

"Yes, he's very good," I tell her. "I just hope I can make him realize how wonderful a man he truly is."

The next morning I wake to a soft knock on my door.

I rise up on my elbows and say drowsily, "Come in."

Lucas opens the door, and Luna bounds in ahead of him, jumping up on my bed and immediately pouncing on Vala like she wants to play. It makes me laugh because Vala looks clueless as to what to do with the pup.

"She thinks you're a real dog," I tell Vala.

Luna goes to the back of Vala and vigorously begins to sniff her backside.

Vala instantly stands up with a yelp and promptly jumps down to the floor.

"Well," Vala says in a huff, "she is certainly going to have to learn her boundaries where certain parts of my anatomy are concerned."

I giggle as Luna pads over to me and lays flat on her back so I can rub her belly.

"I hope you're hungry," I hear Malcolm say as he walks in through my open door. He's carrying a wooden tray with a plate and a full glass of milk on it. I sit up and prop a pillow behind my back as Malcolm sets the tray over my lap. Beautifully arranged on a white plate are three fluffy pancakes in the shape of hearts. Slices of strawberries surround the pancakes outlining them and a heart made out of whipped cream sits in the middle of the top pancake. I smile.

"That's what I wanted to see," Malcolm says, leaning down and kissing me lightly on the lips. "How are you feeling this morning?"

"I'm ok," I tell him. "Let's see how I feel after I eat."

"Take your time," Malcolm tells me. "We're not in any rush."

I pick up the fork and knife as Lucas scrambles onto my bed and Vala cautiously returns, keeping a wary eye on the frisky Luna.

"Do you think it's odd nothing's happened yet?" I ask Malcolm.

I know he understands what I'm really asking by the frown that appears on his face.

"I say we don't worry about it until we have to. They'll make themselves known eventually."

"I wouldn't be worried about it if it wasn't for my papa," I reply as I pour some syrup onto the pancakes from a small glass dispenser.

"We still have feelers out to see if we can find him on our own," Malcolm says, but I can tell from the tone of his voice that he isn't holding out much hope that we'll be able to find my papa by ourselves.

"Hey, Anna," Lucas says, "do you think you could teach me how to fight with a sword today?"

"She might not feel like it today, Lucas," Malcolm warns.

"I tell you what," I say to Lucas. "Let me finish my breakfast, and I'll show you some of the basics. How does that sound?"

Lucas' face lights up with excitement.

"Sounds great, Anna," he says, but I can see some of his happiness diminish.

"What's wrong?" I ask him.

"I feel really funny calling you Anna. Can I just start calling you mommy now?"

I look up at Malcolm. Malcolm looks down at me and winks with a small grin on his face.

I look back at Lucas and cover one of his little hands with one of mine.

"Yes," I tell him. "You can start calling me mommy now."

The cheerfulness returns to Lucas' face which makes me

smile.

"I need to go back downstairs and speak with Brutus about something," Malcolm tells us. "I'll be back up as soon as I'm through."

Malcolm leans down and kisses me again before leaving the room.

"So, when are you and dad getting married?" Lucas asks me point blank after Malcolm is gone.

I chew on the pancake I just put in my mouth slowly to give me time to think of a reply.

After I swallow, I say, "Well, as soon as your father asks me, I would imagine we'll have the wedding not long after."

"Ohhhh, you guys are still courting," Lucas says knowingly. "How long do you think that will take?"

I giggle. "Why? Are you in a hurry for us to get married?"

"Yes," Lucas says, not even making an attempt to hide his true desires.

The honesty of children can be very refreshing.

"I just think your dad wants to take things a little slow," I tell Lucas. "And I think it's sweet of him to want to romance me first."

"I saw Millie sewing your wedding dress," Lucas tells me.

"You did?" I ask, surprised to hear this news. "When?"

"While we were in Cirrus," he says. "I guess she'll have to start all over since we can't go back there yet."

"Could you tell how far along she was in making it?"

Lucas shrugs his shoulders. "It looked almost done to me."

I consider this new information before asking, "Do you know where she put it?"

"It's in that big walk in closet next to your bedroom. She left it there before we went to the desert to meet you and the other Watchers."

"Thank you, Lucas."

"For what?" Lucas asks, looking confused.

"For letting me know my wedding dress is almost done."

"But how are you gonna get it?"

"Let me worry about that," I tell him.

After I get through eating my breakfast, I ask Lucas to leave so I can get dressed.

Once he's out of the room, I quickly put on some of the

clothes Millie bought me.

"What are you planning, Anna?" Vala asks me, knowing I'm up to something.

"I have to go get my dress," I tell her. "You heard Lucas. Millie was almost finished with it."

"You can't go to Cirrus!" Vala shouts.

"Shhh," I tell her. "I'll just phase up there and phase right back. I won't even be gone long enough for you to miss me."

"It's dangerous, Anna," Vala cautions. "At least take me with you for protection."

"I won't be gone long enough for you to protect me from anything," I say in exasperation.

"But, Anna..."

"Listen, I'll go up and be back before you can count to twenty," I promise her.

"If you're not, I'm telling Malcolm where you've gone," she warns.

"Ok, but you won't have to. I'll be right back!"

I phase straight into my walk in closet in Cirrus, which is as big as my bedroom.

The dress isn't hard to find because it's laid out on the table in the middle of the room.

It's a gorgeous white one shoulder gown with a twisted bodice and full flowing skirt. It was simple, classic and beautiful in its design, unlike the monstrosity of a dress I had to wear to my wedding to Levi.

The moment I reach out to pick it up I feel the sharp point of a blade being stabbed into my left shoulder.

"Hello, wife," I hear Levi say close behind me, "I think we need to have a little chat."

CHAPTER NINETEEN

Levi twists the blade until it scrapes against bone, causing me to fall to my knees in agony, but I don't let out a cry. I won't give him the satisfaction.

"Having fun in your little lovers' hideaway with Malcolm?" Levi asks me, bending down as he holds the hilt of the dagger in place. "I wouldn't get too comfortable if I were you, my little dove. Paradise can't last forever."

I grab a handful of Levi's hair and push back on his head as hard as I can. He goes flying into a set of drawers on the wall behind me. I reach up and pull the silver dagger out of my shoulder and keep hold of it. I'm getting really tired of him using it on me.

I stand up and turn to face him.

I immediately see the after effects of Lucifer trapping a soul in a dying body. Auggie's skin was always pale, but Levi looks white as a sheet. There are black and blue bruises on his face that no amount of makeup could ever cover up. The irises of his eyes are turning white making me wonder if he can actually see me at all.

"What are you staring at?" Levi asks irritably, standing to his feet.

"I'm not sure," I tell him, almost feeling sorry for him. Almost.

"What? No clever jest come to mind about my state of decay?"

"If you want me to say that I think you deserve what you got, then yes, I think you deserve it. You were going to kill Lucas even after we gave you what you wanted."

"Not everything I wanted," Levi says. "But I suppose having a child with you isn't really a possibility anymore considering my present state. This body is dead. I can't exactly enjoy the pleasure of yours any longer. I suppose you and Malcolm have consummated your relationship by now anyway."

I hesitate but then say, "That's really none of your business."

Levi stares at me then doubles over in laughter. "You mean to tell me Malcolm hasn't sealed the deal with you yet? What did you do to him?"

"I didn't do anything to him," I say, feeling offended by not only his tone but by the question itself.

"Well, you must have done something. I've never known Malcolm to pass up a free piece of ass before. Are you playing hard to get, my little dove? Or have you decided to keep true to our wedding vows?"

"Our wedding was a sham and you know it, Levi. The only reason I went through with it was to legally become empress."

Levi looks at the dress still lying on the table behind me. Before I know what he's doing, his lightning whip appears in his right hand, and he slashes it towards the table. The dress disintegrates on impact only leaving behind the outline of its beauty in a pile of black ash.

"I don't think you'll be needing a new wedding dress anytime soon, do you, wife? Wouldn't that mean killing me first? Or have you forgotten that I still have Andre?"

I stare at the remnants of the beautiful dress Millie made

for me and feel my eyes tear up. Everything Levi touches becomes ruined, and the reminder that he still holds my papa against his will only makes matters worse.

"No," I answer. "I haven't forgotten about my father. In fact, he's the only thing keeping you alive right now."

"You know what I can't believe?" Levi says incredulously. "I can't believe your real father hid for all these years and then suddenly decides to show back up just when I have everything I need set into place. As far as I knew, he hadn't stepped one foot out of Hell since your mother died."

"Why?" I ask, looking back at Levi. I was told Lucifer hadn't been seen since my mother's death, but the fact that he remained in Hell all that time was never mentioned to me.

"How should I know?" Levi says, like I've just asked an insignificant question. "It's not exactly like we're bosom buddies. I just figured he gave up on living after Amalie died."

"That's quite enough, Levi," I hear Lucifer say.

I look to the doorway connecting my closet and bedroom to see Lucifer standing in the opening.

"Why don't you be a good little emperor and go back to your palace to play."

Levi looks at Lucifer in disgust but doesn't try to argue

with him. He simply phases away.

"Why are you here?" Lucifer asks me, looking perplexed by my presence.

"I came to get something."

"What could be so important that you would risk coming here to get it?"

"Millie made me a wedding dress," I tell him.

Lucifer's eyes find the still smoldering ashes on the table behind me, but he doesn't say anything about it.

"You should go back to Malcolm's home, Anna. You'll be safe there. In fact, feel free to phase anywhere you want in the down-world. None of the princes will bother you if you stay down there."

"Are you ordering me not to come back to Cirrus?"

"I'm advising you to stay down-world. Enjoy your life, Anna. It can be a good one if you forget about the fool's errand my father has sent you on. Just let things go and no one will get hurt."

"Is that a threat?"

"No," Lucifer says shaking his head, "this is my way of trying to give you an easier life than the one my father wants you to have. Simply walk away from His mission Anna or people will get hurt."

"That sounds oddly like a threat to me," I hear Malcolm say from my bedroom.

I phase in there and find him standing by my bed. When he looks at me, his eyes immediately land on the wound on my shoulder.

He phases to me to get a closer look at it.

"Did he do this to you?" Malcolm asks, a hard edge to his voice.

"No. It was Levi."

"Do you have a healing wand here?"

I nod. "There should be one in the bathroom."

Malcolm doesn't hesitate. He walks to my bathroom and returns a few seconds later with the black healing wand in his right hand. I unbutton the shirt I'm wearing to give him easier access to the stab wound. I look up at Malcolm's face and notice his jaw muscles tighten in anger as he passes the device over my injury, healing it instantly.

"I swear to God I'm going to kill that bastard one day," Malcolm grits out between his clinched teeth.

"Not if I get to him first," I say.

"At least you can actually kill him," Malcolm concedes. "I could only hurt him...badly."

Malcolm lets his hand with the healing wand in it fall to his side after the wound is mended. He then turns his attention to Lucifer who has remained silent during our interaction.

"Long time, no see Lucifer," Malcolm says. "I thought you had fallen into a deep, black hole somewhere. It's disappointing to see that I was wrong."

"As witty as ever, Malcolm," Lucifer says with a tight grin. "I can't quite comprehend what my daughter sees in a Neanderthal like you."

"She sees someone who loves her without question," Malcolm tells him. "Too bad you can't say the same."

"You know I told her she could find someone better than you. Surely, you can't disagree with that considering the fact that I know all of your deepest and darkest secrets."

"I have nothing to hide from Anna," Malcolm tells Lucifer. "So you can tell her whatever you want."

Lucifer studies Malcolm like he's trying to silently judge just how much Malcolm truly does care about me.

"If you love her," Lucifer says, "keep her down-world. You've got power down there. You can both have a good life. Stop her from trying to retrieve the seals."

"So you can unleash them one day?" Malcolm asks suspiciously. "You recall I've seen firsthand what they can do when they're broken open. I'll stop you from doing that here in the Origin. Whatever Anna needs me to do to help her get them all back, I'll do it."

"If you love her," Lucifer says forcefully, "I mean *truly* love her. You will stop her from retrieving them!"

"Why? So she doesn't have to kill you?" Malcolm challenges. "Are you saying all this just to save your own skin, Lucifer? Are you that scared of dying? I never thought you would openly show what a coward you actually are."

Lucifer scowls at Malcolm. "Unfortunately, you're just as foolish as I always thought you were, Malcolm. If you don't listen to what I'm telling you, you'll regret it for the rest of your life."

Malcolm takes my hand. "I think it's time we went back home."

Lucifer looks at me. Beneath his scowl, I can see true concern for my welfare. But why? Was Malcolm right and Lucifer was simply trying to prevent me from killing him in the end or was there something else going on that he wasn't telling us about.

"Stay down there this time," Lucifer says to me just before

he phases away.

Malcolm phases us back to his bedroom in New Orleans. I lay the silver dagger in my hand down on the nightstand just before Malcolm pulls me into his arms.

"What were you thinking?" He asks me in a mixture of exasperation and worry. "No dress is worth you risking your life for."

"It was my wedding dress," I tell him, thinking this should be answer enough.

"We can buy you a thousand wedding dresses," Malcolm says, hugging me even tighter. "But you're irreplaceable, Anna."

"I'm sorry I made you worry. I thought I could go get it and be back before you even knew I was gone."

"I'm just glad Vala came and told me where you went. She was sick with worry over you not returning when you said you would."

I pull back from Malcolm. "I should go apologize to her. I should probably apologize to Millie too since what I did made Levi destroy the dress she made me."

I begin to pull away but keep hold of one of Malcolm's hands as I turn towards the door to the room.

"Hey," Malcolm says, squeezing my hand and tugging on it to make me look back at him. "We'll get you another dress. It's not the end of the world."

"I know. It's just that Levi always seems to find a way to ruin things. It's getting really old and tiresome."

"He'll get what he deserves in the end," Malcolm assures me.

"He looked like he was already suffering," I say, remembering how Levi looked in Auggie's decaying corpse.

"Good," Malcolm says without an ounce of compassion for the prince of Hell. "Lucifer actually did us a favor for once."

"Why do you think he was so adamant that I stay here in the down-world?"

Malcolm shrugs. "Who knows? The only thing I can tell you is that the reason benefits him in some way. Lucifer never does anything unless it helps his latest agenda. As soon as we figure that out, we'll understand why he wants you to stay down here."

"It's just that…" I falter because I'm not sure how to explain what I feel.

"What is it that you're thinking?" Malcolm asks gently, obviously seeing that I'm having trouble voicing my thoughts.

"I get the feeling he's trying to protect me from something," I say.

"Lucifer's only ever been worried about protecting himself and his own interest," Malcolm says in disgust. "If you try to get in the way of those things, he'll cut you down as quickly as he can."

"But he wasn't like that with my mother, right?"

I can see the reluctance on Malcolm's face as he admits, "No. He was different with Amalie."

"Then maybe he's being different with me too, Malcolm. I think we should give him the benefit of the doubt for now until we learn something that makes us think otherwise."

"Give Lucifer the benefit of the doubt?" Malcolm asks like this is a concept beyond his comprehension. "Only for you would I even attempt such a feat."

"Come on," I say, gently pulling on his hand. "Let's go tell the others what happened."

We find Millie, Lucas, Vala, and Luna down in the kitchen. I tell Millie about the dress, but she doesn't seem too bothered by it.

"I can make you a new one in a jiffy," she tells me. "Don't you worry about a thing, my sweet."

"Yeah," Lucas say, as he sits at the table eating a cookie, "now all we need is for *someone* to pop the question."

"Hmm, yes, *someone* should do that one day," Malcolm agrees, winking at Lucas which makes our son giggle.

"Mommy," Lucas says in his little high pitched voice, making my heart swell with even more love for him, "do you think you could show me how to use a sword now?"

"Absolutely," I answer.

Malcolm surprises me by having a holo-room like the one I had in Cirrus where my father and I used to spar almost every day. I spend some time showing Lucas how to stand and hold a sword. I even show him a few basic maneuvers, but it doesn't seem to be enough for our little boy.

"Could you show me a real sword fight?" Lucas asks us. "Maybe I could learn something from watching."

I look over at Malcolm. "Up for a little work out?"

Malcolm smiles. "I'm pretty good with a sword you know."

"I hope so because I'm excellent with one."

Malcolm walks up onto the holo-pad while Lucas hops down to sit with Luna and Vala off to the side.

"Sword," Malcolm says, initiating the construction of a

very large broadsword in his right hand.

"Really?" I ask derisively, looking at the gargantuan blade he's holding. "You know it's not the size of the sword that matters. It's how you use it."

Malcolm's smile grows broader.

"Oh never fear, I can use my sword very well. Enough to satisfy your needs anyway," Malcolm teases in a way that makes me think he *isn't* actually talking about the sword in his hand.

"I guess we'll see," I say, catching him off guard by swinging my blade at him and making him defend himself.

I can tell by the way Malcolm starts off that he's afraid he will inadvertently hurt me in some way. Since the swords aren't real, I know he isn't worried about hurting me with his so it has to be that he's worried about using his full physical strength against me. This knowledge just makes me push him even harder until I have him cornered against a wall of the room with my sword pointed at this throat.

"Don't hold back," I tell him, breathing a little hard from the exertion. "Show me what you've got."

"I don't want to hurt you," he tells me.

"You won't," I assure him. "I'm not that breakable."

We begin again and this time Malcolm doesn't hold back. It's exhilarating to fight someone who can almost match me in strength. The only other person who even came close was Amon and that fight didn't last very long before I had to kill him. But Malcolm isn't just good at swinging his blade. He's good at anticipating my next move which makes me think this fight is a little like playing chess for him. He isn't just using brute force to fight me. He's also using his deductive skills to stay one step ahead of me. Finally, I call a truce because it's obvious neither one of us will win this fight. We're too evenly matched.

"Wow," Lucas says to us, his eyes wide in wonder. "Do you think I'll be able to fight that good one day?"

"With a little practice," I tell him, breathing hard from the exertion, "I think you'll be better."

Lucas smiles so happily it makes us all smile.

"You're really good, Mommy," he says to me with pride.

I shrug. "It's my favorite thing to do," I admit. "My papa and I would practice against each other all the time."

"It must have been hard to hold back so much of your strength with Andre," Malcolm comments, and I notice he's also breathing hard from the work out.

"I got used to it," I tell him. "But, it is nice to be able to just let loose and not have to worry about hurting my opponent."

Malcolm loops an arm around my waist and roughly brings me up against him.

"I don't want you to ever hold anything back from me, Anna," he murmurs, "in anything we do together."

From the smoldering look in Malcolm's eyes, I know he isn't talking about swordplay.

"I don't want you to either," I tell him, hoping he understands that when we finally do make love, I don't want him to worry about hurting me. "I can take it."

Malcolm smiles and lets me go. We *are* in the presence of our son after all. Our flirting can only go so far with innocent eyes watching our every move.

"Could we go to your workshop, Dad?" Lucas asks, standing to his feet with Luna cradled in his arms.

"You have a workshop here?" I ask Malcolm.

"I have one in every home," Malcolm says. "Swords disengage."

After our swords dematerialize, Malcolm takes one of my hands into his, and we walk out of the room to his workshop.

This begins a ritual of sorts for the next few days. After the

344

boys bring me breakfast in bed, we work out with a little sword play then go to Malcolm's workshop and work on the family project, a new birdhouse for Lucas. Though, this time we don't build a replica of Malcolm's Lakewood home. This house is just as beautiful but it's one I haven't seen before. Malcolm simply tells me it's a home he designed but doesn't say where it is. After working on the birdhouse, we go down to prepare lunch and Malcolm takes the opportunity to show me how to cook a different dish every day. After lunch, we retire to his study where he reads to us from a book until supper time. After we eat supper, the boys would either play a game of checkers with each other, or Lucas would watch his father beat me in a game of chess.

"I don't think I'll ever get the hang of this game," I confess to Malcolm.

"Good," he says. "That means I'll always win."

I laugh not because of what he said but because I know he's already won the most important prize of all, my heart.

After we tucked Lucas into bed, Malcolm would always walk me to the door of my bedroom and kiss me goodnight. I did remember to let Vala into my room first, however, so we didn't have to subject her to watching our making out sessions against my door. Malcolm remained ever watchful of where his hands were located on my body during these moments.

On this night, however, he let them slip underneath my shirt and to the small of my back. I feel him yank his hands away when they brush against the seal I retrieved from Amon.

As his head lifts from mine, I see a worried look on his face.

"Does the seal cause you any pain?" He asks me.

I shake my head. "No. I forget it's even there most of the time."

"I guess I did too," Malcolm admits, leaning down to drink in my lips one more time before fully pulling away from me. "I've been meaning to tell you that we'll be having guests tomorrow night."

"Guests?" I ask. We hadn't seen anyone other than Millie and Giles in almost seven days.

"Jered, Brutus, Desmond, Daniel and Linn are coming for supper. I told them you would be cooking for us."

"You did what?" I exclaim.

"You can do it," Malcolm says, his voice full of a confidence I don't feel. "I have faith in you. They didn't believe me when I said I taught you how to cook. I want to prove to them that you've broken the chain of horrible cooks in your family."

"But what if I can't? Are you going to help me?"

"No. You need to do this on your own. Like I said, I have faith that you can do it."

"I'm glad someone does," I say, feeling a nervous knot form in the pit of my belly. "I'm not so sure I do."

Malcolm puts his hands on my shoulders. "You can do it. I know you can."

I sigh in resignation of my fate and lean up to give Malcolm one last kiss goodnight.

"Sweet dreams," he says against my lips before walking away.

I watch him walk down the hall away from me, like I've watched him walk away for the past few nights. My eyes are completely drawn to one perfect part of his anatomy underneath his pants, and I am helpless to divert my attention away from it until he's out of sight. The only thing that makes me not feel completely forlorn from his absence is the fact that I know something special is waiting for me on my bed.

Every night, Malcolm has left a note folded on the pillow next to mine. It would always be in the shape of an object or an animal. This night it's in the shape of a heart. After I change into my nightgown and climb into bed, I reach for the note and open it.

To My Love,

My life feels like it should belong to someone else because I never imagined it could be filled with so much joy and happiness. You have shown me through your love that I'm worthy enough to take the next step in our lives. I may not deserve you or deserve to be so blissfully happy, but I'm not fool enough to let this opportunity pass me by either. I want to give myself to you completely, and I hope you will accept what I have to offer.

Sweet dreams, my Anna.

I love you,

Malcolm

After I let Vala read the letter, I ask her, "Do you think this means he's finally ready to propose?"

"I certainly hope so," Vala says sounding as exasperated as I've been feeling the past few days, waiting for Malcolm to 'pop the question' as Lucas put it. "You've been waiting for him to do it all week!"

"I know," I groan. "I thought he would have asked by now."

I hold the note close to my heart as I lay my head down on my pillow.

"I'm sure he'll do it tomorrow," I say to Vala as I close my eyes. "I know he will."

CHAPTER TWENTY

I wake up the next morning well before Lucas knocks on my door, but I stay in bed because I don't want to ruin anything in case Malcolm decides he wants to propose to me first thing that morning.

"Do you think he'll hide the ring inside the pancakes?" Vala asks, her little tail wagging with excitement for me. "I saw someone do that in a movie once."

"Why would he do that?" I ask in puzzlement. "I might choke on it!"

"Well, maybe he won't try to be cute about his proposal. He is old after all. He might just go with something simple."

I giggle. "He isn't that old," I protest. "Plus, I don't think Malcolm does simple."

A soft knock comes from the other side of my bedroom door.

I quickly pull the covers up to my chin and lay back down in bed.

"Come in," I call out, doing my best to sound groggy, like I just woke up from a deep sleep.

Lucas opens the door, and Luna runs in and jumps up on

the bed. She has learned to abandon her efforts to greet Vala by sniffing her backside. All Vala had to do was snap at her a couple of times to make the excited pup rethink her natural instincts. Luna comes up to me and gives me a good lick on the face. Then she curls herself up on the empty pillow beside mine and watches me with her bright aquamarine eyes.

Lucas holds the door open for Malcolm as he walks in with my breakfast and props the usual tray over my legs. He leans down and greets me with a kiss just like he has the last few days.

"Good morning, my love," he says with a smile. "I hope you got a good night's sleep. You're going to need it for today."

"I am?" I ask as I pick up my fork and knife, feeling flush with excitement because I know in my heart Malcolm will propose to me that day, possibly any minute.

"Tonight's the night you show everyone how well you can cook. Remember?"

"Oh," I say. It wasn't exactly the answer I was hoping for but it was certainly true.

With Vala's words still fresh in my mind, I gingerly begin to cut up my heart shaped pancakes into tiny squares, secretly searching for a ring hidden somewhere inside their fluffy goodness.

"Is there something wrong with the pancakes?" Malcolm asks me, watching my odd behavior with open curiosity.

"Uh, no," I say, not finding anything resembling a ring lurking within my breakfast. "Just thought I would cut it all up first," I say, stabbing a section of my pancakes in slight frustration and eating my meal.

It becomes obvious Malcolm has no intention of proposing while I eat my breakfast. So, I wolf down the pancakes as quickly as I can. I don't want to cause a delay in any plans he might have which involve a ring and a certain, life altering question.

While we're in the holo-room with Lucas that morning, I keep expecting Malcolm to fall on one knee at any second during our practice to proclaim his undying love and ask for my hand in marriage… but he doesn't. When we go to his workshop to finish the birdhouse we've all been working on together, I discreetly search through it to see if he's hidden a ring somewhere on it or in it… but don't find one. At lunch time, I begin to wonder if maybe Malcolm's letter from the night before wasn't talking about an imminent proposal at all. Perhaps he was referring to something else?

As we walk into his study for reading time, Malcolm asks me, "Could you grab the book we were reading from yesterday? It's over there on that second shelf."

Malcolm points to the bookshelf on the far wall while he goes over to the fireplace to stoke the dying embers and add a couple of more logs to bring the flames up to keep the room warm while we're in here.

It seems like an odd request which immediately makes me giddily suspicious.

I walk over to the bookshelf and easily find the book we were reading, *Taming of the Shrew* by William Shakespeare. I cautiously pull on its binding to separate it from the other books on the shelf just in case a ring comes tumbling out from some secret spot. But, no ring appears and all I have in my hands is the book. I look at the book and open it to the place we stopped reading yesterday, wondering if Malcolm has hidden the ring between the pages...but I find nothing but words on paper. With a sigh of disappointment, I go over and sit down on the leather sofa. Malcolm soon joins me and gently takes the book from my hands.

"Are you all right?" He asks me with concern. "You've been a little off today. Are you worried about cooking for everyone later?"

"Well, I wasn't until you just mentioned it," I confess, feeling a knot of anxiety form in the pit of my stomach with the reminder.

I'd been so preoccupied with wondering when Malcolm

would propose, I completely forgot about the supper that evening.

"What time are they supposed to be here?" I ask.

"They'll all be here by seven. So, you will probably need to get started at around five."

"And what am I supposed to cook exactly?"

"You already know how to cook a soup, baked chicken, a salad, and fresh bread. I'll handle desert so don't worry about that."

"Will you be in the kitchen with me while I cook?" I ask hopefully.

Malcolm shakes his head. "No, I have faith you can do this all on your own."

"Oh," I say in disappointment. "Do you have a backup plan prepared in case the meal I make is inedible?"

Malcolm chuckles. "I'm sure it will be delicious. You should have more faith in your culinary skills."

I sigh and snuggle up to Malcolm's side as he begins to read to me.

Unfortunately, no proposal comes during our reading time either...

Once five o'clock rolls around, I've pretty much given up on Malcolm proposing to me until the next day. There simply wouldn't be enough time to do it if we were planning to entertain the others that evening.

While I'm down in the kitchen, dicing up the potatoes, Vala asks, "Are you all right, Anna?"

I shrug and try to hold back my tears of disappointment. "I just don't know what he's waiting on, Vala. Maybe he's changed his mind about marrying me."

"Oh good grief," Vala says in exasperation. "Get that thought out of your head right this instant. Of course he wants to marry you! He loves you. Any fool can see that plain as day. Do you want me to go bite him on the ankle for you? Maybe that will give him the incentive he needs to get down on one knee."

I smile at Vala's offer and seriously consider it, but say, "No. I would rather he did it of his own free will instead of being coerced into it."

"How are things going, my sweet?" I hear Millie ask as she walks into the kitchen.

"Just starting the soup," I tell her. "Did you come to check up on me or to make sure I haven't set the kitchen on fire yet?"

Millie blushes.

"A little bit of both," she admits. "Plus, Master Malcolm asked me to set the formal dining table upstairs for the dinner. I came down here to get the silverware and see if you needed anything."

"I think I have everything under control," I tell her, surprised that I actually do feel like can cook the meal planned all by myself. "What are Malcolm and Lucas doing?"

"I'm not entirely sure," Millie tells me, walking over to a set of cabinets and pulling out a medium size polished wood box which must contain the silverware she came down to get. "I saw them head into Master Malcolm's workshop, but they didn't tell me what they were up to."

That seemed a little odd to me. We had finished building the birdhouse that afternoon. But, I didn't have time to ponder what else they might be doing in there. I had a supper to prepare.

About an hour later I had everything cooking. The soup was practically done. It just needed time to simmer on the stove. The chicken was baking in the oven, as well as the bread. I had already prepared the salad. There really wasn't anything else to do but wait.

"It smells delicious in here," I hear Malcolm say as he strolls into the kitchen. His cheeks have a rosy hue, evidence that he's been outside in the cold for a while.

"I'm just waiting for things to cook," I tell him.

He walks up to me and sweeps me off my feet and into his arms. The smile on his face as he looks at me is filled with so much love and happiness I have to kiss him.

"I have a surprise for you," he tells me as our lips part.

"You do?" I ask, wondering if this is the moment I've been waiting for all day.

Malcolm begins to walk out of the kitchen with me still cradled in his arms. We ascend the grand staircase to the second floor, and Malcolm takes me into his bedroom.

"Do we have time for this?" I ask, assuming Malcolm is absconding with my person for a playful romp on his bed.

"Yes," Malcolm says, not stopping by his bed like I had hoped. He heads straight into his bathroom. "You have plenty of time for a bath."

The white claw foot tub in the room is filled with water and brimming to almost overflowing with bubbles.

Malcolm sits me on my feet.

"Take your clothes off," he tells me.

"Have you finally come to your senses and decided to put me out of my misery?" I ask him, hoping this order for nakedness is going where I want it to go.

Malcolm smiles. "I haven't changed my mind," he says resolutely. "I do have some modicum of self-control, even though there are others who would argue otherwise."

I wrap my arms around Malcolm's neck.

"How much longer are you going to make me wait, Malcolm?" I pout, effectively I hope.

"Haven't you ever heard the age-old adage that all good things come to those who wait?"

"No," I say. "Whoever said that was a complete idiot."

Malcolm laughs and kisses me on the lips, but it's only a quick peck. He picks up a hairclip from the counter by the sink and turns me around so he can pile my hair on top of my head and secure it there. Presumably so it doesn't get wet during my bath.

"Get undressed, my love," he says, kissing the side of my neck. "And let me know when you're in the tub."

I look over my shoulder only to see him turn his back to me.

I sigh, feeling slightly frustrated and disappointed, but I do as I'm told and strip off my clothes.

Once I'm safely underneath the camouflage of the bubbles,

I say, "You can turn back around now."

Malcolm faces me while pushing up the sleeves of the shirt he's wearing above his elbows. He saunters over to the tub and kneels down beside it. He reaches over me and grabs a bottle labeled soap from the metal holder hanging on the side of the tub. I watch him pour some into his cupped hand and then place the bottle back in its spot in the tray. He rubs his hands together to spread the soap onto both.

"No wash cloth?" I ask, finding it hard to breathe because I have a feeling I understand Malcolm's intent.

"I don't think I need one," he says, looking up from his hands to meet my gaze. "Do you?"

I shake my head, not able to find any words to say.

"Lie back," Malcolm tells me.

I do as he says, watching him as he leans forward to place his hands near the base of my throat, massaging the soap up the sides of my neck and across my shoulders. He takes my right arm into both of his hands and gingerly runs them down the length of it to my fingertips. He lets it slide back into the water and pays the same loving attention to my left arm. He reaches for the bottle in the tray again and pours some more of the liquid soap into his hand.

"Raise one of your legs, Anna," Malcolm says, his voice sounding hoarse this time.

I raise my right leg and he wraps his fingers around my ankle to hold it up for me while he uses his other hand to lather the soap it holds across the sole of my foot and between my toes, making me giggle from the ticklish sensation. I see Malcolm smile at my laughter as he continues to slide his hand down the length of my calf, over my knee, and along my thigh underneath the water, causing me to catch my breath as the tips of his fingers graze across my hip.

Malcolm rests my leg back into the water.

"Now the other one," Malcolm requests, his voice a low whisper this time.

I raise it out of the water and watch Malcolm's face as he gives it the same gentle treatment. I notice his breathing is a little more labored now than it was when he first started and see my opening to end the pleasurable torment we've both been suffering through practically since we met.

As his fingers glide down my leg and dive beneath the water again to reach my thigh, I say, "Malcolm…"

The sound of his name passing between my lips isn't just me saying his name. The word is filled with a desperate request that he not take his hand away from me. It's a quiet plea for him to continue along the natural trail my inner thigh leads to because I feel like I might die on the spot from want if he doesn't touch me there in that instant. The ache has become more than I can bear, and it would be so simple for him to satisfy my physical torture, to finally help me find release.

I see Malcolm swallow hard as his hand gently massages my inner thigh, but he doesn't give into my desires. Instead, he gently glides it across the sensitive flesh of my belly and between the valley of my breasts until it emerges out of the water, sliding up to behind my neck. In one quick motion, he leans in and at the same time pulls me forward until our lips meet. His mouth ravishes mine telling me without words how much he yearns to oblige my request. The kiss is almost savage in its intensity, making me want him even more.

Malcolm suddenly pulls away, leaving me longing for so much more from him.

He stares down at me, and I can see a war raging behind his eyes. It's so plain to see that he desires me as much as I desire him. Why does he keep denying us both so much pleasure?

"I'm here, Lady Anna!" I hear Millie call from the bedroom, breaking the intimate connection between us with her arrival.

Malcolm leans in one more time and kisses me again, but

it's different now because we both know our moment has passed.

"Millie will help you get dressed," Malcolm tells me as he stands to his feet. "I should go get dressed myself. They'll be here soon."

I don't say a word because I know it would simply come out sounding like a plea for him to continue what he started.

Malcolm phases. I notice his phase trail leads out to the courtyard for some reason. Why would he go out there to get dressed for a dinner party?

I lie back in the tub and try to purge myself of the pent up desires his bathing of me has induced.

What was he thinking? How much torture was he trying to put me through before he finally relented and gave into our mutual desire for one another?

"Lady Anna?" Millie says, cautiously peeking into the bathroom. "Are you ready to get dressed, my sweet?"

"Give me a minute, Millie," I say, trying to hold onto my last bit of sanity and pull myself together enough to make it through the dinner party we were hosting that evening.

I stand from the tub and grab a towel that's been left on a nearby stool. After I dry my body, I go to the bedroom and see Millie fussing over a gown lying on Malcolm's bed. It's a deep red, full length dress with a crystal beaded waistline and shirred bodice. An extra swath of fabric cascades down from the one-shoulder strap to gently sweep from front to back across the upper arm.

"Did you make it?" I ask Millie.

"Oh dear me no," Millie says with a small laugh. "I bought it the other day when I went shopping for your clothes."

"Why haven't I seen it before now?"

"Master Malcolm asked me to keep it hidden until tonight. I guess he wanted it to be a surprise."

Millie helps me dress and styles my hair into a classic loose bun.

By the time I'm ready, I realize it's time to go back down to the kitchen and finish preparing the meal.

"Oh, don't worry about it," Millie tells me. "Giles and I will handle the rest. You've done all the hard work. Let us worry about serving it. And Vala has volunteered to stay down in the kitchen with Luna to keep the pup from disturbing your evening."

A quick knock resounds on the other side of the door just before Malcolm pokes his head in and asks, "Are you decent?"

Seeing that I am fully clothed, he opens the door the rest of the way, and I see my two men dressed rather sharply for our evening together.

Malcolm and Lucas are dressed in matching tuxedos. The jacket and pants are made out of a dark grey pinstripe material with silver cravat ties and matching vests and pocket squares. The picture they make standing together instantly brings a smile to my face.

"Well, don't the two of you look dapper this evening," I say as I walk over to them.

"Wow," Lucas says looking at me with his eyes as wide as saucers. "You're beautiful, mommy."

"Thank you."

Malcolm holds his hand out to me. "Shall we go greet our guests?"

"Are they here already?"

"No," Malcolm says. "But they'll be here in exactly five minutes."

I laugh. "How on earth could you know that with such precision?"

Malcolm shrugs as I reach out to take his proffered hand. "It's a Watcher trait. We have internal clocks that make it almost impossible for us to be late or early anywhere."

His words explain how all of the other Watchers phased to the spot where we met Levi for the trade at the exact same time.

"You look lovely by the way," Malcolm says as we make our way down the hallway to the staircase. "Have I told you lately what a lucky man I am?"

"Yes, but I don't think you can ever say it enough."

"I'm a very lucky man, Anna," he says again, gently squeezing the hand he holds to emphasize his words. "Very lucky indeed."

Malcolm escorts me into the formal dining room, a room I haven't been in yet.

It has a very tall ceiling, nearly twenty feet, with dark wood wainscoting and walls painted a warm light yellow. Hanging on the walls are portraits of women, some of whom I actually recognize. The most prominent one is of Lilly which hangs on the wall behind the head of the table. It's at least five feet tall and shows her in a black dress standing in a rose garden.

"Brand painted that portrait of her," Malcolm tells me. He points to a slightly smaller portrait to the left of Lilly. "That's Caylin when she turned eighteen."

I look around at the other portraits in the room. "Who are

the other girls?"

"The descendants who came before you," Malcolm says looking at them all.

I search the portraits but see one descendant missing from the bunch.

"Where's the one of my mother?"

"You had that one," Malcolm says. "Andre took it to Cirrus so you would always have her near you."

"Oh," I say, remembering Levi destroyed my mother's portrait with his lightning whip the night he revealed himself to me. "Maybe I can paint another one of her from memory to replace it."

"I'm sure you can," Malcolm says full of confidence in my untested ability. "All of the descendants painted their own portraits."

"You could practice with me," Lucas volunteers. "I promise to sit real still while you do it."

I hug Lucas close to my side. "I would love that."

"They're coming," Malcolm says, just as our guests phase into the dining room.

I feel my forehead crinkle as I look at them all.

366

They're all dressed in the same exact tuxedo as Malcolm and Lucas.

I want to ask why they're all dressed alike but feel such a question would seem rude. Only Linn stands out amongst the group in a traditional Chinese evening gown. It's made of royal purple silk with a gold lace overlay, mandarin collar with frog button, and short cap sleeves.

They all walk over to us.

"You look lovely, Anna," Linn says to me as she leans in and kisses me on each cheek.

"And you are simply gorgeous," I tell her. "That dress is stunning."

I look at the other four Watchers in the room. "You all look very handsome…in your matching suits."

"Matching?" Jered says, feigning ignorance as he looks down at himself and then to his brothers. "Oh, I guess we do, don't we?"

"Yes…" I say, seeing them all smile at one another in a conspiratorial fashion. But, I still refrain from asking why they're all wearing the same suit. I assume if they truly wanted me to know the real reason someone would say it.

"So," Brutus says to me, "Malcolm told us you were

cooking the meal we'll be eating this evening."

"Yes, I did," I say proudly.

No one says another word. They all just stare at me looking somewhat worried over this fact.

"Well," Desmond finally says, breaking the silence in the room, "this should be…interesting."

Before I can ask why they all seem so sure I've failed miserably in my attempt, Millie enters the room with Giles following close behind her, rolling in the meal I prepared on a wooden cart.

We all sit down at the table as they serve us the potato and sausage soup I made.

I watch the men, except for Malcolm, around the table as they all peer into their bowls with apprehension, like the soup is alive and might eat them instead of the other way around.

Linn shakes her head at their behavior and picks up her spoon to take the first sip of the soup.

The others watch her closely like their expecting her to have an adverse reaction after eating it.

After she swallows, she looks over at me and smiles.

"Delicious, Anna," she compliments.

I audibly hear a collective sigh of relief as the others reach for their own spoons and tentatively begin to eat the soup. After a couple of bites, the boys dig in with gusto and even ask for a second helping of it from Millie.

I feel Malcolm place a hand on one of my thighs underneath the table and give it a gentle squeeze. I look over at him, and he winks at me.

Millie quickly serves us the baked chicken, salad and rolls I made while Giles refills everyone's crystal goblets with white wine, except for Lucas, of course, who gets some white milk instead.

This time no one seems concerned about surviving the meal I've prepared and eat while we have casual conversations about what's going on in their respective lives.

"Well, I have some interesting news to report," Desmond tells us while he butters his roll. "Something very odd is going on with Lorcan Halloran."

"Why?" Brutus asks, obviously interested in what his soul mate's brother is up to. "What's he done this time?"

"Nothing bad," Desmond is quick to tell Brutus to ease his worries. "He's actually been rather generous the past few days. He's sent more supplies to the down-worlders in the past two days than the Hallorans have during their whole entire reign of Stratus."

"Do you know the reason why?" Malcolm asks, I can tell from the tone of his voice he finds this uncharacteristic behavior of Lorcan's suspicious.

Desmond shrugs. "Haven't got a clue. All I know is that they were desperately needed. Maybe the drugs he's been taking have actually transformed him into a real human being."

"Is Kyna all right?" Brutus asks.

"I haven't heard from her in a while," Desmond admits. "I'm sorry. I wish I had more to tell you."

"But you would know if she were in trouble?" Brutus presses.

"I'm sure word would have reached me if she were," Desmond tries to reassure Brutus.

Brutus nods, accepting Desmond's assumption, but I can tell he's still worried about her. I silently hope we can resolve the situation with the princes quickly so we can all get on with our lives.

"I can't believe this meal," Jered says in amazement. "Did you help her do any of this, Malcolm?"

"Not a bit of it," Malcolm answers succinctly.

"Well, you certainly are a miracle worker then," Daniels

says with a shake of his head. "I didn't think you would be able to do it. Congratulations!"

"I knew I could do it if I put my mind to it," Malcolm answers modestly.

I just stare at them all as each of them congratulates Malcolm.

"Wait a minute. You do realize I'm the one who actually cooked this meal, right?" I ask them, not seeing why they're giving all the credit to Malcolm.

"Trying to teach one of you descendants to cook has been tried before," Brutus tells me. "Every attempt was a wretched failure. We had little hope it would work this time. Though, Malcolm protested that you would be the one who broke that particular tradition of your lineage."

"You did a wonderful job, Anna," Linn says. "I think we're all simply proud of your accomplishment. Who would have thought the Empress of Cirrus would be cooking for a poor woman like me?"

"Thank you, Linn," I say, grateful that at least one of them is appreciative of my efforts.

The guys then start to tell me what a great job I did, and I graciously accept their accolades, even though they are a bit belated.

When dessert rolls around, I wonder what Malcolm has prepared for us to eat.

Millie and Giles bring in plates with little blue boxes wrapped with white ribbon.

I stare at mine when it's placed in front of me.

Could this be it? The box was certainly big enough to hold a ring inside and then some.

"Ok, I tried to remember what everyone's favorite was," Malcolm tells us. "And for sweet Anna, I had to make an educated guess. Please open your boxes now."

We all begin to open our boxes, and I can feel Malcolm watching me closely. I slowly pull on the white ribbon, letting it fall on either side of the box before I lift the lid.

It's not a ring. There are three pieces of chocolate candy in the shape of hearts lying within the box.

I hear Desmond laugh across the table from me as he lifts the treat out of his box.

"An Irish potato candy," he says. "I haven't seen one of these in ages!"

I watch Daniel and Linn both pull out what look like dense

little cakes with strange symbols on their tops from their boxes.

"A moon cake!" Linn says with joy, quickly taking a bite out of hers and looking like a kid who has just been given her most favorite treat in the world.

"I bet I can guess what's in mine," Brutus says, lifting the lid of his box. A slow smile spreads his lips as he peers into it. "Just as I thought."

"What did you get, Uncle Brutus?" Lucas asks.

Brutus pulls out a piece of candy. "It's honey sesame seed candy. Would you like a taste?"

Lucas doesn't have to be asked twice. He promptly gets out of his seat on the other side of Malcolm and goes to Brutus to sample his treat.

Jered opens his box and smiles.

"How in the world did you find Jelly Babies?" Jered asks Malcolm.

"I have ways of getting things," Malcolm says mysteriously.

Malcolm looks over at me smiling. "I wasn't completely sure which flavors you would like best so I put in three different ones, strawberry, caramel and vanilla."

I try to smile convincingly, but I can't help but feel a bit let down that I didn't find a ring inside the box.

Malcolm must notice my disappointment because he asks, "Are none of those flavors your favorite?"

"Strawberry is my favorite," I tell him, trying to pull together a convincing smile. "Thank you."

Malcolm picks up what must be the strawberry filled candy from my box and brings it to my lips. I accept the sweet confection and eat it while he cups one side of my face with his hand.

"I love you," he mouths, but doesn't say out loud in front of our company.

I nod, letting him know I understood what he said.

After everyone eats their special treat, Malcolm says to me, "Why don't you take Linn to the sitting room? We'll help Millie and Giles clean up the table."

"Well, I don't mind helping."

"No," Malcolm says to me. "You cooked the meal. You shouldn't have to clean up after it too."

"I don't mind," I protest.

"Oh, let the boys handle things for once," Linn says to me. "It's been ages since I was able to talk to another woman without little ones being around. Let's not pass this opportunity up, Anna."

Linn simply wasn't someone you could say no to.

We leave the dining room, and I notice that even Lucas stays behind to help.

"So," Linn says as we walk to the sitting room across the foyer from the formal dining room, "how has your time here been?"

"It's been the happiest time in my life," I admit.

Linn smiles at me. "I don't think I've ever seen Malcolm so happy either. It's nice to see him like this." Linn is quiet for a moment before asking, "What's it like to be with your soul mate?"

Knowing that Daniel and Linn aren't soul mates, I have to ask, "Why do you want to know?"

Linn shrugs. "I've always wondered if Daniel gave up on finding his too soon."

"But Daniel loves you, Linn," I tell her. "Anyone who spends time with the two of you can see that."

Linn nods. "Yes, I know he loves me. I love him too. But, seeing you with Malcolm makes me wonder if he should have waited. I fear he might come to regret his decision to marry me and settle for what we have."

"You should never think that," I tell her. "If you ask me, he's lucky to have met someone who loves him so much. I haven't seen an ounce of regret in Daniel's eyes when he looks at you, only love."

We enter the sitting room and sit on the plush, evergreen sofa in front of the fireplace. A roaring fire is blazing giving the room a soft, orange glow.

"I'm not sure why the lights aren't on in here," I say, making to get up to find the light switch, but Linn places a hand gently on my arm to stop me.

"Why don't we just sit here and enjoy the fire?" she suggests. "It makes things so nice and cozy."

I remain seated.

"All right," I say. "I'm sure the guys will be in here soon anyway. They'll probably turn the lights on when they come in."

We sit in silence for a moment, but it doesn't last past a few seconds before I hear someone singing right outside the room.

I look towards the entrance of the sitting room and see Desmond walk in while he sings about having sunshine on a cloudy day. He comes to a stop in front of me and Linn with the glow of the fire at his back.

A deep voice joins Desmond's as Brutus walks in next

singing about it being cold outside and comes to stand by Desmond's side.

Daniel walks in next singing about the month of May and comes to stand with the two already in front of me.

Jered saunters in singing the next line and comes to stand with the other three. As they hit the chorus of the song, it acts as a cue for Lucas to join the group as he jumps into the room and points his little index fingers straight at me singing 'my girl' with gusto before twirling around and dancing over to stand by the gathering of Watchers in front of me.

The whole scene makes me giggle with delight, and I have a hard time suppressing my mirth at their impromptu song and, believe it or not, dance as they start swaying back and forth in unison to sing the next few lines of the song and the second chorus.

A new voice joins the singing group as Malcolm strolls in singing that he doesn't need money, fortune, or fame. He stands a couple of feet away from the others as they all continue to sing and dance their coordinated routine, and I finally understand why they were all dressed in the same suit.

Near the end of the song, Malcolm walks out of the room, still singing, and walks back in with a red ribbon in one of his hands which trails out the room's entrance. He comes to kneel in front of me and takes my left hand into his. He ties the end of the red ribbon around my ring finger into a bow just as he sings the last two words of the song while looking into my eyes.

He leans up and kisses me gently on the lips before saying, "Find me, my love."

Malcolm rises to his feet and walks out of the room.

"Go, go, go!" Lucas says excitedly, waving me out the door to go after his father.

I'm smiling so wide my cheeks begin to hurt, but I don't care because I know what all this means.

I rise from the couch and follow the red ribbon trail.

As I walk out of the sitting room, I notice a small white note card tied to the ribbon. I pick it up and read it.

To My Love

I look further down the ribbon and notice there are a few note cards tied to it in regular intervals. As I follow the ribbon, I read them in sequence.

My life has simply been a string of moments

Moments leading me up to this time in my life

A life filled with pain and heartache

378

Only now does my heart understand the true meaning of loving someone

And being loved

My deepest desire is to make you the happiest woman in this world

And I hope you give me the opportunity to do just that

I'm standing beside the door which leads to the outer courtyard now. The red ribbon leads out past the door, but someone has hung a thick wool cloak on the door handle. I drape the cloak across my shoulders hastily and pull up the hood over my head. Sticking out from the doorjamb is another note.

Beyond this door stands a man who wishes to give you all of him. Find me, my love. I want to ask you the most important question of my life…

I place my hand on the door handle and hesitate. I don't hesitate because I don't want to hear Malcolm's question to me, but because my heart is beating so rapidly inside my chest I feel like I might pass out. I close my eyes and take a few steadying breaths before I turn the handle and open not only a door to the outside world, but the way into my future.

It's snowing outside. The ground is covered in a light scattering of white so I know it hasn't been coming down for very long. The red ribbon in my hand leads out to the middle of the courtyard where I see Malcolm standing, waiting for me.

Beside him on a wooden pedestal is the birdhouse he, Lucas and I spent the last seven days building together. The end of the red ribbon leads to the small front porch of the house. I follow the ribbon up to it and find a ring tied with the other end of it to one of the front posts. I drop the ribbon and note cards in my hands to the ground and gently untie the other end of it to release the ring into the palm of my hand.

It's a beautiful three diamond ring where the diamonds are arranged vertically instead of horizontally along the band. Smaller diamonds surround the three larger ones and extend down the band on both sides. As I'm looking at the ring, I'm faintly aware of Malcolm lowering himself beside me onto one knee. He takes my free hand into his as I meet his gaze with my own.

"Anna," he says, "there has never been anyone like you in my life before. For the very first time in my entire existence, I want to share all that I am with someone else. The three diamonds in the ring you hold represent my past, my present and our future. I ask that you accept everything I ever was, everything that I am, and everything I hope to be for you and our children. If you can accept all of that, please say that you will marry me and not only become my wife but my partner in this life and the next."

As I look at Malcolm, I can't believe the uncertainty I see in his eyes as he waits for my answer.

"Of course I'll marry you, Malcolm," I tell him like my answer should have simply been a foregone conclusion. "What took you so long?"

Malcolm smiles and stands to his feet. He takes the ring from my other hand and slips it onto my finger.

He brings me into his arms, and I hear him let out a long sigh of relief.

I hug him tighter wanting to make sure he understands how much I love him, how much he truly means to me. It's then I realize I'll have the rest of our lives to do just that.

CHAPTER TWENTY-ONE

"I have something else to ask you," Malcolm says, pulling away from me as he places an arm around my waist and faces us towards the birdhouse we built as a family in his workshop.

"There was a reason I wanted all three of us to work on this birdhouse together," he tells me. "It's a house I intend to build for us one day, and I want you to decide where it should go."

"That's easy," I say, instantly knowing the exact spot I want it built. "I want you to build it where the old beach house is."

"Really?" Malcolm asks in surprise. "I would have thought that place held too many bad memories for you."

"Not really," I tell him, remembering back through what happened there. "It holds a certain significance for me because it's where I met Will, God, and Lucifer for the first time. I also got to learn more about you while I was in your dream world. It might not have been the best way to learn what I did, but it still made me feel more connected to you. It was the first time I truly understood why Lilly means so much to you."

"If that's where you want me to build it," Malcolm says, bringing me into his arms, "then that's where it shall be built."

I raise my hands and smooth out the collar of Malcolm's tuxedo while I ask, "Malcolm, now that we're officially engaged, how long do you intend to make me wait for a wedding?"

"We can have it anytime you want."

"Then let's go have it right now," I suggest eagerly, grabbing one of his hands and practically yanking him off his feet as I make my way back towards the house. "It's the perfect time! Everyone is already here."

Malcolm laughs at my eagerness but doesn't make any protest. He runs beside me as we make it back into the house.

We find everyone in the sitting room, but we also find a guest neither of us could have expected to see.

Olivia Ravensdale, Empress of Nacreous, stands in the middle of the room with everyone around her listening to whatever it is she's saying.

"I just don't know what to do," we hear her tell the others as we enter the room. "That's why I'm here."

"Olivia?" I ask, remembering she insisted that I call her by her first name at the wedding reception in Cirrus. "What in the world are you doing here? Is something wrong?"

From the look on the faces of everyone else in the room, I can only assume something is terribly wrong.

"Anna," Olivia says, relief in her voice to see me. She

glances at Malcolm by my side. "Overlord Devereaux, I'm so sorry for barging into your home like this, but I needed to see Anna to seek her guidance on a matter."

"You're welcome in any of my homes at any time, Empress Olivia," Malcolm says graciously.

"How can I help you?" I ask her as we come to stand in front of her.

"When we were at your wedding to Augustus, everyone in Cirrus was commenting on how different your husband was now compared to how he used to be. I need to know…what was different? Why did he change from the sweet, loving, respectful Auggie we all knew to the creature who was standing by your side at the reception?"

"Why do you ask?"

Olivia's eyes drop to the floor for a moment before she meets my gaze again.

"Something is wrong with my husband, Horatio. He is most definitely *not* himself."

Olivia's statement suddenly causes tension to fill the room. I can see the strained looks on the other Watchers' faces. When I look at Malcolm, I see a tightness in the set of his jaw now that wasn't there a few minutes ago. I know exactly what it means.

"When did he start acting differently?" I ask Olivia, needing to get as much information as possible from her to confirm our suspicions.

"Oh, let's see," Olivia says, her eyes becoming a little unfocused as she thinks back. "About a week ago, I guess. I noticed a difference in him one morning. Horatio normally gets up early to go for a run through the city, but that morning he stayed in bed until almost noon! When he finally did wake up, he immediately left the palace and began a week long drinking binge. And…" I can tell what Olivia has to say next is difficult for her. "He has been spending an inordinate amount of time in establishments he has never visited before for female companionship. I don't know who that man is, but he is certainly not my husband. Considering how differently Auggie was when we last saw him, I thought you might be able to lend some light on the situation and help me find a way to change my husband back to the man he used to be."

I look to Malcolm because I'm not sure how much we should tell Empress Olivia about what's actually going on. If one of the princes has indeed taken over the body of her husband, I feel an obligation to tell her that he's dead.

"Empress Olivia…" Malcolm begins.

"Oh, just call me Olivia, Malcolm. I think we can dispense with the formalities."

"Olivia," Malcolm says instead, "I think you better sit down for the explanation we're about to give. There's a lot you need to know to fully understand what's happened to your husband."

Olivia looks alarmed by what Malcolm has said, but she also looks somewhat relieved that he has the answers she's looking for.

Almost an hour later, we've all tried to ease Olivia into our world of angels and demons and the dangers we face. She held in her grief when she learned her husband was dead. I think the reality of how her life just changed simply hadn't sunk in yet. Unfortunately, she wouldn't have much time to get used to her new situation. If one of the princes of Hell was indeed in possession of Horatio Ravensdale's body, then it was more than likely I would have to kill him.

"We need to go to Nacreous as soon as possible," Malcolm says to us all. "Once we see Horatio, we'll be able to tell who he really is."

"Well," Olivia says, "my eldest son is having his eighteenth birthday party this evening at the palace. I've invited all the royals from the other cloud cities to attend but thus far no one has responded."

"Isn't that odd?" I ask Olivia.

"No, not really," she says with a melancholy smile. "Nacreous isn't rich enough to be considered part of the inner circle. Sending the invitations was more of a formality than anything. But, you are still Empress of Cirrus so your presence wouldn't be considered out of the ordinary to those in attendance. The party will provide the perfect excuse to have you there. It will seem a little odd that you come with your lover by your side instead of your husband, but we in Nacreous have always been rather non-judgmental when it concerns matters of the heart."

"My lover?" I ask, somewhat taken aback by this news. "Is that what people think Malcolm is to me?"

"Well, he did whisk you away on your wedding night from your bedchambers. What else did you expect people would think?"

I didn't have an answer for her, and I'm not sure why the thought bothers me so much.

"When is the party?" Jered asks Olivia.

Olivia lifts her hand and a holographic clock, presumably on Nacreous time, hovers in the air above it.

"In about an hour," she tells us. "Gracious, I didn't realize I'd been here so long. I need to get back before it starts."

Olivia stands causing us all to stand out of respect for her. She leans in towards me and gives me a hug.

"Thank you for helping me, Anna," she says. "And thank you for telling me the truth about what's going on."

When she pulls away, I warn her, "We may have to kill him. Are you prepared to handle the fall out if that happens?"

Olivia nods. "Yes, I can handle it. My husband is gone, and I want the bastard who killed him to pay for taking him away from me. You do what you have to. I'll handle the political fallout of it all."

I nod, satisfied she understands what needs to be done.

"We'll be there soon," I reassure her.

"Thank you for helping me," she says to all of us just before she uses her personal teleporter and returns to Nacreous.

We finalize a plan for us all to make the journey to Nacreous together.

"I think we should all change out of these clothes," Desmond says.

"Agreed," Daniel replies taking off his cravat.

"I may have something that will fit you, Brutus," Malcolm tells him. "I'll go up and get it for you."

"I'll take care of Desmond and Daniel," Jered volunteers. "I'm sure I have something in my room that will do."

"Remember, this is Nacreous," Malcolm reminds them. "And this is a teenager's party. I can only imagine what they'll be wearing. So try to pick something that might have a chance of blending in."

Malcolm grasps one of my hands and phases us directly to his bedroom. Once there, he pulls me against him roughly, deftly coaxing my hair out of the loose bun it's in. He runs his fingers through the now free strands and holds the back of my head as his lips ravish mine. I feel him lift me into his arms and take me to his bed. Gently, he lies me down and straddles my hips, cradling me against his warmth. He kisses me with an urgency that makes thinking impossible. The sweep of his tongue against mine makes me melt from desire, and all I know is that I don't want him to stop kissing me.

His lips make a slow, wet trail down my neck to the tops of my breasts as his hands squeeze them gently upward over the top of my dress to receive his singular attention. I feel him press himself against my center, slowly moving back and forth causing my heart to race into my throat, making it hard for me draw in a steady breath. Just as quickly as he started this foreplay, he ends it by returning his lips to mine for small, chaste kisses and ceasing the rhythmic movement of his hips against mine. I'm finally able to take in a steadying breath as he pulls away to look down at me.

"Why are you stopping?" I ask, feeling completely

unfulfilled and in desperate need of satisfaction.

"For one, we don't have time to go any further," he tells me, leaning down and kissing the corners of my mouth. "Two, we're not married yet."

"We're practically married," I say, flashing the ring he gave me in front of his eyes. "And I'm sure we have a few more minutes left before we have to get ready."

Malcolm smiles at me. "Anna, when I'm finally able to make love to you, I'm going to need more than just a few minutes," he says, sliding one hand down over my breasts until it comes to rest on the side of my hip. "I'm going to need a *lot* more time than that to pleasure you."

"You drive me insane when you touch me like that," I say, wondering if he truly understands how his caresses make my body ache for release.

"I was hoping we would be able to take things further this evening," he admits with a disappointed sigh. "I'm not sure I can wait much longer either. I'm shocked I've lasted this long, if you want to know the truth. Especially with you practically begging me to bed you."

I slap him playfully on the arm which makes him laugh.

"I have not begged," I say, trying to sound offended but

knowing he's playing with me. "Would begging have worked?"

Malcolm laughs even harder and rolls onto his back, pulling me on top of him.

"Oh Anna," he says, looking up at me with more love in his eyes than anyone has ever looked at me. "You are my match in every way possible I believe."

"Hmm, yes. Jered did mention that you like to have a lot of sex."

Malcolm looks confused. "Why on earth would he tell you something like that?"

"He didn't say it in so many words. But I did just to clarify what he was insinuating when I asked about your relationship with Celeste."

The mention of Celeste's name visibly diminishes Malcolm's happiness, making me regret mentioning her name, and it reminds me to keep the promise I made to her when she helped me get to New Orleans.

"Celeste asked me to tell you she was sorry about what she did. I don't think she understood that she was putting Lucas' life in danger. There was no way she could have known Auggie wasn't himself anymore. She simply took his word that he wouldn't harm us."

"It doesn't matter," Malcolm says, his voice suddenly cold. "She's dead to me now."

It was as I thought. I assumed Malcolm would never purposely seek Celeste out again for any reason because of her betrayal. Once his trust in a person was broken, I seriously doubted it could be earned back easily or possibly at all.

"Come on," he says, gently pushing me off him. "We should get dressed to go to Nacreous."

"What do you think I should wear?" I ask.

Malcolm takes my hand and pulls me off the bed.

"I have just the thing."

He walks me over to his walk in closet and turns on the light. He goes to the back of the closet and reaches up for a large white box sitting on the top shelf. After he pulls it down, he hands it to me.

"It was a backup one JoJo made just in case something happened to Jess' before you were born."

I take the box from his hands and walk over to the bed. I lift the lid to find a complete white leather outfit, including boots, like the one I used to wear. After Levi burned Malcolm's Lakewood home and all of its contents to the ground, all I had left of the outfit was the jacket.

"And you think I should wear this type of outfit to a royal function?"

Malcolm crosses his arms over his chest. "Have you ever been to a teenager's birthday party in Nacreous?"

"No," I admit.

"Then trust me. Even with your sword strapped to your back you'll be one of the most conservatively dressed people in attendance."

I have to giggle. "Now you have my interest piqued. What are you going to wear to blend in?"

"I figured I would just wear my overlord get-up."

"Do all the overlords down here wear the same outfit?"

"Yes."

"Well, at least you have the body to fill yours out."

Malcolm smiles. "Does it turn you on, my love?"

I feel myself blush and quickly pick up the box.

"I'll be back," I tell him and phase to my room to change, but not before I hear Malcolm laugh at my hasty departure.

I quickly change into the new leather outfit and find that it fits just as perfectly as the last one. I grab my sword and strap it onto my back. Malcolm seems to think it won't make me stand out in the Nacreous crowd which is fine by me. I will need it if Horatio turns out to be a prince of Hell. I think we all assumed he would probably be one. It was just a matter of finding out which one. To me, it didn't matter. They each possessed a seal that I needed to recover. I didn't want to know too much about them because getting to know them wouldn't really benefit me in any way. The less I knew about them the easier it would be for me to assassinate them.

And that's pretty much what it boiled down to. I was, in effect, God's assassin. I could take the princes' lives without much effort. One simple touch. One single thought was all I needed to strike them down and take what I wanted. I stopped myself from over thinking matters. I had things to do and now wasn't the time to start doubting my mission.

I left my room and walked down the stairs to find the others. Everyone was standing in the foyer, presumably waiting on me.

The boys were all dressed in some variation of black outfits either in cloth or leather. They each had swords swinging from their hips which made me even more curious about the dress code for this party. I feel a bit conspicuous in my all white outfit in the circle of black.

Lucas runs up to me when I get to the bottom of the stairs and hugs me tightly around the hips.

"Be careful, mommy," he says, hugging me even tighter.

I bend down on one knee and look him straight in the eyes.

"I don't want you to worry," I tell him. "I'll be back before you even get up in the morning."

Lucas nods but doesn't look completely convinced.

Vala walks up to me.

"Do you need me to come with you?" She asks. "I'm a lot bigger now. I might be of some use."

"You would be of more use to me here. Keep an eye on Lucas and Luna for me," I say, hoping Vala understands that I want her to stay and give Lucas comfort while I'm gone. If anyone had experience in comforting a child, it was Vala. She certainly had enough practice with me.

"Don't take any unnecessary chances," Millie says, giving me a hug. "Just do what you need to do and come back home to us."

"We won't be long," I tell her.

I look at Giles over Millie's shoulder and tell him, "Protect my family while we're gone."

"I will, Anna," he assures me. "You have my word."

I go to stand beside Malcolm.

"Are we ready?" I ask them.

"I think the important question is," Malcolm says, "are you ready?"

"As ready as I'm going to get," I admit, taking in a deep breath. "Let's go."

Malcolm takes hold of my hand and phases us to Nacreous.

CHAPTER TWENTY-TWO

We phase in near the entrance of the palace.

Before now, I'd only seen videos and pictures of Nacreous. I knew the basics about their architecture and culture, but physically being inside the most intellectually advanced cloud city is an experience beyond anything I could have ever imagined.

Nacreous is the epitome of modern technology and free thought. Every building within the city is built with a polymer which adjusts its opacity to let in as much natural light as possible. The material is also polymorphic and can assume any shape and mimic any type of material that the owner wants. It is also engineered to absorb the energy from the sun itself to run most everything which needs power. The architectural design of the city itself is an eclectic mix of the new fused with the old. Somehow the combination melds perfectly together to form a cohesive community of buildings. The citizens of Nacreous are encouraged to broaden their imaginations and experiment with different concepts not only in their architecture but also in their everyday lives. New ideas are the hallmark of their society. If you wanted to expand your mind in literature, the arts, and sciences, Nacreous is your cloud city of choice.

"I thought you might like to see the city before we went inside," Malcolm says to me. "I know you haven't been allowed to travel much."

"The only travelling I've done has been with you and Jered," I tell him. "This is...spectacular! Beyond anything I could have imagined from the pictures I've seen."

I let my eyes drink in the city before allowing myself to study the majesty of the palace's breathtaking design. The exterior looks like it's made of polished mercury. Its silver curves extend out in a random pattern like the rays of the sun, and I can imagine it looking almost golden when the sun shines against its metallic surface.

Even though Nacreous is situated above Antarctica, the citizens are still able to have a day and night cycle provided by the special shielding properties of the protective dome covering the city. It's night time now, and the palace is lit up with artificial lighting to accentuate its fluid lines.

There is a throng of people present standing outside the glass entrance of the palace, waiting for their turn to enter and join the festivities.

"Come on," Malcolm says to me, squeezing my hand. "We should probably get inside now. I just wanted to show you the city first."

We all phase into the palace arriving within its center, at least that's what I assume. I find us in a circular atrium. I look up at the glass ceiling, and notice its design is that of an abstract representation of the sun. A white, walled off ramp circles around the periphery of the room leading all the way to the top level of the palace. We make our way up the ramp with the other people present.

On our way to the top, I immediately see why Malcolm said I wouldn't stand out in my leather outfit amongst the other party goers. Almost everyone is dressed in either some sort of form fitting leather outfit or they're dressed in minimalistic black clothing. Many of them are carrying swords or daggers at their sides, but I get the impression their function is completely decorative unlike mine. I feel like the most overdressed person there considering how scantily clad the younger people in the crowd are.

Once we reach the top of the ramp, it's easy to find where we're supposed to go. Near the entrance to the grand hall, I see Empress Olivia and Horatio greeting their older guests while the younger ones bypass the traditional greeting of the empress and head straight for the birthday celebration.

"What the hell?" I hear Malcolm say beside me as he comes to an abrupt halt and stares at Horatio in bewilderment.

"When did he come up here?" Jered asks as he glares at Horatio too.

I see that all my guardians are glowering at Horatio Ravensdale.

"Which prince is he?" I ask, wanting to know why they all seem so surprised to see him. Surely they expected him to be one of the princes of Hell. Why look so shocked?

"That's not one of the princes," Malcolm finally says, explaining their reaction to what they see. He looks down at me. "That's Botis. He's one of Lucifer's generals, but he normally isn't allowed up here on the surface. Lucifer keeps certain demons on a tight leash in Hell and Botis has always been one of them."

"But why place him here?" Jered asks. "Why not place one of the princes at the head of Nacreous society?"

"I don't know," Malcolm says. "Let's go see if we can find out."

We stand in line to greet the empress and her consort. I see Botis glance furtively down the line at us a few times as we make our way forward. He looked a bit alarmed when he first saw us, but he quickly wiped that expression from his features and now wears a mask of indifference as we approach. Once it's our turn to be greeted, Botis bows to me.

"Greetings Empress Annalisse," Botis says through his human mask of Horatio Ravensdale. "It's an unexpected pleasure to have you here at our little soiree."

400

"Thank you for inviting me, Iggi," I say, knowing the real Horatio would have hated the use of the nickname, but since I'm talking to the demon who pushed his soul out of his body, I feel sure Horatio would get a small amount of satisfaction by my use of it.

Botis looks at Malcolm and the rest of my Watcher contingent.

"Expecting trouble gentleman?" Botis asks.

"Depends," Malcolm answers. His eyes narrowing on Botis. "Are you planning to start any?"

Botis smiles. "Not me. I'm just here to enjoy the revelry. As long as certain people leave me alone, I'll leave them alone."

"I would wager the odds are against you," Malcolm tells him. "So many against one. It really doesn't seem fair."

"No, it doesn't," Botis agrees, eyeing us warily, especially me. "Then again, I guess it all depends on the cards you have in your hand like in any good game of poker. I suppose I should warn you that I have an ace up my sleeve in case anyone tries to cause trouble."

"An ace…" Malcolm muses, sounding like he's trying to figure out what Botis could possibly have that would prevent us from killing him on the spot.

Botis smiles. The action instantly sends chills up my spine.

"A little present from my superior actually. I had a brother break something once that he couldn't repair. His only recourse was to give up at the time. I wonder what would happen if what he tried to stop was suddenly let loose again."

I have no idea what he's talking about, but from the look on Malcolm's face, I can see that he does.

"That was a very generous gift," Malcolm agrees.

Botis smiles even wider now that he knows Malcolm understands what ace he holds.

"Yes. Yes it was," Botis agrees. "I think he understood my life might depend on it one day. Now, if you don't mind, we have other guests to greet. You should probably move along now."

We move down to Empress Olivia who looks clueless about what the entire exchange between Malcolm and Botis was about. She isn't the only one.

"It's so good to see you, Anna," Olivia says, leaning into me like she's kissing me on the cheek.

"Is he one of the princes?" She whispers in my ear before pulling away to kiss my other cheek.

"No," I whisper in her ear. "But he is a demon. I assume

you still want me to kill him?"

Olivia pulls back and says, "That would be lovely, Anna. I would be forever grateful. Please, enjoy the festivities we have planned for this evening and let me know if you need anything."

My group moves into the grand hall where the music is so loud it reverberates against the crystalline walls. The decor for the party is that of a gothic ice palace. The icy theme seems a bit redundant since Nacreous is situated directly above one of the polar ice caps. A thick layer of white mist conceals the floor and tall, skeletal trees festooned with glass ornaments in the shape of icicles act as the only decorations.

I lean up and whisper into Malcolm's ear.

"She still wants us to get rid of him," I say.

Malcolm nods his head acknowledging that he heard and understood what I said even over the loud music being played in the room. He looks over at the rest of our group and holds up a fisted hand. Apparently it's a prearranged signal because Malcolm grabs my hand, and we're suddenly standing right outside the palace again in the same spot where we first arrived.

"Olivia still wants us to kill Botis," I tell the others.

"Can we?" Daniel asks Malcolm. "If he has who we think he does, he'll use it against us."

"What was he talking about?" I ask them. "What ace does he have up his sleeve?"

"He has Asmodeus," Malcolm tells me looking slightly frustrated by the fact.

"Do you remember when we were in the desert with Levi," Jered says to me. "And when Christopher came back with the first prince Levi said he was the defective one?"

"Yes," I say with a nod of my head. "I remember."

"Years ago," Malcolm says. "Asmodeus and Caylin had an altercation. She crushed his seal and accidentally broke it open. Asmodeus stabbed himself with one of the daggers to stop the seal from opening completely."

"What does his seal do?" I ask.

"It will cause major earthquakes to erupt all over the world if it's fully opened," Desmond tells me.

"We can't leave him in control of something that powerful," Brutus says. "I say we kill Botis before he can do any more harm to these people and grab Asmodeus back from him."

"I agree," Malcolm says, turning to me. "Are you ready for this?"

"Yes," I say. "I'm ready."

We phase back into the party and bide our time. It's not until almost an hour later that we see Botis enter the grand hall with Olivia by his side. He kisses her on the cheek, and I see Olivia involuntarily flinch from the contact. Although she tries to cover up her reaction with a smile, it's too late. It's obvious by the look on Botis' face that he knows she understands what he is and that her knowledge of him might just be reason enough to end her life. For me, his reaction just adds to my motivation to kill him before he has the chance to do more damage.

Botis leaves Olivia's side and mingles with some of the guests present.

"How are we going to get him away from all these people?" I ask Malcolm.

"I don't think that's something we'll have to worry about," Malcolm replies keeping his eyes on Botis.

We soon see him sneak out a side door of the grand hall. It is either an invitation to come find him, or he's trying to escape. Either way, we have no other alternative but to follow him.

Malcolm looks around the room to find our friends and lifts his fist into the air to gain their attention. It only takes a few seconds before they're by our sides. We make our way to the exit Botis used and find that it leads to a long hallway with numerous rooms leading off of it.

"Check all the rooms," Malcolm orders.

As I reach for the panel which leads to one of the rooms, I notice something bright flash at the end of the hallway. I look down the corridor to the full length window there and see something flash again far off in the distance. I walk over to the window and look outside.

Standing on the circular roof of a building in the far distance is Botis. He's holding a large sword in one hand which gives off a bright blue glow and Asmodeus in the other.

"Malcolm!"

Malcolm and the other Watchers come running down the hallway.

"What's wrong?" Malcolm asks before following my gaze to the scene outside.

"How are we supposed to get over there?" Daniel says.

"Can't you just phase over?" I ask.

"We can only phase to places we've been," Jered reminds me, sounding frustrated by the situation. "And none of us have been on the roof of that building.

"I can fly over," I say.

"Not without taking me with you," Malcolm says. "You

406

can carry at least one person with you while you fly."

I nod because I know no amount of arguing is going to change Malcolm's mind.

"Break the glass," I tell him.

Malcolm takes a step back from the window and releases it from its casing with one swift kick. I grab him to me and hover above the floor a little.

"Malcolm," Jered says, "phase back and get us as soon as you get over there."

Malcolm nods, and I fly us out of the broken window.

"Don't take any unnecessary chances," Malcolm tells me as we fly over.

"I won't," I reply.

In no time at all, we're on the roof of the building where Botis is.

Malcolm phases away but phases right back with the other Watchers in tow.

"So nice of you all to join me," Botis says arrogantly.

He's standing near the edge of the roof with Asmodeus lying on the ground at this feet. The large sword he holds at his side glows a bright, ominous blue.

"I should have known the lot of you were just too stupid to not let things remain the way they are. As you can see, I wasn't lying about the ace I hold. If you leave now, I won't have to play it."

"That's not happening," I say, drawing my sword out which signals the rest of my party to draw theirs as well.

Botis shakes his head at me.

"Lucifer underestimated you. He felt sure you would choose to live the easy life he was offering you. How disappointed he'll be that you've chosen to ignore his warnings and disrupt his plans."

"I can't leave you alive," I tell him. "You would corrupt this city and most likely kill Empress Olivia so you can rule it on your own."

Botis smiles. "So very perceptive, Anna."

"Why didn't you just take over her body in the first place?" I ask. "She's the one with the real power."

"It might sound petty," Botis tells me, sounding like he's about to divulge a secret, "but I didn't want to be in a female human's body. Your hormonal activity is very erratic, to say the least. No, much simpler to be a man in this world. Women are too high maintenance with your constant primping and worrying over what outfit to wear. I'd rather stay in Hell than do all that just to fit in."

"Well, I could certainly send you back there," I offer.

Botis laughs. "No, thank you. I much prefer it up here. The air is far fresher. In fact, I intend to stay here for a very long time."

"I'm afraid your visit will have to be cut short." I say. "I can't allow you to stay in that body. I promised Olivia I would kill the person who murdered her husband, and I always follow through with my promises."

"I know you can kill me," Botis says. "I've been warned about your powers. But, I wonder. Which will you choose to do? Kill me for a single act of vengeance or save millions of lives instead?"

Botis quickly reaches down and pulls the silver dagger out of Asmodeus' hand. He kicks Asmodeus' body off the roof and phases away.

It only takes a second before we feel the trembling of the earth beneath our feet as the effects of the first earthquake caused by the seal opening begins.

I instantly know what I have to do. I throw my sword down, run to the edge of the roof and jump off. I faintly hear

Malcolm cry out my name as I allow myself to freefall.

I angle my body forward, head first with my arms close to my sides to increase my speed. My hands ignite with the blue flames of my power as I reach out and grab one of Asmodeus' hands. He opens his eyes and looks up at me. The fear on his face after waking up from a thousand year sleep and finding himself in such a precarious position saddens me for some reason. I don't know what he's done in his life as a fallen angel to deserve such an end, but I can't help the pity I feel for him in his last moments. His life is a danger to not only the ones I love but to the world at large, and I have no other recourse but to end it.

"I'm sorry," I yell to him, just as I silently wish for his death.

Asmodeus screams out in pain as his body is reduced to ashes in the wind.

The agony accompanying the burning of Asmodeus' seal into the skin at the small of my back makes my plan of flying to safety impossible. I immediately feel incapacitated as my body is wracked by wave after wave of excruciating pain. I close my eyes as I approach the ground and pray that my own personal guardian angel is watching.

I taste the sweet breath of life, but it doesn't seem to be

enough to pull me back from the black abyss I'm in. I languish in the darkness until I taste it again and again, but each time it just doesn't seem to be enough to lift my soul out of the chasm between life and death.

Time passes, but I have no way to judge how much has gone by. It silently watches me and waits to see what the outcome of my fate will be. My heart yearns to be with those I love, but my memories of them seem to be fading, becoming more distant the longer I remain in death's shadow.

Finally, I feel the pull of life urge me to return into its arms. I reach out in the darkness, feeling the tips of my consciousness push against death and grasp onto life.

I wake, taking in a deep, hard fought for breath.

I look around me and see that I'm lying in Malcolm's bed in our New Orleans home.

I feel a gentle hand cup the side of my face. I look over to the person sitting beside me on the bed and smile.

"You had me worried," Will says, his eyes filled with that very emotion as he looks down at me.

"What happened?" I ask, my voice raspy like I haven't spoken in a while.

"You died...again," he answers in mild exasperation. "I

thought I told you we needed to stop meeting like this, Anna."

I feel a small smile tug at the corners of my lips.

"Where's Malcolm?" I ask, not seeing him in the room.

"I had to order him to get out," Will tells me. "He was going crazy because I couldn't resurrect you, and he was making it impossible for me to concentrate."

"Why were you having trouble bringing me back to life?" I ask.

"I don't know," Will says, as his brows furrow together, making him look even more troubled. "It's always worked on the first try with the others. Even with you the last time, it worked like it should. But, something was wrong this time... I had to do it twenty times before you came back. I almost gave up, Anna."

I reach out and grab one of Will's hands.

"Thank you for not giving up," I tell him. "I have a lot to live for."

"Yes, I see you finally got your man," Will says with a small laugh. "I can't tell you how tired I got of you asking me questions about Malcolm while we were in Heaven. It almost drove me insane."

"Really?" I ask, Will's words confirming what Lilly told

Malcolm about me already knowing him even before I was sent to Earth. "I wish I could remember the time we spent together."

"And I wish I could forget *that* part of it," Will laughs. "Malcolm and I have had a very strained past with one another."

"Could you get him for me?" I ask Will. "I need to see him."

"Yes," Will says. "I know he needs to see you too. He's been beside himself with worry."

Will stands up and leans down to give me a kiss on the forehead.

"I'll go get him, but then I need to return to Heaven. Do you think you could do me a favor, Anna?"

"What?"

"Please stop dying. I'm not sure I'll be able to pull you back next time."

"I'll do my best," I promise him.

Will steps out of the room, closing the door behind him.

Just as he does that, I see someone else phase in.

"Didn't I tell you to leave things alone?" Lucifer says to me in agitation, walking closer to the bed.

I sit up and immediately regret the quick movement. My back aches from receiving the second seal, but I push through it and face Lucifer.

"You know I can't do that," I tell him.

"If you want to live a long, healthy life, you have to," Lucifer says angrily. "How much more of a warning do you need? You almost died for God's sake!"

"But I'm not dead," I try to reason. "I'm perfectly fine."

"Leave things alone, Anna! If not for your own sake, then do it for that big buffoon you protest to love. Or do you want to hurt him? Do you want to cause him so much pain he'll wish he were dead? I've been on the receiving end of self-sacrifice in the name of God's plans. If you truly love Malcolm, don't do that to him for something that doesn't have to be done!"

"Are you saying that for my benefit or for your own?"

Lucifer runs an agitated hand through his shoulder length blonde locks.

"There are things going on that you simply don't understand, Anna."

"Then tell me. Help me understand why you're so adamant that I not complete the mission God gave me."

"Just do as I say, daughter! Stop questioning my motivations! If you truly want to have a long and happy life with Malcolm, leave things alone!"

Lucifer phases. I know by his phase trail that he's gone to hide out in his unholy domain. A place no sane person would follow him to.

I stare at the black hole he left, peering into its darkness but not seeing even a pinpoint of light. It's a place empty of hope and love.

I swing my feet off the bed and stand up.

I realize Lucifer is the only one who can answer the many questions I have about not only my mother but also about my future. What is he trying so hard to warn me about? What is the real reason behind why he doesn't want me to retrieve the seals? I need more information so I can fully understand what's happening, and my only opportunity to find the answers I need is about to disappear.

"Forgive me, Malcolm."

I reach out for Lucifer's phase trail... and follow him straight to Hell.

17003467R10234

Made in the USA
San Bernardino, CA
26 November 2014